MY FATHER'S SHADOW

P. M. Smith

WestBow
P R E S S®
A DIVISION OF THOMAS NELSON
& ZONDERVAN

Copyright © 2019 P. M. Smith.

All rights reserved. No part of this book may be used or reproduced by any means, graphic, electronic, or mechanical, including photocopying, recording, taping or by any information storage retrieval system without the written permission of the author except in the case of brief quotations embodied in critical articles and reviews.

Scripture taken from the King James Version of the Bible.

WestBow Press books may be ordered through booksellers or by contacting:

WestBow Press
A Division of Thomas Nelson & Zondervan
1663 Liberty Drive
Bloomington, IN 47403
www.westbowpress.com
1 (866) 928-1240

Because of the dynamic nature of the Internet, any web addresses or links contained in this book may have changed since publication and may no longer be valid. The views expressed in this work are solely those of the author and do not necessarily reflect the views of the publisher, and the publisher hereby disclaims any responsibility for them.

Any people depicted in stock imagery provided by Getty Images are models, and such images are being used for illustrative purposes only. Certain stock imagery © Getty Images.

ISBN: 978-1-9736-2212-3 (sc)
ISBN: 978-1-9736-2214-7 (hc)
ISBN: 978-1-9736-2213-0 (e)

Library of Congress Control Number: 2018902672

Print information available on the last page.

WestBow Press rev. date: 01/24/2019

"He that dwelleth in the secret place of the most High

shall abide under the shadow of the Almighty."

Psalm 91:1

PROLOGUE

Why does it always seem to rain on the day of a funeral? Today was no exception and presented an unrelenting rainstorm that I thought would never end. The raindrops were so falling so fiercely that I could hear each drop as it fell against the windowpane of the car. The closer we got to the cemetery, the faster the rain fell from the sky. The downpour came so quickly that the windshield wipers worked overtime to keep the glass clear of precipitation. It reminded me of how my mother loved the rain. She loved the scent in the air after a torrential downpour and the sound of splashing raindrops on the rooftop. I must admit I did not share my mother's love for rainstorms…especially today of all days. Funerals and rain storms seemingly go together…under my breath, I whispered a little sunshine would have been nice.

As the cars pulled into the cemetery, we gathered inside the mausoleum to escape the cold persistent rain. It was not a large building, barely enough room for everyone to enter. The immediate family led the way into the mausoleum first, of course, followed by those who were fortunate enough to come in out of the storm. After everyone was settled, the minister began reciting the Lord's Prayer. He spoke slowly in a low monotone voice that brought no attention to him or the words proceeding from his mouth. After the recitation of the Lord's Prayer, without pausing, he moved onto the twenty-third book of Psalms. Then a beautiful lone soprano voice began singing, "Nothing between My Soul and the Savior," one of my parent's favorite hymns. I too loved the lyrics of this song as it has so much meaning. The words repeated in my head:

> "Nothing between my soul and the Savior,
> not of this world or my fondest dreams.
> I have renounced sin and all of its pleasures,
> Jesus is mine there's nothing between."

As the mourners sung the old hymn, I turned my attention to the outside and silently counted the dancing black umbrellas emerging from the many vehicles making up the funeral procession. As the words from the second verse filled the air, the cemetery workers made their way into the building.

> "Nothing between, like worldly pleasures;
> Habits of life, though harmless they seem,
> Must not my heart from Him ever sever;
> He is my all, there's nothing between."

Without uttering one word or disturbing the bereaved, the men dressed in their overalls and muddy boots powered up a small electric lift and slowly hoisted the first casket into the walled tomb. My knees went weak. Everyone continued singing as if they didn't notice a casket containing my father's body was being laid in its final resting place.

I was focused on a spot on the ground when my brother Russell came from behind me. "Hey," he whispered. "Let's move a little closer to say our last good-byes." I looked up just in time to see the workers slide the second casket into the tomb in the wall. Just when I felt I could no longer maintain my composure, Karen, my older sister collapsed right into my arms. It took every bit of strength to keep her from falling to the floor. "Give me strength, Jesus," I whispered. "Lord give me strength!"

The Lord must have heard my prayer because one of the deacons came to my rescue. He gently lifted Karen out of my arms and sat her safely on one of the benches provided nearby. Overcome with grief, I slid into the seat next to her. She laid her face on my lap and uncontrollably we wept in each other's arms.

This was a day I've dreaded, but knew would happen sooner or later. My parents were getting older, and they were moving a little slower, and it was becoming more and more apparent that they were not as mentally sharp or as physically quick as in times past. But, truth be told, we, my brother and sister and I, never anticipated God taking them both on the same day and in such a horrific manner.

The scriptures are so right when comparing the brevity of our lives to a vapor. We are given a few days on this earth. The days and years disappear as swiftly as a faint mist of steam evaporating into thin air. We're here today and sometimes gone today. That's how I felt about losing my mom and dad. One day we're laughing and talking with them, planning the future and before we know it, their lives are snuffed out never to be seen again. Never again will I hold their hands or lay my head on my mother's lap or hear my father call me "baby girl" or watch him play with his grandchildren.

I will never forget the night of the accident. I wasn't in the car with my parents. I wasn't even in the vicinity at the time of the crash. What we saw was the aftermath of two vehicles colliding at high speed. What I do have is a vivid memory of the state trooper who came to our house that night to give us the unfortunate news. He mentioned something about a driver losing control of his car, crossing the median..... *"Man was drunk as a skunk, blood alcohol level registered at .016,"* I remember him saying in his thick southern drawl. My husband held my hand tightly as we drove in complete silence to the scene of the accident. Our children begged to come along with us, but we thought it best that they remain at home since we did not know what to expect when we arrived at the scene of the accident. During the long drive, I silently prayed for a miracle. Hoping it was not as severe as the state trooper had made it sound over the phone. But my reasoning quickly kicked in------ *if it wasn't so bad why did the state trooper make a visit to our home late at night? A telephone call would have been sufficient. And why escort us to the scene of the accident, if it wasn't so bad?* Something in the back of my mind said to prepare for the worse.

Unfortunately, the worse thing I could have ever imagined had come true ----a head-on collision. Both cars burst into a mass of flames upon impact. When we arrived on the scene, paramedics had pulled Mom and the driver from the other car out of the charred wreckage. Their bodies lay on the side of the road as paramedics worked frantically to save their lives. Firemen were putting out the smoldering flames and using the Jaws of Life to free Daddy from the mess of scorched metal.

Russell, my older brother, immediately took charge. "You and Karen ride with Mom to the hospital," he said. "I'll stay with Dad until they cut him loose." Without a word, Karen and I followed his instructions. In the ambulance, mother was in and out of consciousness. Looking at her were painful. The skin on her arms and face badly singed from the fire and scorching heat. Her constant moans from the agonizing pain were tearing me up inside, as I could do nothing to alleviate her physical discomfort. I held her hand sobbing, praying, hoping for a miracle. Even though the ambulance was traveling as fast as humanly possible, it seemed to take forever to reach the hospital. As Mother uttered incoherent sentences, I continued to stroke her hand and begged God to spare her life. Just as the ambulance pulled in front of the hospital, she breathed her last breath.

Daddy survived long enough for the doctors to operate and for us to talk with him one last time. The injuries to his head and body were too severe to allow him to live through the night. The other driver, we were told, also died the next morning.

I find it amazing how God gives us bits and pieces of our lives. I imagine He doesn't give us all the details because we lack the emotional strength to handle knowing every aspect of our short time here on earth. What would we do if we knew every injury or each little offense we would experience? It would be impossible to live a typical everyday life, anticipating every moment of satisfaction or every moment of pain. Life would not be as enjoyable as God intended, if you and I faced every day expecting something specific to occur, anticipating *how* it would happen and *who* the offender would be. Jesus is the only person I know who walked this earth knowing every minute detail of His life. He was fully aware of *how* and *when* His earthly life would end. He knew at the age of thirty-three He would die a horrible death by crucifixion, yet Jesus still went to Jerusalem and allowed himself to be arrested, unjustly tried and then He willingly laid down His life. My parents would have been devastated, to say the least, had they known that drive on I-75 would be their last night on earth.

"God has a million ways of doing things." This was one of my father's favorite sayings. It was an expression he used to explain how the omniscient God does not have to do things as *we* expect nor does He have to repeat actions that He has performed in the past to prove He's God or that He's more than capable of achieving the impossible. God is not deficient in any way. My father's point was that God is so mighty and full of wisdom that He has an assortment of creative ideas and methods that will never enter our finite minds, to accomplish His will. From the very simple to the extremely profound, one never knows just how the Lord will bring a vision or a promise you've been holding in your heart to fruition. I had to concur, its true God has a million and one ways of doing things. In one single night, with one memorable act, He set things in motion that instantly shifted my world and changed my life forever.

My father, Charles P. Woods was born and raised in Oakdale City, Alabama. Oakdale is a rather small southern town. It is not known as a popular tourist destination. There are no historical landmarks, no famous monuments, no fascinating or exciting natural or man-made attractions to lure travelers. And as far as I can tell not one public figure either famous or not so famous was born there or resided within the city limits. Oakdale is your every day, ordinary rural community. It's a nondescript country township that sits about seventy-five miles north of Birmingham, Alabama. It has never been a bustling, energetic city with folk rushing around town or speeding down city streets in their fast cars. It resembles any small community with a meager population and three or four mid-sized buildings that make up the downtown landscape. You know the kind of small town where the post office, the gas station and the justice of the peace are all housed in the same building and operated by one lonely man? That's the kind of unremarkable place my father called home.

Despite its ordinary qualities, my father loved everything about his hometown. Vast, sprawling, metropolitan cities with people scattering about from place to place, oblivious to their surroundings and to one another had minimal appeal for him. Sure, he had read about the Eiffel Tower, the Grand Canyon, Detroit's Motor City, and many of the world's well-known landmarks. He hoped to one day visit those and other fantastic sites that everyone gushed about, but he was in no hurry to travel or see the world. In fact, he would have been quite content had he never left his beloved Oakdale.

If someone were to ask what he loved most about Oakdale, it would not take much for him to go on and on about the town's beautiful landscapes, the natural sceneries of God's green earth. He would talk about the sparkling blue lakes and streams were where he spent hours fly fishing and swimming. Or the rolling green hills and the over-abundance of tall, flourishing pecan trees growing in every other yard. The densely wooded areas he loved to explore and the gigantic trees that spread their branches across the land. He may tell you how he listened for the whistle of the afternoon train as it rolled through town alerting the residents that lunchtime was near. Or he would go on and on about the crooked dirt roads where he learned to ride a bicycle. The schoolyard playgrounds, where he did his best to avoid fistfights, and later when he grew older, those same play-grounds became playing fields for him and his friends to enjoy baseball in the summer and toss a football around as the brown leaves on the trees signaled fall's arrival. He might even tell you of the peculiar odors that occasionally emitted from the soap factory of the neighboring town and seemed to linger over Oakdale for hours. It was such an unpleasant smell that, as it hovered in the air simultaneously all of Oakdale's residents would close their windows and slam shut their doors to prevent the foul odor from creeping into their homes. If you happened to be outdoors during this drift of stale air, you would quickly reach for a hankie or use your hand to cover your nose to avoid inhaling the factory's unusual aromas. These are just a few of the quirks and peculiarities that made Oakdale for my father and its citizens such a loveable place to live. It wasn't a city full of noise and energy or activities, but it was home, and nothing and no one could convince my father that there was a better place to live or a better way of life.

MY FATHER'S SHADOW

My father's parents were Percy Lafayette Woods and Margaret Jean Woods. I did not have the pleasure of meeting my grandparents but was told numerous stories about their lives in the south. What I remember most was that they were both extremely religious people. They were the kind of church-going people whose entire lives centered on God and His Word. Their conversations almost always included a quote from the Bible, and before making any decisions for their family, either big or small, they inquired direction from the Lord. They weren't the holier than thou type but seemed to be a loveable couple devoted to one another and committed to serving their God.

It was said that my grandfather, Percy had two loves that he cherished more than life, well maybe three; the farm he started as a young man, his Bible and his wife and children. Those were the things he treasured most in this world, probably in that order. Reading his Bible was his favorite past time. The book he read and studied most was the Old Testament book of Job. Grandfather Percy chose Job because of his unusual faith, a faith that was in fact very secure for Job to continue trusting in a God, who without rhyme or reason, disrupted his life by abruptly snatching away from him everything he treasured and enjoyed. I thought it a bit strange to pattern one's life after a man who is known for suffering and misery, who wants that in their life? My father explained that his father sought after that kind of steadfast faith and reverent fear, even if it meant extreme hardships.

Like Job, my grandfather prayed regularly for himself, his wife and the souls of his children. My father described the daily prayers of repentance that Percy prayed on their behalf for known and unknown acts of evil they may have committed against God. And if that was not enough, every morning before school, my grandfather held a short prayer meeting with his children, taking the time to utter a prayer for each child as my grandmother smeared their foreheads with a dab of "blessed oil" from a small bottle my grandfather kept in his shirt pocket. This was a tradition that even my own parents adopted and performed on my siblings and me when we were young.

Every morning when he came to the breakfast table, my dad would find his father drinking a cup of hot coffee, pouring over his daily local newspaper and/or his well-worn Bible. At night before laying down, my grandparents gathered their children to read from the family Bible. Each child was expected to select and read a passage of their choosing. To please his father, my Dad would choose a passage from the book of Job. He barely understood Job's troubles, nor did he care. The odd phrases and strange sayings of Job and his friends made the book all the more difficult to understand. But, that did not matter, every night, without fail, young Charles would choose a verse from that strange book because it was his father's favorite. And he hoped one day his father would notice, and shower him with some much-desired fatherly love, perhaps a pat on the head, a brief smile or even a hug to express what a smart boy his son had become.

My grandmother Margaret Jean, who my grandfather playfully called "MJ" fell in love with Percy when he barely had two nickels to rub together. She was instrumental in helping Percy build his farming business. Grandmother Margaret took pleasure in managing the business end of the operations while Percy oversaw keeping the workers in line and coaxing the vegetables to grow from the ground.

Margaret enjoyed supporting Percy in his work, but she did not relish digging through rocks and worms in the hot sun, she knew without a doubt this was not her forte in life. Her enjoyment came from being a housewife, mother and when time allowed developing her artistic talents. When the children were at school, and Percy was busy in the fields, that's when grandmother sharpened her artistic creations. She would take pen to paper and painstakingly transcribe her favorite scriptures using her calligraphy like penmanship. Once selecting the scripture of choice, she would write the verse on cardboard, wood or paper in her fancy script. Then, Margaret drew flowing swirls, curls or flowers around the verse and placed it in a frame for hanging on the wall of her choice. When she tired of using framed artwork, she got the bright idea to use the bare walls of their home as her canvases. Of course, not every wall in their house was filled with her artwork, she knew Percy would not allow that, and it would be overkill. She wisely selected a few walls facing the east and the ones that received the most sunlight. Whenever the radiance of the sun hit the colors of her artwork just right the scriptures covering the walls seemed to shimmer and glow.

Her creative, artistic works made their home a one of a kind showpiece. The unusual artwork was an instant conversation piece whenever visitors stopped by. As soon as they stepped over the threshold of the front door, her work of art would be the first thing to catch their eye, and everyone would immediately want to meet the artist in the family. This, of course, opened the door for her to discuss not only her love for art but also her love for God. My father's favorite of his mother's artwork was a small piece that she painted and adhered to a magnet and stuck on the door of their refrigerator. The scripture was taken from 2Thessalonians 3:10, "…if any should not work, neither should he eat." I grew up looking at that exact piece of artwork every time I opened our refrigerator door.

As you can see my grandparents were fully committed to holy living, and so was everyone who lived under their roof whether they wanted to be or not. Several times a week my father and his siblings found themselves in the house of worship. All day on Sundays. Every Wednesday without fail they would attend Bible class. Friday nights prayer meetings and Saturday afternoons were designated for choir rehearsal. As you can see attending church services was a significant part of their life. Bible reading was as essential as partaking of their daily meals. Prayer time was also a must in the Woods household both family prayer time, and individual prayer was expected of every member of the family.

Whenever I hear this description of my grandparents, their godly lives and holy ways, I am always reminded of my own father. I never knew the worldly Charles Woods. The man with no enthusiasm for a religious lifestyle. I am sure I would not have recognized him at all. It is tough to imagine my father and mother prancing around on the dance floor with a drink in one hand and a cigarette clenched between their lips. The Charles Woods that I knew and loved was someone who had wholly given himself to the Lord. A man whose life and beliefs strongly resembled what I heard of my God-fearing grandparents.

With all this spiritual teaching, holy living and church-going, one would think that my father would have continued his relationship with the Lord as he grew older, but for him, it did not turn out that way. His connection to God came later in life and through a circuitous route that he never dreamed would have occurred. It seems that God wanted my father to develop a relationship with Him on his own not one that was compelled by his parents. Because he had no other choice my father, obediently attended church services and read his Bible along with the family reading time. At that period in his young life, he had no desire in his heart for God or the church.

For no particular reason, as my father grew older, he slowly allowed himself to gradually drift away from the church. He didn't turn to a life of crime or anything that drastic. When he became of age, he made a choice to sleep in on Sunday mornings and skip the daily Bible reading sessions. It was a hard and risky decision. One that he knew would create tension in his father's household. Of course, Percy and Margaret were disappointed. Charles' decision to reject the church did not come as a surprise for them, especially his father. Percy saw his son's increasing disinterest in the church as he grew older. As a father, Percy knew it was his duty to teach his children not just about life, but how to live for God. He took time with Charles and his siblings to explain what he called "good Bible living." He guaranteed his children that a successful and prosperous life would be theirs if they took to heart the teachings of that extraordinary and holy book. Charles politely listened but did not completely take in all he heard. For him the way to success was to get the best grades he could, earn a college degree and hope that would be enough to start the career he desired. It was just that simple. He felt at the time that God and all those rules was not necessarily needed to succeed in life. All one needed to achieve success was determination and hard work.

Percy saw his son's indifference towards the ideologies of the Bible, but he did not give up on him. He understood that everyone has a different style of learning. Some learn through hearing about the experiences of others. Others learn by observation and then there is that select group of people who are destined to learn the hard way, by experiencing things for themselves. His son Charles was of the latter group.

Until he graduated high school, my father lived with his parents. He was the youngest child, the last one to leave home and the only Woods offspring who chose not to make farming a life-long career. He was thankful for the years he lived off the farm, but he was not bound to it like his siblings and his parents.

Soon after completing high school my father decided to enroll at Alabama University. During his junior year of college, he met the love of his life, Ms. Iris Elaine Whitman. An attractive young graduate student working at AU as a teaching assistant. He was

P. M. Smith

drawn to her smile, confident manner and those piercing brown eyes that seemed to be looking only at him. Unfortunately, for Charles her being a few years older was a deal breaker for Iris, and it did not help that he was from a small farming town. These were all valid reasons for Iris not to give him the time of day. Somehow my father's charm, good looks, and flattery won her over because a year or two after they met Iris Elaine consented to become his wife.

After a small wedding ceremony and graduation from college Charles took a teaching position at City College. My mother had already begun her career in the nursing field. They hoped to start a family and build a life together in Oakdale City for the rest of their lives. He was content with the small, town life. Whenever asked if he thought about moving to the north his reply was: "I was born in the south and plan to stay here until I die." My father loved the south more than anything, he loved the slow-moving way of life. He enjoyed good, simple, country living, the food and the clear, clean country air. If my father had had his way, he would have stayed in Oakdale City until the day he died, but that was not to be.

A few months after they were married an incident erupted between my father and a family friend, named Reed Johnson or Cousin Reed as he was called. It was said that Cousin Reed was supposedly related to our family on my grandfather's side. No one knew for sure exactly how he and my grandfather were related, and no one took the time to research his people or the supposed connection between the two families. It was believed that Reed himself started this rumor to ease his way into my grandparent's lives for reasons unknown. My grandfather had met Reed when he was a young boy and always called him cousin, so it stuck. There didn't seem to be any harm in his desire to be a part of their family. As Reed grew into a young man he connected with a wrong crowd, my grandfather hoped some of his Christian ways would rub off on him, but this never happened. It got to the point where my father's parents did not like having him around, but they did not prevent Reed from participating in family gatherings.

Some say that hindsight is the best kind of vision because it's not until *after* an incident has happened one can clearly see things as they should have been. Hindsight helped my father understand how God used Reed to prompt him to leave his beloved Southland. I was never told the entire story, from what I gathered my father and Reed got into a heated argument about a remark he made concerning my mother. When Daddy confronted Reed, asking him to apologize for his rude words. Reed refused to apologize, and the argument became more and more intense until on impulse my father struck Reed in the jaw, knocking him to the ground. They ended up tussling in the dirt and had to be pulled apart. It was this incident that forever banned Cousin Reed from any future Woods' gatherings, and it also caused my parents to move from their beloved Alabama southland.

My father like most men loved his wife, and the idea of someone belittling her, especially in his presence, family or not was hard for him to stomach. Mother, on the other hand, was much more tolerant. She had heard of Reed's reputation. She never cared for him. He seemed to be of the sneaky sort. The way he leered at her, seemingly checking her out from head to toe made her nervous, and she hated being around him. She pleaded with my father to ignore his insulting words. She was afraid of what Reed and his cohorts from the streets might do to her husband if he retaliated in any kind of way. My mother's pleading caused daddy to leave Reed alone, but he swore within himself that he would rue the day those words came out of his mouth.

A few weeks went by, and there was no more talk about the incident with Reed. My father no longer spoke of it to my mother, but he had not forgotten and apparently, neither had Reed. Several weeks after the incident my grandparents came to my parent's house in the middle of the night. They informed Daddy, how they heard through the grapevine that Reed was planning to retaliate against Charles striking him in the jaw. Just what Reed planned to do was left to the imagination. Daddy remained unmoved, he felt Reed's threats were empty, meaningless words. Reed was just mouthing off with no real inclination to harm him. Besides he wasn't afraid of Reed or the thugs, he called friends, and my father wasn't going to run from him. He had friends as well, good friends who were ready and willing to come to his aide.

My grandparents pleaded and argued with my father, hoping he would understand that the best way to avoid any confrontation with Cousin Reed was to get out of town. Leave Oakdale? My father hated the idea of running from a fight and he certainly did not want move from his hometown. He responded that he was well prepared for an attack on his home or his family. My grandparents could not get through to their son until my grandmother said to him, "Charles, the Lord gave me a dream last night."

On occasion, my grandmother was known to have dreams or visions. Her dreams and visions saved many from unnecessary dilemmas and helped others to solve difficult problems of life or understand how to properly handle or rid themselves of a sticky situation.

Even though Charles knew of his mother's reputation of dreams, he was in no mood to hear about her latest night vision. "Mama, I don't want to hear about your dreams right now, this is not the time----besides I'm capable of handling myself." He said abruptly. "Reed is all talk. You know that mama, he always has been. I know exactly how to deal with him and his low life friends. I'm not going to run from Reed, he's always been a loud-mouth, who talks too much and can't back up his foolish talking. You and I both know that. Besides, I have friends who are ready to help me if necessary, and I'll be prepared for him if he comes around talking crazy. I'm prepared to handle him. Trust me." He said boldly.

My grandmother patiently waited until he was finished, "Oh you're prepared huh?" she asked removing her glasses.

"Yes, I am." He said confidently. "I'm prepared to handle anyone who tries to make trouble for Iris or me. I'm well prepared."

"Alright, then let me ask you this….." Charles interrupted her before she could ask her question.

"I know what you're going to say, Mama. You want to know how I've prepared myself right?" He asked.

Grandmother calmly sat on the couch, pulling Charles to sit down beside her. She held his hand in her hands and in a quiet voice she said. "No, Charles I wasn't going to ask how you plan to protect yourself. I was going to ask if you were prepared to live alone?"

"Live alone?" Evidently, he was not expecting to hear those words. With a nervous laugh, he asked his mother to explain what she meant by living alone.

"I'm saying the dream wasn't about you Charles-----." There was no need for her to complete her sentence. She slowly allowed her gaze to turn to Iris, my mother. Charles jumped up from the couch and vehemently began insisting how he would never let anything to happen to his wife. Percy grabbed him by the shoulders, looking him square in the face. Percy could see the pressure and stress this was situation causing his son.

He shook his son, "Calm down boy, get ahold of yourself... I know what you're thinking, but violence is not the only way to solve a problem. Besides, there is no way for you to be with Iris every waking moment, come on man you know that. More importantly, you don't want your wife to live in fear, constantly looking over her shoulder, disturbed by every little noise she hears if she's alone in the house. Or worrying about you if you come home late. I wouldn't try to scare you or Iris because I love you both, but the vision your mother had... I believe is a warning from God."

"A warning?" My father said in anger. "What about protection? I thought God was this great, protector….. ?" He said sarcastically. "Isn't that His specialty, preserving the righteous? That's what you taught me. What's the matter don't you have faith in your prayers? Don't you trust *your* great and powerful God to come through for you when you need Him most?" He said mockingly. Knowing he had taken things a bit too far. Charles knew how much his parents revered their God and to speak of Him in such a cynical manner was not only blasphemous but also taking a chance with his life. But Charles didn't care anymore, nothing at this point mattered to him more than taking care of Reed Johnson once and for all.

"Charles, watch your mouth!" Margaret cautioned him. "Remember Who you're speaking of…and you're right the Lord defends those who love Him and sometimes those who don't.""

"You and Dad are always preaching how God is this mighty, powerful force, which no one can stop. Haven't you said that He's the only God who can do anything, and He shows up in the nick of time? Well, don't you think we need Him right now?" He said looking at his parents with contempt. "Where is our protection?" he hollered. "Where is my solution to this problem that's about to drive me to do something I may regret? Why don't you answer me?

Why is it that I have to run away like a scared, little ….." he was unable to finish the sentence.

Percy, listened in silence until Charles ended his outburst against God. He talked a good game about being prepared to protect his home and his young wife, but deep down inside Charles was deathly afraid. As much as he tried he could not fool his parents they knew him too well. It was evident, they could hear the fear in his voice and see it in his eyes. There was no hiding it from Percy, as a man, a husband and a father he understood. This kind of fear was typical and expected of anyone who faced an uncertain threat. Reed was unpredictable, my father nor his parents had any idea how or when he would retaliate. Charles was scared to death and too proud to admit it to those who loved him most.

"To everything, there is a season…." Percy began.

Charles waved him away. "Awwww, not now Dad. I don't want to hear that Bible talk right now. God doesn't care what happens to me, if I lose my life or something happens to Iris. If He cared, He would send an answer, the cavalry or something. Dad, I need you to talk to me man to man, tell me what you would do if you were me. If you were in my shoes." He looked Percy square in the face. "Talk to me like you're my father, not some preacher."

"I'm trying to help you if you would shut up, and hear me out," Percy said. "Sit down," he motioned for Charles to sit on the couch next to his mother. "Don't ever get it in your thick head that God has not come through for you. Who do you think provided for you down through the years? Clothing and food, a roof over your head? How do you think you went to college or got that job? Every time we called on God or when we had a need, He sent an answer, or the provision, mostly at the eleventh hour, but He still came through.

He has never, ever let us down. That's how this family has survived because God provided."

"Son, fear and, retaliation are not your only options, …you want to know what I would do if I were you? Man, I would fall on my knees and ask God for help and direction. That's what I would do if I were in your shoes. It's not about being a man or getting revenge or stocking up on weapons to handle your business. It's not about that at all. If you want me to talk to you like a man, I will talk to you like a godly man. Cause that's all I know."

"A real man takes his son to the Word of God where all of life's answers can be found. Before you cut me off, I was quoting Ecclesiastes, ….*to everything, there is a season and a time to every purpose under the sun*. That may not mean anything to you now, but it will one day, I guarantee. Because I know God did not allow this to come for no reason. Everything He does is intentional This is your day, your season."

"Season…what do you mean?" Charles looked at his father quizzically.

"To know God."

"I already know about God," Charles responded. "Heard about Him since I was a child."

"No son you don't *know* Him not yet, but you will. Son, don't be too proud to avoid trouble by running away from those who want to do you harm. There is nothing wrong with eluding danger if possible, any way you can… sometimes running from trouble doesn't mean you're weak or cowardly it could also mean you're wise. Sometimes God's way of providing safety is to warn us that danger is ahead. He gives you an out, a way to escape the danger coming your way. Intelligent people know how to elude danger. Listen to God's guidance. It's wise to *avoid* things and people who are too strong for you to handle."

Charles glared at his father. He didn't like hearing that Reed was too much for him to handle. He was about to voice his disagreement, but Percy held up his hand signaling Charles to keep quiet.

"I know you *think* you can handle Reed. It's true, he's smaller than you, in weight and height...but he's scrappy, and he doesn't fight fair. Everybody knows you're not afraid of Reed. We all know you're not one to back down from a fight. And how you like to face your fears head-on. But it's not just you anymore. You're not living for yourself, you have a wife to consider. All your major decisions must be made with her in mind. Sometimes it's best to avoid a troublesome situation altogether than to confront it, especially if a way of escape is provided."

"I understand what you're saying dad, but it would help if I knew what the dream was about, Mama, please tell me about the vision." He turned to Margaret. "Tell me what you saw."

"I'm not going to tell you I think you can figure it out for yourself. Trust that God is saying take your wife and leave Oakdale. Even Jesus steered clear of those who wanted to harm Him. If He had the good sense to avoid those who wanted to take His life what about you?" She hugged her son tightly by his shoulders burying her face in his chest. Charles put his arms around his mother and held her close.

With tears in her eyes, she looked up at him. "It's not easy to walk away from your family. I know how much you love the south and this city. It's hard for me to say it, but I promise that leaving is the best thing for you and Iris. Everything your father said is true, there is a purpose for this interruption in your young lives."

Charles concluded whatever the vision his mother had could not have been good. Especially since his mother would not disclose any details. He didn't want to leave his family and his beloved Southlands. But he also did not want anything to happen to his lovely Iris. He looked at his young wife who was trying with all her might to be strong. She had been quiet through the whole conversation. He didn't even have to ask her what she thought. The look on her face said it all. With all the talk about how ruthless Reed could be and his mother's dream, he knew it was making her extremely uncomfortable. Considering the well-being of his new wife Charles made the hard decision to do something he never imagined he would do in life, relocate to the north.

That same night packing only essential belongings and giving the rest of their possessions to their families, like thieves in the night my mother and father slipped out of town to migrate to the northern states, to a city known as Macklin County, Michigan. My parents had no idea they would never again set foot in Oakdale City, Alabama either for sad or joyous occasions. This relocation would be the beginning of a new life.

Saying goodbye to his parents and his hometown was one of the most difficult things my father had ever done. Tears flowed as they all hugged and kissed each other goodbye. Percy pulled his son to the side and held him as though it would be the last time he would ever see him. Charles could not understand the intensity with which his father hugged him. "Hey Dad, we'll come back to visit. Maybe one day after all this blows over we'll move back home." Percy silently squeezed his son's shoulders and shook his head, tears welling up in the corner of his eyes. All the years he had known his father this was the only time Charles saw his father cry.

MY FATHER'S SHADOW

Before they drove off, my grandfather stuffed a wad of cash in daddy's shirt pocket and planted a small Bible in his hands. "Remember what I always taught you ....*a good man obtains favor from the Lord.* Live a good life son, and you will always have God's favor. Live a good life and never forget our family verse Job 36:11." He said it with such finality that it made Charles even more reluctant to leave. He started to say so, but changed his mind and continued packing their things in the car.

As he and my mother drove along the dark highway every so often daddy glanced in the rear-view mirror until he could no longer see his father and mother standing on the side of the road watching the car's taillights fade into the darkness.

Days before my parents arrived in Michigan, my grandfather arranged for mom and dad to stay with relatives until they found jobs and suitable housing. It was difficult for my parents to adjust to months of freezing weather, the fast-paced lifestyle and the unusual ways of city folk. There always seemed to be loud noises coming from the streets. Screaming sirens, car alarms, loud music from passing cars that caused your windows to shake. Kids playing in the streets and the continued busyness of the people coming and going that never seemed to stop. A painful adjustment for both Charles and Iris that would generally cause a strain on any marriage, but they grew closer because of the simple fact that they had no friends or acquaintances in Macklin County. A result of not knowing anyone other than their distant relatives, Charles and Iris spent time together taking long walks around the city streets checking out the people, the scenery, observing the culture and lifestyle. After some time, Charles

P. M. Smith

purchased a car, and the long walks turned into long drives exploring the suburbs and quaint Michigan towns.

Within a few days, Charles found a job, to his disappointment it was not in the education field as he had in Alabama. He found work with an automobile company. He was promised a call when a teaching position became available, but the call never came, so somewhat out of desperation to provide for his family, he took a position as a supervisor of workers in the factory. It was far from his dream job, but he was making three times the money he made as a school teacher, and it more than paid the bills. Soon he and my mother purchased a moderately sized home and by the fall of that year welcomed their first child into the family, a baby boy they proudly named Charles Russell Woods, II.

When Russell turned three years old mother discovered she was going to give birth to a second child. It was during this time my Daddy began to get restless with the life he was living. He realized he was going nowhere. Working during the week and getting drunk on the weekends with some of the men from his job became mundane, boring and predictable. He saw there was no end to it. No end and no purpose. The guys he worked with were content leading a life filled with partying, drinking and chasing foolish women who wanted nothing more from them than their hard-earned pay. He was becoming weary of it and fed up with the group of guys determined to waste their earnings and their lives. It wasn't long before he discovered he no longer enjoyed their company. So, he abruptly ended their friendship and befriended a new group of guys. Several semi-intellectuals, who drank cheap wine, argued about their favorite jazz musicians and speculated on the current political situation. Soon he saw the futility in that activity as well. This sorry group of men was worse than the last. They were educated men, smart enough to make something useful of themselves or help uplift others. He soon realized their conversations were pointless and his friendships with them soon dissolved. Forcing my father to sit at home on the weekends reading, sulking or playing with his kids. No matter how hard he tried, he could not ignore the emptiness he felt inside.

One morning my father woke earlier than usual. He laid on the bed listening to the quiet of the house, no one was stirring, even his wife an early riser was still snoring softly beside him. after lying under the covers, staring at the ceiling and listening to the birds singing and the occasional cars passing by. He finally jumped out of bed, started the coffee maker and sat on the back porch in his robe with a hot cup of coffee. This was the only time the city reminded him of home when it was deathly quiet. When one could hear nature. Birds chirping in the trees, crickets making their unusual noises and dogs howling in the distance. No one was rushing to get anywhere. He could not hear car horns blowing, brakes squealing or children yelling for their friends down the street. This was the peace that he missed and enjoyed. It was quiet because it was just before dawn. The sky was still dark but in the distance, he could see the sun was slowly emerging from the clouds. He thought of the consistency of nature. How the sun always rose in the east every morning never failing. The moon and stars made their appearance every night and darkness covered the earth at the same time every day. The four seasons always arrived on schedule, just like clockwork. No one could be that consistent but the Almighty God. As he watched the sun rise it resembled a bright orange and purple ball, as it slowly surfaced from the clouds. It was a most beautiful sight. Although he had seen the sunrise before, this was different in ways he could not explain. For some reason, he thought of the power of God and his father's words as leaned in the car window, "live a good life." He wasn't sure what he meant by those words. He knew his father meant something specific by it, but he still did not understand. Slowly his eyes watered. He could not understand why he felt emotional at this moment. It wasn't because of sadness or pain. Maybe it was because he knew his life was far from good in the way his father meant. The splendor of the sun and the power and consistency of God only accentuated his feeling of being lost and empty. Right there on those porch steps as the sun rose, with tears streaming down his face he asked God to help him. Help him find fulfillment in his life. Help him find what he was searching for --- to fill the emptiness he felt in his soul.

Being an observant person, mother noticed the difference in Daddy's behavior. How frequently he changed friends. The strange sleep patterns, his limited appetite, and his unusually quiet manner. Her husband was not a quiet person. He loved to make her, and the kids laugh. Always entertaining them with a joke he heard or mocking a quirky person he met on the job. This was not the man she knew and loved. Whatever was bothering him, he kept it to himself. His unusual behavior worried her, and she began to wonder if he was depressed, or on the verge of a nervous breakdown.

While coming home from work one day, Daddy was approached by a young man passing out pamphlets on the street corner. The young man was wearing a bow-tie and what he looked like an expensive suit. His hair slick and shiny as though it was plastered to his head. Daddy wondered what new gimmick he was peddling. Was it a get-rich-quick-scheme or some other tactic to finagle his paycheck? The man forced a small booklet into his hand. The black and white pamphlet spoke of a new kind of following that taught a better way of life. He decided to check it out by himself before exposing mother and the rest of his family.

Maybe this was God's way of helping him in his search to find meaning and purpose in his life. He went to one of their gatherings and was immediately impressed by the promptness of the people, the friendly atmosphere and the love they seemed to have for one another. They addressed each other as Brother or Sister. He thought it odd that the men sat on the main floor while the women sat in the balcony. The men were all dressed in their suits and ties while the women and little girls wore long white dresses covering themselves from head to toe. Soon the speaker was introduced whom Daddy assumed was also the leader. He spoke very eloquently of lofty ideas of raising humanity to another level. The speaker roused the audience with his powerful words of disdain for the establishment which sought to control them. As my father walked home from the meeting he thought long and hard on the speech he heard. It was a strange religion to him. There was no mention of God, the Bible and too much talk of hatred and very little said about love. He turned to God once again and said: "Lord I feel like I'm dying inside. If you don't help me, I think I might lose my mind."

One day out of the blue, Daddy's cousin Earl and his wife Gracie stopped by for an unannounced visit. The relatives my parents stayed with when they first moved to Michigan. They wanted to see how they were faring and visit the new baby girl. Uncle Earl asked if baby Karen had been dedicated to the Lord. Daddy and mother were unfamiliar with this ceremony. Uncle Earl explained it was a blessing that the preacher prayed over every new-born child. Daddy liked the sound of it and promised to come Sunday to dedicate his children to the Lord.

The church was a small building. In another life, the midsized building had been a restaurant or retail store, because of the enormous glass windows and doors. The windows were covered with thick curtains to prevent outsiders from peeking in and to keep the cold breeze to a minimum in the winter. Instead of pews, rows of folding chairs were lined up in the small room. Hard folding chairs that made it difficult to find comfort. An upright piano sat in the corner beside a small organ and a two-piece drum set. The congregation was not large consisting of mostly adults who were the same age as my parents and a few teenagers and some young children running about.

"Praise the Lord." Seemed to be the greeting for this warm and friendly congregation. Immediately Charles saw the kindness and felt the love among them as they accepted him into their fold. The men were dressed in the usual Sunday suits, and the women wore dresses that left everything to the imagination. The dresses were well below the knee, sleeves to the wrist and collars covered their neck. Mother felt underdressed as her sleeves were short and her neck exposed. She recognized immediately that this was one of those holiness churches. She could tell by the way the women were plainly dressed, faces free of any mascara or make-up. She wanted no parts of these "holy rollers" as they were called. She was well-aware of the many stories of pastors who controlled their congregations, telling them what to wear and how to raise their children. She said nothing to dad, but she planned to dedicate the baby and never return to this holiness church again.

The service began with the small choir offering several musical selections. The music was enjoyable as the singers and musicians were in sync. When the singing and rejoicing concluded a big, burly man with graying hair and a white beard approached the lectern. He looked at the small congregation who was eager to hear a Word from the Lord. He leaned over the small podium and said, "Praise God from whom all blessings flow! Let everything that hath breath praise ye the Lord!" The entire congregation jumped to their feet and began clapping, dancing and shouting for joy.

After the congregation settled down the preacher made several announcements about upcoming services. Then he opened a large black Bible. Turning the pages rather swiftly he said, "This morning we're going to talk from one of my favorite books." His voice was rather raspy but strong. The storefront church was not very big, so there was no need for a microphone as his voice was strong enough to carry over the entire room. "To honor the reading of God's holy Word let's stand to our feet and find in your Bibles the Old Testament book of Job. Job chapter thirty-six, verses eleven and twelve."

It didn't take long for my father to blend in with this small congregation. Perhaps it was because some of them reminded him of people from his hometown. Or maybe it was the preacher's love for God that reminded him of his father's relationship with God. He could not exactly state what it was that drew him to this church. But that didn't matter to him, he was just glad he found a place where his soul could be satisfied.

From the word 'go' he was sold out to the Lord. Voraciously he read his Bible. Studying day and night to understand and soak in all that was written by the prophets and apostles. When he came home from work, he would read Bible stories to Russ and Karen animating the stories to hold their interest. On his lunch break, he read. Early morning hours before going to work he read, prayed and cried and then read some more. It was beginning to sink in why his father loved the Word of God so much. He found it difficult to believe anyone could reject God's love. He found reading the Bible to be more satisfying than anything he had ever experienced. For some, the Bible was merely words on a page. Words that made no sense evoked no emotions and had no effect on the reader. But Charles found an unusual amount of peace and joy in those words. Words authored by God Himself and spoke directly to into his life.

Mother was a little slow in accepting Daddy's new lifestyle. She was skeptical about the whole thing and watched him closely waiting for him to become dissatisfied with yet another crowd of friends who failed to meet his high standards. But this never happened. In fact, the longer she waited, the more his discontentment with life disappeared.

Mother did not know how deep my father was into the Bible until one Saturday afternoon when she was returning from her a trip to the market. It was a weather-perfect day, so she decided to walk to the supermarket. The sun was warm on her arms, every so often a slight breeze blew through trees. As she and the kids walked along the busy street she noticed a crowd of people gathered near the park. The crowd was cheering and clapping loudly. She stopped with the children to see what the ruckus was all about. They were too far away to understand what was being said or to see what or who had captured the crowd's attention. Mother was about to ignore it and take her children home when she decided to stop one of the little boys nearby and ask him what was going on. "It's just some man reading from the Bible." Some man … reading the Bible? Immediately mother had a sinking feeling in the pit of her stomach. Charles? It couldn't be. Grabbing her children by the hand she ran across the street, pushing her way through the crowd to get closer. She almost dropped her bag of groceries when she saw her husband standing on a milk crate, reading from the Bible. Her first thought was he must have lost his mind. Mother could not believe her eyes or ears. She had no choice but to call her father in law because her husband had become a religious fanatic. She looked around to study the reaction of the crowd. Did they think he was crazy? Were they just standing there seeing what he would do next? To her surprise, their reactions were none of these. The small group of people gathered around him seemed to be enjoying what they heard. They seemed to be captivated as he read the words from the Bible. To her surprise, the crowd was enjoying his reading, especially the adults and elderly folk. Some had Bibles in hand reading along with him. An occasional comment such as "that's my favorite part' or 'read that verse again' could be heard from the crowd.

She turned her attention back to my father to listen and observe him as he read. My mother had never seen my father give any kind of talk in front of a group of people before. Teaching was his profession back in their hometown, but he had not taught in years. Besides this was different, he wasn't just teaching or just reading, what he was doing could be considered a performance, not play acting. Charles was very serious about every word that flowed from his lips. He read with expression and meaning, as though he penned the words himself. She had not recalled his voice being so full of passion and power.

Suddenly he was shouting loudly his fist raised in the air saying "Repent! Repent for the kingdom of God is at hand!" The small crowd applauded and shouted "Praise God! It's time to repent" and "Tell the truth!" Even little Russell and Karen joined in on the applause clapping their little hands for no other reason than they were excited to see their father, but he did not see them. It seemed that Charles and his audience were oblivious to the fact that they were in the middle of the sidewalk of a busy city where people walked by talking, laughing, playing music none of this bothered them or interrupted their Bible reading session. They were either unaware or unconcerned about the rest of the world walking by shaking their heads or the car horns blowing, kids playing ball in a nearby park. None of these sounds of the streets seemed to interfere with their reading.

She watched as some of the people leaned in closer when he lowered his voice at the tender parts of the passages. Other times he would lift his voice as loud as possible when reading passages that addressed man's sinfulness and the blessings God desired to provide to those who loved Him. He had the crowd's attention, and he knew it. There was a passion and softness in his voice that Iris had not seen until now. My mother closed her eyes and listened as he read verses from the book of Matthew: *"Blessed are the poor in spirit: for theirs is the kingdom of heaven. Blessed are they that mourn: for they shall be comforted. Blessed are the meek: for they shall inherit the earth."* The voice was her husband's but how he spoke was unlike him. She had never heard him talk so affectionately, so lovingly… maybe it was the words he was reading that made him sound different, it had to be the words because her husband was not really the tender or gentle type.

The small crowd interrupted his reading with applause and shouts of praise when hearing these words of blessings flowing from his lips. It was like God Himself was speaking to them. Mother was uncertain how to react to this unusual event. Part of her was proud. She was pleased that her husband could make the Bible *sound* so exciting and alive that people would stop what they were doing and listen to a man read to them. Something they could do for themselves. But there was another feeling bothering her, a feeling she found difficult to ignore. There was an uneasiness that caused her to be concerned for her husband. She had heard of people who became religious fanatics—literally lost their minds from too much studying. They lost sight of reality and became obsessed with understanding biblical mysteries—they abandoned their normal lives, family, friends, jobs. She didn't want this to happen to her husband. She thought her husband had avoided this part of the Woods' family line. She didn't want her children to lose their father. Overcome with anxiety she grabbed Russell and Karen by the hand and took them home before daddy spotted them among the crowd.

She could not wait until this phase of his life was over and done with. He was driving her crazy with his constant talk about the Bible or what the pastor said in his sermon or what did she think of this doctrine or reading various verses and asking her opinions. When he wasn't talking about church, God or the Bible, he was trying to get her or their friends to attend church services with him. It was a never-ending conversation, he was like a man possessed with a one-track mind. Now she finds him in the street standing on a box reading the Bible and screaming at the top of his lungs as though he was Jesus or John the Baptist himself. She was so upset she was almost in tears. She longed for the day when he would finally tire of this church stuff or find some flaw with the pastor or the Bible and move on to something else.

When he came in later that afternoon, smelling of the streets, his skin tanned from the hot sun and his heart on fire for the Lord. He found my mother waiting for him in the kitchen. The house was filled with the sweet aroma of a cake baking in the oven. Mother was leaning against the kitchen counter sipping a cup of coffee. She refused to look his way as he entered the house. An immediate sign to my father that something was amiss. If something was not quite right, if he had upset her in some way, all he had to do was simply observe his wife's body language. Without her saying one word he could determine if she was happy, sad or angry. She had, what he thought were some definite tells that manifested in her body language. A quiet demeanor and her trying hard to ignore his presence were indications that he was in hot water. All the telltale signs were there; she had not greeted him or acknowledged his presence in any way. When she was angry with him, she would become very polite and her words terse. He decided to defuse the potentially volatile situation before it turned into something ugly. Without warning, he walked into the kitchen and grabbed mother around the waist and smothered her face in kisses. If she hit him over the head with the coffee cup or pushed him away he knew it was serious trouble and he would have to take it like a man.

"I don't know what smells better you or that delicious cake baking in the oven." He hugged her tightly. Coffee spilled on her dress, but she didn't mind. Mother allowed his affection and sweet words to disarm her unpleasant mood.

"Charles, you're spilling coffee all over me." She tried her best to retain her anger. But he noticed she did not try to pull away from his embrace.

"I'm sorry honeybun, guess I got a little excited to see you. Here let me wipe it off." He reached for the dish towel, but mother had already retrieved it from the rack and was busy wiping the coffee stains from her dress.

"I sure could use a nice cup of java," he said pouring himself a cup of the lukewarm coffee and watching Iris out of the corner of his eye to assess her temperament and mood. "Where are the kids?" He asked taking a sip from his coffee cup.

She took her time answering his question. An indication that the odd mood had quickly returned. She wanted him to notice that she was more engrossed in wiping off her dress than answering his simple question about their children's whereabouts. The coffee stains were minimal and did not threaten to ruin her dress. Knowing better than try and force her to speak before she was ready my father waited until she was ready to respond. Finally, when she had removed all the coffee stains to her satisfaction mother decided to answer his questions. "Napping." She said avoiding eye contact. She folded the dish towel and placed it on the rack above the sink.

Opening the refrigerator and she removed a package of chicken. Without looking in his direction, she ripped open the package of chicken, and calmly said, "We saw you on Crane street."

Now he was beginning to understand the reason for the cold reception. Apparently, Mother did not approve of what he was *doing* on Crane street. "Oh really? I didn't see you at all, you should have said something or waved at me." He nervously took another sip from his coffee cup, preparing himself for a barrage of questions.

Mother held her peace long as she could when she couldn't stand it any longer, she placed the chicken in the sink and tore into him with one question after another, giving my father no opportunity to provide an answer or explanation.

"Had he gone mad or become a religious fanatic?"

"What would your children think of their father standing on the corner making a spectacle of himself?"

"What sense did it make reading on the streets from a book?"

"If people wanted to hear somebody read the Bible let them go to church."

Remembering she had a cake baking in the oven, mother removed the hot cake pans and placed it on the rack to cool. Setting the potholders on the counter, she continued her tirade. "I don't understand Charles why you would do that? What on earth made you do something as ridiculous as that?" she asked sharply. The look on her face was of disappointment and puzzlement. "I was so embarrassed, for you and our children. I'm so glad they are too young to understand what's going on with you. Don't just stand there looking silly, answer me, what made you do such a foolish thing?"

"God." He answered allowing it to sink in for a minute. He was certain she was not expecting that response. It was true, he wasn't trying to be smart or flippant. "It wasn't me Iris. Wish I could take credit for it, but it wasn't my idea. The Lord said to me one morning 'Get your Bible and go to Crane Avenue.' I did exactly what He said, grabbed my Bible and walked over to Crane. As I stood on the corner watching the people go by, wondering what to do next. He said, "Read." And that's what I did. I opened my Bible and began to read. Starting with the book of Luke, reading all about birth of the Savior of the world, Jesus Christ. On one of the busiest streets in the city. Hottest days of the year. Seemed like the whole city was outdoors getting some sun, shopping, trying to cool off, kids playing in the streets. He could not have picked a better time for me to share His Word with the world."

"Just how long have you been carrying on like that in the street? She asked.

"I'm not sure, I haven't been keeping track ……a few times I would say." He answered hesitantly.

"You should be ashamed of yourself."

"Ashamed? Nothing to be ashamed of. I admit at first, I felt foolish reading out loud on the sidewalk. The more I read, the better I felt. I believe it was the love of God just burning in my heart and I started reading louder and louder. That's when people took notice and stopped to hear what I was saying. After I gave some thought about who I was reading for, and who gave me the assignment, I didn't feel foolish any longer. Iris, I was elated, thrilled that God would ask *me* to do something for *Him*. The average person doesn't think about reading their Bible. Hearing someone else read it to them could motivate them to go home and read it for themselves. I know you think I'm crazy or something, trust me I haven't lost my mind—" He stopped in mid-sentence and thought about what he just said and let out a little chuckle. "I guess I have lost *my* mind, cause now I have the mind of Christ and that's a good thing, not a crazy thing."

He sat down at the table with his half-filled cup of coffee and watched as she quietly continued to prepare their dinner. She did not try to hide her anger as she vigorously stirred pots and chopped vegetables. He knew she did not appreciate or understand his relationship with God, but he was determined to make her understand his love for God if that was possible.

"Iris, I'm doing better than I ever have in my entire life. I have a good job, and a wonderful family that I love coming home to ....but I discovered that's not all there is to life… I now know what life is all about. Russell and Karen will know they have a father who loves God. You're right they don't understand what's going on with me, but one day they will because I'll make sure they understand how their father fell in love with God. That's the most valuable thing I can give to my children, teaching them to love God, just like my father taught me."

Mother removed a knife from the utensils drawer and laid it next to several small onions she had placed on the kitchen counter. She didn't mind her husband going to church and even reading the Bible. She was concerned that he was taking things too far, that he would one day become like his father, a total and complete fanatic. She turned to him, "This is not the life I expected to have with you, Charles. Remember our conversations, the plans we made, the kind of life we planned to have?" she said slicing onions. "You were so worried about forcing religion on our children. The way it was forced on you and your brothers and sisters. You said you wanted to be different from your parents. You said we weren't going to raise our children like your parents raised you – *making* you and your brothers read the Bible, *making* you go to church seven days a week. What happened? Did you forget what we talked about?" Removing several jars of seasoning from the cabinets, she sprinkled various spices, slivers of chopped onion and green peppers over the pieces of chicken and shoved the pan into the oven slamming the oven door so hard it shook the stove and entire countertop area.

"Charles, if you've changed your mind then just let me know. Because that kind of life is not for *my* children or me…in church all day, every day. That's way too much church for me." She sat down at the kitchen table and pulled a bowl of green beans close to her. One by one she angrily snapped the beans in half. "There is more to life than going to church, reading the Bible, praying and talking about Jesus all day. If you aren't careful, you'll have a mental breakdown just like your …... "

"I'm not having a mental breakdown, I'm changing, that's all Iris, growing, evolving. If I were losing my mind, I'd rather be crazy for Jesus.than anything else. Listen to me, I haven't forgotten how we agreed to raise our children. I remember the conversation and I plan to keep my word. I will *not* force God on them. You and I will *teach* our children how to love God. A love that's coerced is not real love." He took a few beans out of the bowl snapped them and removed the strings. "I do think we, as parents must teach our children about God, don't you?" he paused to allow her to answer his question.

She thought awhile before responding. "I guess so----if that's what we believe. But, you know… I'm not much of a believer." She said quietly. "You knew that before you married me."

"You *can* become a believer." He said thoughtfully. Mother gave no response.

"I never imagined that I would become a godly man. Not in my wildest dreams did I see that coming at all." He shook his head in disbelief. "Can you imagine me singing hymns? Can you believe that?" He closed his eyes humming softly.

"No, I can't imagine that." Mother muttered under her breath.

Dad smiled ignoring Mother's remark. "When I was a young man I could care less about God and the church. I had a perspective on God, and it wasn't good. I didn't know the loving, kind God who I'm learning to love more and more. I think it was because I was looking at God through my father's eyes. Through my father's eyes, I saw God as this stern, constricting, uninteresting high and mighty being -----that I wanted no association with at all. But now that I'm a grown man, I see the Lord differently, and I see life from a different perspective especially how mama and daddy raised us. It wasn't so bad. We had more than enough of whatever we needed and even some things we wanted. Sometimes it was sheer torture…so many rules, so many endless nights praying and reading that book they loved so much. Names we could not pronounce, and places we weren't sure if they existed or not. Strangest sayings and the oddest stories. It was a lot of stuff I did not understand nor did I *want* to understand. But now that I'm much older, and I'm on the Lord's side, in retrospect, I see my childhood from a totally different perspective. It's funny how things change once you get a better understanding. My parents didn't have much to offer us in the way of material things. But they made sure we got what they valued most. A love for God. My parent's mistake, although they meant well, was imitating other people in our congregation by forcing us to go to church, pray, read the Bible and pray some more. We were kids, so I guess it was natural to reject it….no one likes anything forced on them. If they had taken a different approach, things might have been different. Guess they were doing all that they knew to do at that time."

Mother sighed and smiled. "Who would have thought, that you would resort to religion. If I close my eyes, I swear I'm talking to Percy Woods. Every day you sound more and more like your father."

"Like my father? Me? Like my daddy?" He laughed at his wife having the nerve to compare his spiritual life with his father's spiritual life. "The Percy Woods you saw was the public side of him, but I lived with the man. And Iris I can only hope to come close to having the kind of discipline my father had in pursuing God and living a righteous life. I have never seen nobody go after God like that." He shook his head in amazement as he reflected over his father's lifestyle. "I was so ignorant about God. I mean I didn't know nothing, went to church three or four times a week and all day on Sunday since I was a boy and I was so uninformed about who God was and what He required of us. I *chose* to be ignorant cause back then I didn't care about God and had no desire to be like my father ..... but I would give anything to talk with Daddy or my mother about their walk with God...... it's too late for that conversation." He said sighing. "Had a living example of Ecclesiastes 12:13 right under my nose and I didn't have a clue."

Mother stopped him, "What is that? What are you talking about?" she questioned.

Without one word, daddy opened his Bible and began flipping the pages until he found the place he wanted and began to read: *"Let us hear the conclusion of the whole matter: Fear God and keep his commandments: for this is the whole duty of man. Ecclesiastes chapter 12 and verse 13."*

Mother rolled her eyes, "I should have known it had something to do with that book." She said flippantly.

My father continued reflecting on his childhood days. "My parents gave their all trying to live out this very scripture, the whole duty of man…fearing God and obeying His commands. As far as I could see that was their whole purpose in life. They weren't the kind who talked a good game and lived a raggedy life, no, no, no, every morning at 4 am I heard them praying and calling on the God. Never heard either one of them lie, cheat or steal. They weren't perfect but awfully close." His voice trailed off as he thought about his father's ways. "Iris my dear I am nowhere near like Percy Lafayette Woods. I do have some of his ways, can't help that because I'm his son, some even say we have the same shape head." He chuckled.

"But I can't touch his spiritual life, no ma'am it was second to none. If you're going to be extreme about something, might as well be for God. He and mother had a zeal and passion that was unstoppable. Seemed like they could not live without God. He was always reading his Bible or praying, and she was somewhere painting scriptures on the walls." He laughed. "What an unusual couple they were. You know, Iris if it's possible, I believe scriptures flowed through their veins if there is such a thing. That's just how committed and passionate they were about their faith. I have a long, long, long way to go before I come close to their level of dedication."

"Almost there if you ask me." Mother said smartly

"Not hardly, not hardly," he said shaking his head. "Got a ways to go." He stood up and stretched his arms. "I sure could use a nap before dinner." He turned to look out the kitchen window at the neighbor's kids playing in the backyard. He smiled as he watched them toss the baseball back and forth.

"You know Iris I have to admit," As he returned to his chair. "There were more times than I care to remember how I felt my parents were a bit obsessive, overdoing it just a bit with the religious beliefs. When I was a boy, my father, grandfather, and uncles and a few of the brothers from the church would come to our house. You remember the pecan tree that grew in our backyard? The one near the barn, that tree was their spot. They used to gather under the shade of the pecan tree with their cups of coffee or soda pop and talk for hours. You think they were talking about who hit a grand slam, or the latest political uprising, or debate who was the fastest running back at Alabama University?"

He laughed, "Are you kidding me? I hoped that their conversations would turn to regular everyday events going on in the world, but they rarely did. Sports of any kind was a waste of time. Percy Woods didn't have time to chase after a ball or spend hours watching Hollywood's latest offerings of what he called fantasies and foolishness."

"Iris, I watched them sometimes for hours on end sitting around that tree debating about what *I* thought was fantasy. Everything they read in the Bible they believed and debated about it. Did the flood cover the whole earth or just part of the earth? Or did Jacob wrestle with an angel or with God? One of their most heated arguments was about the identity of Jesus. Was He God, the Son of God or all three in one? Back then I thought who cares? Who gives a hoot? Nobody cares about that stuff in the Bible. Even if they knew the answers to what I thought was outlandish fairy tales, it wouldn't do anybody a bit of good."

He took another green bean from the bowl and stuck it in his mouth. He chewed on it for a while.

"I was wrong for what I thought back then because I didn't understand them or what it meant to love God. When I was a kid, about eleven or twelve, I came close to hating my parents and despising the church and even God. My heart swelled with bitterness every time I saw my father choose to spend time with his friends talking about the Bible and would not spend ten minutes teaching me how to catch or throw a ball or how to do anything outside of learning about the Bible or running that farm. That used to hurt me so ….." His voice cracked with emotion, Mother sensing his pain, squeezed his arm. He patted her hand and forced himself to smile.

"I promised myself I will not raise my children like that. I'll be committed to God for sure, but life will be different for Russell and little Karen. We'll play ball together. They will learn how to fish if they want to. We'll ride our bicycles together, all four of us. I'll take my children to a movie every now and then. We'll live balanced lives, it won't be all church all the time. I'll make sure Russell and Karen know who God is and how much He loves them. But I'll take time with my children and teach them other things as well. I'll make sure they understand the significance of having God in your life because that's the greatest legacy a father can pass on to his children, the whole duty of man…..fearing and obeying God."

He reached for mother's hands and cupped them in his. "The four of us will enjoy Jesus and life together side by side. What do you think of that?" He kissed her hands.

Mother shrugged her shoulders and turned her attention to her bowl of green beans.

"If I had stayed in Oakdale just one day later, I wonder if I would be the man I am today." Daddy said thoughtfully.

Mother dropped several beans on the table, "The man you are today?" She said incredulously. "Charles, there was nothing wrong with you. I loved you just as you were when I met you a little country bumpkin. You're not perfect, but the Charles

P. M. Smith

Woods I fell in love with is not the man I'm looking at right now. You're so different it's scary….obsessed with God and the Bible, I hear *you* praying and carrying on every morning." Mother began picking up her beans from the table one by one throwing them into the bowl.

"And every time I turn around you've got your nose stuck in that book. And then I find you standing on a milk crate in the middle of the street reading at the top of your lungs in the blazing hot sun like you've lost your mind. This is not what I expected in our marriage, this is not the life I thought we would have together."

"Get it right," Daddy interrupted. "I was not standing in the street. I was standing on the sidewalk, and I wasn't screaming, I was projecting my voice so everybody could hear what I was saying."

Mother pursed her lips and allowed her eyes to slowly roll towards the ceiling.

"There is nothing more important, for me at this point in my life than learning all I can about a God who loved me enough to give His life for me. It may sound corny, clichéd or whatever…. I realize now that my father was right about that scripture he used to quote all the time…*Oh taste and see that the Lord is good. Blessed is the man who trusts in Him.* I just hope that one day you too will see how good God is to you, me and the entire world."

Mother took her bowl of green beans to the sink, pouring them into a pot of cold water.

"Didn't you wonder why we had to move north so abruptly? It was so strange, why our lives were so suddenly interrupted by something that seemed so foolish, -- -- it took a long time for me to understand, but, now I think I get it… I believe God's purpose was for me to discover God for myself, on my own, not through my parents."

"And that *book* as you call it has given me a peace I've never known and I finally have direction for how to live on this God-forsaken earth. The Lord told me to share His Word, and I will continue doing that until He tells me to stop. I want the world to know that God is alive. And this book" he pointed to his Bible lying on the table. "This book is alive, and it's alive in me." He pointed to his chest as he spoke. "God's Word is alive in me, and this precious book, that I love more than life itself is teaching me how to live. I finally know *how* to live, I wasn't living before, I was existing, now I'm truly living."

He began turning the pages of the Bible. "Let me show you something, here read this verse. Read it out loud." He gently took mother's and pulled her from the sink to his chair. She dried her hands on her apron and began reading from the page Daddy had selected.

"Therefore, if any man be in Christ, he is a new creature, old things are passed away behold, all things are become new." She looked at him uncertain of what she read.

"So, you're a new creature? Is that what you're trying to tell me?" She asked hesitantly.

"That's right, once you let God in your life, He slowly and lovingly transforms you from the old person you used to be into the person He planned for you to be from eternity past. That's when real living begins. It's a combination of the Word and God's love making you over until Christ is formed in you. Don't you love the way that sounds….until Christ is formed in you?"

Mother was entirely unmoved by anything he said, but dad continued talking. "That's from the book of Galatians...I'll show it to you later."

"That's okay, I'll take your word for it," she replied softly.

"You remember the night we left Oakdale? Before we drove off, my father told me to live a good life. I never forgot those words. I didn't have a clue what he was talking about. I thought he meant taking care of you, finding a decent job or making a lot of money. I don't think that's what he meant. He didn't say live *the* good life, he said to live *a* good life. There is a difference. Society teaches that *the good life* is fame and fortune and doing everything that pleases the flesh. But what they don't know is the secret to living *a good life* is found in the Bible. It's a secret that's in plain sight. All they have to do is open this book and discover an answer to all of life's problems."

"And when we went to cousin Earl's church, and the preacher read from Job 36:11, the very scripture daddy told me not to forget. I thought I would fall off my chair. So, honeybun, get used to it because this is the way it's going to be for the rest of my life I'm going to serve the Lord."

Mother had never heard my father talk so much about God before in his life. He was never one for religious things. Dad did love to read and discuss things he learned, but this was different. Not only was he reading and learning he was allowing what he read to drastically change his way of thinking and his way of life. She knew he was serious, it was no put-on. There was no way he could turn back into the man he used to be, the man she fell in love with.

""Charles," she said. "I'm a little confused, you told me many times that the "religious gene" was not in your blood, now this... I'm sorry, but I don't understand how could you do this to me, you promised, and now you're letting this religious stuff drive us apart."

He corrected her, "No, it's making me better, and we'll be closer, you'll see. God has given us a better life. For the first time in my life Iris, I have real purpose. All I wanted to do was teach about world history and American history. Now I can teach the world God's history! I love the sound of that. The history of God! Sweetheart, I'm doing something that matters. Not drinking my life away or spending my time listening to foolish men talk about foolish things, that don't amount to a hill of beans. You should have heard the comments from the people when I finished reading. They didn't want me to stop. People *want* to hear God's Word. They want to know that God loves them, that He has not forgotten about them, that He cares about what they're going through and I want to tell them about His goodness long as He allows me."

Mother knew in her heart of hearts this was real. Whenever he talked about his God or the Bible, the excitement in his voice was unmistakable. My father's love for God was genuine. He sounded more sensible and somehow wiser than before. In the past, he had an unpleasant habit of flying off the handle over the smallest things. Always trying to settle arguments with a fist fight or never knowing when to let a quarrel or disagreement go. Maybe Charles had really and truly found religion as the saying goes. Some of his undesirable qualities that disturbed her like his short temper and his proud ways had begun to disappear. There was a noticeable difference in how he interacted with her and the children. He was much more tender, patient and gentle with them. She loved him deeply and didn't want to lose him to the church, nor did she want him to leave her behind.

"Charles sometimes I think about us, you and me, the children... I wonder what's going to happen to us...if we might lose you."

"Lose me? What on earth are you talking about? Lose me to what?"

"To God...and those people at the church," she said hesitantly.

He smiled at the thought of her concern over losing him. "Iris, you're not going to lose me. I promise you this is going to make our life better. This is going to make our love stronger. I promise." He took her hands in his to reassure her.

Maybe it was the fear of losing her husband to the church. The possibility of her husband choosing God and the church over her and their children was always lurking in the recesses of her mind. This is what bothered mother. It wasn't that Charles had found religion, it was the likelihood that she may have to deal with living without him or her husband becoming distant because of his newfound faith or one of those fanatics who sheltered his family from the world.

She knew that Charles was not crazy or had become over excessive with his beliefs. He remained loving and kind to her, and the children and on occasion he invited her to join him at the services, proving he desired her and their family to be involved with his love for godly things. He wasn't trying to exclude her or their children, this was all in her mind.

Mother made up her mind to join him in his quest for this godly lifestyle and to understand his newfound love for the life of holiness. Seeing his passion and love for God made her feel terrible for bad-mouthing his faith, and she told him so. "Charles I'm sorry for criticizing your religious beliefs... but a lot of it I don't understand. Help me. Please help me. Show me how to love God." She asked him. Daddy held her close and promised that he would.

With her mouth, mother said she wanted to know God and promised to attend worship services the next time Daddy planned to go to church, but her actions spoke otherwise. Whenever Daddy asked her to go church with him, there was always an excuse. Either the baby was sick, or she had to work or she was tired from working too much. Soon he stopped asking because he knew she would have an excuse for why she could not attend church with him. Every Sunday morning, daddy and little Russell drove across town to the small store-front church.

But God has His own unique way of getting our attention. One Sunday afternoon Daddy and Russell came home from church. Mother noticed Russ wearing a red wool cap she had never seen before. When she asked Russell who gave him the hat, he replied, "A lady from the church gave it to me." She snatched the cap from his head and inspected it, wondering what lady had the nerve to give *her* child gifts. Then Russell said something that really, set her mind on edge. "Mommy, she gave daddy a gift too. Isn't that right daddy?" Little Russell pointed at his father. Charles let a half smile come across his face. Iris was not amused to learn that an unfamiliar woman was giving gifts to *her* child and *her* husband.

Little Russell pulled on his father's coat jacket insisting that he show his mother the gift he had received from the mystery lady. "Show mommy the gift she gave you daddy." He said innocently.

Of course, Russell an innocent child had no idea the kind of friction he was causing between his parents. Mother looked at Charles who had been observing the interaction between her and Russell and the effect it was having on his wife. Daddy attempted to make light of it all saying it was nothing. Mother held out her hand demanding to see this *gift*. He knew it was wrong to laugh at her or to provoke her in this way, but he could not help but be tickled by her unnecessary anger and jealousy. He removed a small package from his suit jacket. The gift was wrapped in plain white tissue paper and held together with a red ribbon. He laid the poorly wrapped package on the dining room table and walked over to the bassinet, picked up baby Karen and watched mother as she unwrapped the small gift. She tore open the tissue paper and pulled out two blue and white handkerchiefs that reeked of sweet smelling perfume. He knew his wife well enough to understand the look of contempt in her eyes. Still, he made no attempt to calm her down, or ease her troubled mind. Mother threw the package on the table and stomped out of the room. She was enraged at the thought of some woman, church woman or not attempting to encroach on her family and ply her husband and child with cheap drugstore gifts. She was steaming hot, and Daddy knew it. Not wanting to laugh in her face, Daddy took the baby into the kitchen and softly chuckled. The very next Sunday morning Mother was out of the bed before the crack of dawn. She was wearing her prettiest dress and had both children dressed and ready for church.

Unlike my father, mother did not instantly take to the church very quickly. It was a long while before she allowed herself to become comfortable around the congregation. She was slow to embrace their doctrines and beliefs, she wanted to get a complete understanding of what she was getting into. Some of the members made small attempts to show her friendliness, mother was polite but aloof. Eventually, the efforts to befriend her came to an end. The people seemed kind enough, even the woman she suspected of ruining her happy home turned out to be a grandmotherly type who had fell in love with little Russell and enjoyed treating him like her own.

Mother explained that she wanted to fully understand the biblical principles being taught before she gave any thought to becoming a member of the small congregation. The best way to do that was to ask questions and to study the church's literature, which of course was mainly the Bible. Charles gladly took her to the store and allowed her to select a Bible of her choice. She not only selected an excellent study Bible, but she also purchased several theology books on general topics to aid in her studies. On quiet afternoons while baby Karen was napping and little Russell was at school Mother would sit down at the kitchen table with the Bible in one hand and her afternoon drink in the other. Slowly, she began to appreciate and long to apply biblical principles. It gave my father extreme joy to see his wife gradually learn to love God more and more. And for that reason, his love for her grew even more.

That's how it all began my parents love for God and a desire to win souls. With a desire to serve God and help faltering souls everywhere my parents, Charles and Iris Woods became a dynamic team, who from a small band of followers created a flourishing work that began in their living room. Whenever they encountered friends on the street, at the mall or even strangers at PTA meetings or the local grocery store these chance meetings always morphed into mini Bible sessions as they skillfully weaved God's love, kindness, mercy, patience, wisdom, and even judgment into everyday conversations. There was not a person they would not attempt to evangelize telling them of the goodness of God. Rich, poor, small or great if your path crossed Charles and Iris Woods you were destined to hear the salvation story.

After a while, Charles and his former pastor knew the time had come for my father to branch out and start his own work for the Lord. He gladly gave him and mother his blessing. Thus, began the birth of First Deliverance Christian Church. If my father had his way, their church would have been called: THE CHURCH OF HOLINESS,

TRUTH, GRACE AND LOVE. Thankfully, Mother talked him out of using such a long and wordy name. She gently encouraged him instead to *teach* holiness, truth, and love as the standards to live by. She suggested a church should have a memorable or appealing name and reveal that it was a Christian congregation. Daddy took her advice, gave it some thought and much prayer and decided First Deliverance Christian Church would be the name of their newly formed congregation.

The congregation of First Deliverance Christian Church got its start in my parent's living room. It began as a small group of people, comprised mainly of family and friends. Over the years the small group of people steadily multiplied into a substantial congregation of souls dedicated to holy living. One of the reasons for the burgeoning growth of the upstart church was my father's tell-it-like-it-is preaching style. He was not the kind to beat around the bush, he had a straight to the point personality, and it came through in his teaching and preaching. He was the kind of person you didn't ask a question unless you really wanted to hear the truth. If you were looking for flattery or sugar-coated-sweet talk, Charles Woods was not the one to waste your time or his breath.

Since my father was such a direct person, it would stand to reason that his sermons would be hard-hitting, straight talk, no beating around the bush or sugarcoating things. He did not believe in "playing church" if you were going to give your life for God, then do it wholeheartedly or not at all. If someone felt that the rules of First Deliverance were too strict, he would kindly suggest they find a church where they believed in casually serving God. He took his charge as a leader of souls as a serious responsibility. If one was serious about their salvation, there was no such thing as an easygoing walk with God. Philippians 2:12 was his life's mantra. "Work out your own salvation with fear and trembling." He would quote this verse almost every time he got up to preach. He especially emphasized the "fear and trembling" part.

Such hard preaching meant the sermons he delivered were difficult to hear at times. But the people seemed to appreciate his willingness, to tell the truth because they kept coming back for more and they didn't come back alone. Family members, friends, strangers walking down the street were invited to hear the dynamic preaching of pastor Charles P. Woods. They anticipated hearing good gospel preaching that was not watered down and would not only satisfy their souls but also keep them in line with holy living.

Soon after the church was started, word quickly circulated that this church was the real deal. Friends warned each other if you had one foot in the church and the other in the world, then First Deliverance was not the place for you because Pastor Woods was no joke when it came to holy living. If you didn't want to risk being embarrassed as he called out sin and downright ungodliness, you either got your act together or avoided this church until you were good and ready to give up worldly living.

The philosophy of First Deliverance in its infancy was holiness and love. Back then Daddy's favorite scripture was I Peter chapter 1: 15-16 *"But as he which hath called you is holy, so be ye holy in all manner of conversation; Because it is written, Be ye holy; for I am holy."* Almost every sermon he preached was centered around the doctrine of holiness or hell. His straightforward preaching drew people to the church, rousing the hearts of both young and old, the well-off and the not-so-well-to-do. Everyone enjoyed his energetic style of preaching. The ladies would throw their hats and hands in the air, and the men lost all semblance of style as they ran up and down the aisles in exuberant praise of their gracious God. First Deliverance became known around Macklin County as a church where they believed in holiness or hell and Bible living.

By the time, I came into the world, my brother Russell was seven years old and my sister Karen was a five-year-old little girl whose sole purpose in life was trying to keep up with her older brother. I was what some people would call an "oops baby" meaning, my parents had no intentions of having a third child. I was a total surprise to them both. Years later when I was much older and had children of my own, my mother confessed how miserable and depressed she became when discovering she was having another baby.

Of her three pregnancies, she said I was the most difficult. My constant shifting around in the womb caused her much physical discomfort. I changed positions as though it was my mission to find the quickest way out of her belly. Consequently, she got very little sleep and eventually became concerned about the child she was carrying. She thought my constant movement in her stomach could mean one of two things; either I would be an unruly child or her middle-aged body was too frail to handle another pregnancy. She feared she would not carry me to term.

As it turned out her body was in fantastic condition. She delivered a healthy bouncing baby girl weighing six pounds and three ounces. And for the record, I was not an unruly child. In fact, I always believed that I was the joy of my parents' middle-aged years.

MY FATHER'S SHADOW

Before I was born Mom and Dad decided to get the entire family involved when it came to choosing a name for the newest addition to the Woods' family. Everyone wrote down a name they favored and placed it inside of one of Daddy's Fedora hats. Daddy and Mom preferred the name, Vanessa. Karen wanted to name me Rosalind and Russell chose the name Earline, a girl in his class on whom he had a crush. I don't know exactly how it came about, but when Mom pulled the name from the hat, I was destined to be Vanessa Elaine Woods.

Growing up as a young child, one of my favorite things to do was hang around my father. If my mother were busy in the kitchen, I would sit at the table and talk with her or help her in whatever way I could. But, when my father came home, I dropped whatever I was doing and ran to the door to greet him. He would give me a peck on the cheek and at the same time place his oversized fedora on my head. The hat was so large that it completely covered my entire face and Daddy would have to be my "eyes" directing me around the house, to prevent me from bumping into the furniture. Every time I would eventually stumble over something which would make us both laugh then he would pick me up and carry me into the kitchen to say hello to mother.

My favorite part of hanging with daddy would come after his evening nap. When he finally woke up I would locate my picture Bible, a little notepad and make a beeline to his office, eagerly waiting for him to start his work. Daddy would come into the office, place his coffee cup on the desk, let out a loud sigh, stretch his arms, yawn and then take a seat at his desk. I would sit legs crossed on the floor, in the corner watching his every move. The corner floor of his office was my place to sit until my mother purchased a child-sized desk at a yard sale. It was a lovely white junior roll top desk. The handles on the drawers were painted pink and it came with a matching white chair. At the time, I thought it was the most beautiful thing I had ever seen. I loved pulling down the roll top to conceal my books, artwork, various scraps of paper, dolls and other things I treasured. I kept pencils, crayons inside the drawers. How I loved that desk. It holds so many childhood memories. I promised my parents I would never get rid of it. (to this day it is stored away in my attic). When my mother and father brought the desk home, they were going to put it in the room I shared with Karen. I asked if the desk could be placed in daddy's office. At first my mother started to turn down my request, but my father knowing how much time I spent with him in the corner on the floor, he knew that's where the desk should be. He pulled me close to him, patted me on the head and said he and Russ might be able to find a place for my little desk.

I now realize how much of a sacrifice that was for him to allow me to invade his privacy. Most people prefer studying alone, in a secluded spot where they can think, meditate and not be bothered by undesired noise. But my father allowed his little girl to intrude in his space. Of course, I had to promise to be quiet, I was not to bother him with questions, I was not to touch anything on his desk or make any loud, disturbing noises. Complete silence all the while I sat at my desk in the corner of his office. For a young child that was hard, but I did it, all because I wanted to be near him.

So, while he studied from his numerous Bible commentaries or prepared his sermons, I would quietly pretend to read and when he wrote something on a pad. Imitating his every move, I would take out my little notebook and scribble something on a page. After what seemed like several hours, my father would look down at me and say "Sweetpea, let's take a break. My eyes are getting tired." Break times were the best because it usually meant one of two things; either he would tell me a story about his life as a boy in the south or the five of us my mother, brother and sister and would go for a walk. My father said a stroll in the crisp air would help him think. Our family walks almost always ended up at the ice cream parlor.

MY FATHER'S SHADOW

As I look at it from an adult point of view, my relationship with my father as a little girl was the absolute best. Daddy and I were at times inseparable. I wanted to be like him in so many ways. I loved his passion for studying the Bible. I loved his natural ways with people. He made it appear effortless to reach people and help them see the need for God in their lives. My relationship with my mom remained strong and steady and began to flourish after I matured into a young lady. We had a close and loving relationship that lasted well into my adult years. Yes, I was a sheer joy to mom and dad as a youngster.

Although it's been a year or two since we lost them. I still think of mom and dad almost every day. I reminisce about the stories of my grandparents, my parent's life in the south before moving to Michigan. I still mourn their loss. I still miss them both deeply. I miss my mother's friendship, her words of wisdom and her warmth. I would give almost anything to hear my father tell one of his corny jokes and watch him shake with laughter, slapping his knee with every chuckle.

I love them both despite our differences and disagreements. Like my brother and sister I thought they were taken from us way too soon. But who am I to question God and His wisdom? As scripture teaches we are to trust Him in all His ways because God is just and He never makes mistakes.

I must confess my parents were blessed to live very full lives. They didn't suffer long illnesses or battle a prolonged physical disease. My siblings and I did not have to watch them slowly waste away as some incurable illness decayed their bodies or caused their memories to fail. Mom and Dad lived on their own, not in nursing homes, rehab facilities or assisted living complexes. They were both in great physical shape and still had their mental faculties. Dad was just a year shy of turning seventy-five and Mom who never liked to tell her age had just turned seventy-seven. As I look at their lives from a positive perspective, I see just how blessed my mom and dad were. They were blessed to see their grandchildren before they departed this earth. Blessed that they knew God and that He used their lives to fill His kingdom with souls and they were blessed to have three loving children who chose to follow in their footsteps serving in God's kingdom.

Rather than think of the pain and the emptiness that lingers in my heart I force my mind to focus on the good parts of their lives. Of course, we don't see it at the time because we are focusing on the loss or the gravity of the situation we're dealing with —often it's not until years later that we see how good can emerge from bad. In my heart of hearts, I know the Lord had a purpose for taking mom and dad away from us. Although their death was sudden, came without warning for my brother, sister and I it was still heartbreaking and tragic. I knew I just had to trust God's wisdom in this situation.

My husband and children were still asleep I took advantage of this quiet Saturday morning. I was enjoying my second cup of coffee, reading about Elisha's pursuit of his mentor Elijah, in the second chapter of the book of Kings. Typically, my habit was to read a passage or two from the Psalms in the morning. But for some strange reason, I woke up with the prophet Elisha on my mind. Maybe it's because I dreamt of him standing on the banks of the river crying "My father, my father" as his mentor Elijah disappeared in the whirlwind that took him into heaven. Suddenly the dream changed and I was sitting the sanctuary of our church while my father stood behind the lectern. Instead of wearing a suit or his clergy attire, he was wearing a bathrobe. He was pointing and gesturing wildly. I looked around, and I alone was his audience.

This part of the dream startled me, and I awoke with aghast. I wasn't sure what this meant. Why would I dream of my father wearing his bathrobe in the pulpit? And why would I be the only person sitting in the sanctuary?

The unusual dream caused me to turn to the Old Testament book of 2Kings to refresh my mind on Old Testament prophets Elijah and Elisha. I had gotten just past the part where Elijah smote the river with his mantle and was reading of his translation to heaven when I thought I heard the doorbell sound. "Did you hear something?" I questioned Brownie, our little brown and white Jack Russell Terrier. Apparently, he heard nothing because he continued to lie as still as a bump on a log. I listened again to be sure, hoping that it was our next-door neighbor's bell or some stray sound from the streets. I waited a few seconds, when I didn't hear the noise again I settled back on my chaise lounge, took another sip of coffee and admired the red rose trees that lined our patio garden.

Most summer mornings, my family knew exactly where to find me. When I had the opportunity to be alone, our patio became my private outdoor retreat. All I needed was my journal, my Bible, and a hot cup of coffee. Our ground-level patio that spanned the rear of our modest home was a perfect place to de-clutter my mind. Besides the bedroom suite that I shared with my husband, the patio was without question my favorite area of our entire house.

Whenever family or friends visited we would fire up the grill for a backyard barbeque, watch the children play in the pool and just enjoy each other's company. On those really, rare occasions when time permitted, my husband would light a fire in the fire pit, and we would sit under the pool-side pavilion for a quiet, romantic evening. Talking, watching the fire burn and gazing into each other's eyes. It was a perfect getaway right in our own backyard.

P. M. Smith

Winter months, I would seek the Lord's face in a particular corner of our spacious family room. An area by the bay window was a perfect place for prayer, Bible reading and writing my thoughts in the pages of my journal. Early morning hours I could be found in my corner of solitude, pouring out my heart to God.

Sitting here in my patio garden I began to reflect on my life one day in particular. It was a day that my mother and I had an unusual encounter with our own modern-day prophet---we called him our "grocery store prophet." I had not given any thought of the incident in years. "Special gift" were the words the man used many years ago to prepare me for God's plan for my life. I was around ten or eleven at the time. My mother and I were leaving the grocery store when we encountered a strange man who we would later realize was actually a messenger from the Lord. He didn't look anything like you would expect someone sent from God to look like, his clothes were ragged and dirty, covered with stains as though he had been sleeping on the ground. The thin gloves he wore exposed the tips of his fingers to the brittle cold. I felt sorry for him, so I remember asking Mother if we could give him some money. She reached into her purse and gave the man a few dollars.

"Thank you," he said. Then he did something totally unexpected. He said, "Now, I have something for you, little Vanessa."

I had never seen this man before in my life. "How do you know my name?" I asked him.

"God knows everybody's name, even yours." He replied.

Mother cautiously pulled me close to her body not knowing what was on the man's mind. Sensing my mother's apprehension, he said: "Don't be alarmed I'm not going to harm you Mrs. Woods or your child." He kneeled to the ground, his face just a few inches from mine. But I was not afraid. I had no idea what he was going to say or do, but I remember not feeling any fear of being that close to a strange man. He placed his hand on my shoulder, "You are very special in God's eyes and God has given you a very priceless gift, a love for His Word and His people. He is going to use you to save many lives from destruction." *I looked up at mother to see what all this meant. By the look on her face, I could tell she was no longer afraid.*

Continuing to kneel the man directed his next words to my mother, "Your child is destined for great things. God has appointed her to work for Him. There will be those who will try to prevent her or do the work themselves, but it won't fit because God has ordained her to carry on her Father's work." *When he said those last words, he placed his hand on my head. I looked intently into his eyes, and he smiled at me. I glanced up at my mother to see if she understood what he was saying. She was speechless her arm still protectively across my shoulder. But her eyes were fixated on the man as he continued to speak.* "This child has been placed in your care, she is in your charge, never forget that. The Lord has put her in your care for as long as you are alive."

He stood up and said to my mother, "Mrs. Woods, your sister Laura is bedridden, she's been ill for months—don't worry any longer about her health. She's going to live. God has heard your prayers, and your sister is healed of kidney failure. Her healing is proof that my words about your little daughter are true. If you both remain faithful to God, He will do some amazing things in your life." *The mysterious man said nothing more. He thanked mother again for the few dollars and disappeared into the crowd of shoppers.*

On the way to the car, mother was talking to herself and appeared to be crying. Once we were inside the car I asked, "Was that man an angel?"

"I'm not sure sweetheart, I think so----."

"Mommy, how did he know Aunt Laura was sick? Did God tell him?" *I asked.*

"Yes honey, God told him, and God has healed your auntie." She took out a tissue from her purse and cried into the tissue. "Praise God, praise God. Thought I was going to lose my only sister. Oh, thank you, Lord. Thank you, Jesus!"

As a young child, I wasn't sure what it all meant or how to react to the whole situation, so I mimicked my mother and clapped my hands saying "Thank you Jesus" along with her.

"Vanessa," she said looking in the rear-view mirror. "You are never to tell anyone about this or what he said to us. You understand?" She turned around in the seat to look me in the eye. "I just think its best that we keep this between you and I. Alright sweetheart?"

"Not even Karen or Russell?"

"No one Vanessa." She said sternly. I got the message loud and clear. I was not allowed to divulge any of the information to my older brother or sister. They probably wouldn't believe me anyway. But I did want to share the experience with somebody. Certainly, it would be okay to tell Daddy about our encounter with the strange man. He would be excited. He would want to know all the details.

I asked mom, "What about Daddy? God wouldn't mind if we told him, right?"

"Vanessa," she said turning around in her seat again. "If God wants your father to know He will tell him. Now you must promise you will keep this to yourself. Do you understand me?" from the tone of her voice and the look in her eyes I knew she meant business. So, I agreed to keep it to myself.

"Yes, ma'am," I said in a disappointed voice. "I promise not to tell." I really wanted to tell Karen. I promised Mother that I would keep our little secret trusting that she knew what was best. I kept it in my heart for years and years never telling another living soul until years later after I met and married my husband.

The words of the grocery store prophet were forever stored I my heart: *"Destined for greatness"*, *"carry on her Father's work…"* *"special in the eyes of God."* and *"destined for great things"* Every time I recalled his words to me I'm amazed me how the God of this universe selected *me* of all people to serve Him. Back then I was too young to understand the meaning of it all. For weeks, maybe months afterward I remember feeling excited and confused all at the same time. Excited because he said I was destined to do "great things" but what kind of great things? What does that mean? Just how does one prepare for greatness? I knew it was a good thing, but I didn't know what it all entailed. What was I supposed to do? What was my father's work? How should I act and what was so wrong about telling others about it? For the answers to these questions, I relied on my mother. Unfortunately, she was just as unsure as I was, but mother did her best to answer my unending questions. Thankfully, as the years went by the fragments of my life slowly unfolded until I began to see my life heading along a path over which I had no control.

"My Father, my Father," I said out loud. Brownie lifted his little head and tilted it to one side. "I'm not talking to you." I reached down to rub the small brown and white patch on his head. He inched forward and laid his head on my lap.

Looking up at the cloudless blue sky as I pondered about the dream I had of my father. "Lord, what is that about, what does it mean?" I questioned. Why would Dad have on his bathrobe in the pulpit and why would I be the only one sitting in the pews? The way he was flailing his arms and preaching as though the sanctuary was filled to capacity. As hard as I tried, I could not remember one word he said in the dream. What could it mean? Perhaps it had no meaning. Maybe it was just a dream. Thoughts from my subconscious mind coming to surface. Or maybe, just maybe it was God's way of gently nudging me, *be ye also ready* …..

I returned to writing some thoughts in my journal. Just as I began to write, I heard the doorbell again. This time it was much longer and seemed slightly louder. Brownie stirred, lifting his little head, looking up at me as if it was my fault his mid-morning nap was interrupted. Placing my pen in my book I sighed, hating to bring my quiet time to an unexpected end. *Who could be ringing my doorbell this early on a Saturday morning?* I thought as I sauntered through the kitchen. I noticed the clock over the stove said 9:45 AM, way too early for Calvin and the kids to be up and about.

Brownie brushed against my legs as he trotted to the front door. Slowly and cautiously I eased the living room curtains back just a bit so I could see outside the window without my early morning visitors, whoever they were noticing the curtains moving.

As I peeked out of a corner of the curtain, I saw my nine-year-old niece, Zoe leaning against the porch railing. She was struggling to balance an oversized garment bag in her arms. I pulled the curtains back further to see Karen, my sister, my childhood friend Kendra and Karen's friend Tara in the driveway. They knew I would look out the curtain before opening the door so they were all leaning against Karen's car waving and smiling. I opened the door to relieve little Zoe of the large garment bag and to find out what these women wanted this early Saturday morning.

The moment I opened the door Brownie started barking. "Be quiet Brownie, you'll wake up the entire household with your noise." He quieted down and began scraping the screen door with his paws, anxious to get outside.

MY FATHER'S SHADOW

As soon as the door swung open Brownie was all over Zoe, she was just as glad to see him, as he was to see her. "This crazy little dog is so excited to see you, Zoe. Here, give me that garment bag, it's obviously too heavy for you to carry."

"Hi Aunt Vanessa," Zoe said smiling, "Mom said this is for you." She shoved the garment bag at my waist, relieved to get it out of her hands. Then she began playing with Brownie. Taking the garment bag from her, I asked, "What is this Zoe?"

"Mom said she'll call you about it later." She barely glanced my way, her attention was focused on playing with Brownie.

There they stood three grown ladies making a little child strain to carry a heavy garment bag almost twice her size. Seeing the three of them standing in the driveway looking so goofy I couldn't help but laugh out loud.

Karen, my sister, inherited our mother's good looks, my father's sense of humor and his shoot from the hip personality. It seemed the older she got, the more she resembled our mother. Just like Mother, she was tall and had a head full of jet-black curly hair, that was starting to show some signs of graying. I was tall too because height ran in our family. However, I knew I was not blessed with my mother's beauty. I was always told how much I favored my father, his sandy colored skin, the wide-flat nose and the trademark Woods' greenish-gray eyes. I guess I wasn't a bad looking person, just never thought I measured up to Karen or my mother's beauty.

If I had to choose one person as my best friend, I would have to honestly say it is my sister Karen. Although we are entirely different in personalities, I've always felt it was our differences that allowed us to bond from sisters into friends. She can be loyal to a fault, at times brutally honest. We are often each other's emotional support.

P. M. Smith

Our conversations are at times therapeutic because of the level of trust developed over the years into our relationship. We trust each other with our deepest, darkest secrets. Sometimes she makes me laugh until my stomach aches and other times she has the distinct ability to wear on my nerves. Next to Calvin, my husband, I think she knows me best.

Tara was someone I met through Karen. She was Karen's age, and they befriended each other while away at college. Tara was a very lovely, gregarious woman, who never met a stranger. With her sociable and friendly ways, one would never guess she had wealthy parents. Tara and Karen were in some ways alike. They had the same quick wit. Karen had been instrumental in Tara becoming a Christian during their junior year in college. Tara's conservative parents were not exactly excited about their daughter aligning herself with organized religion. They hoped it was a phase in her life that would soon pass. So far, the "phase" has lasted for over thirty years.

Kendra Rogers and I were the same age. They say opposites attract, well sometimes those with similar personalities and interests can also become close lifelong friends. I met Kendra after she and her family moved across the street when I was around nine years old. It's surprising that we became friends at all because we absolutely did not hit it off when we first met. In fact, it took some time for our personalities to click. Kendra was an only child, and I was the youngest in the family, so we were both somewhat bratty, self-centered and used to having our way. Once mom and dad evangelized Kendra's parent's, and they became members of our congregation Kendra, and I saw each other more and more forcing us to learn how to get along.

One day my father got the bright idea that Kendra and I should serve on the youth outreach ministry team. He made sure the leaders placed us both on the same projects, he thought that by working together we would become friends. Our duties were to serve meals to the elderly, assemble and distribute care packages for the homeless and underprivileged children. Witnessing people, especially children our age in such heartbreaking situations caused us to quickly forget about our selfish lives and become more concerned with the needs of others. We had no alternative but to learn how to work together. My father's plan worked it wasn't long before we not only enjoyed working together but also started enjoying each other's company. Our work relationship slowly grew into a friendship. Dad was pleased to discover that she and I made an exceptional evangelizing team.

We were so young and inexperienced back then. We didn't know our left hand from our right so to speak. But we were looking for opportunities to test what we read in the scriptures. It may sound trivial, but we were eager to step out on faith and attempt some of the miraculous acts we read about in the Gospels and the book of Acts. We didn't just want to read about it, we wanted to see God's Word in action. We believed every word Jesus said, if He said we could do what He did, we wanted to try it out and *see* the Holy Spirit at work.

Little did we know that an opportunity to "practice" our undeveloped ministry skills would soon arise and that it would hit close to home. It occurred one summer when Kendra's grandmother, Mrs. Eva Crutcher arrived in town for her yearly vacation. Mrs. Crutcher was the epitome of the word "grandmother." She was your average grandmotherly type, small in stature, bifocal glasses hung on a chain around her neck, her forte was cooking and crocheting. What I remember about her the most is her colorful wig collection. She owned an array of curly wigs in almost every color imaginable. One day her hair would be grey the next day black, then brown, reddish brown. Whenever I visited Kendra, I could count on seeing Mrs. Crutcher in one of two places, either standing over the stove in the kitchen preparing some elaborate meal or sitting on the back porch with a glass of ginger ale, her crochet needles and a bag of yarn. She was a woman of few words. Whenever I came to their home she'd put on her glasses to get a good look at me, after recognizing who I was, she'd smile approvingly, nod her head and go back to whatever she was doing at the time. I used to wonder why she would visit Kendra's family if all she would do was crochet and cook. Who travels hundreds of miles to cook and crochet? She never went anywhere other than church and occasional trips to the store. Day after day she'd be cooking and crocheting. I thought it was such a waste of time, but apparently, it made her happy because this is what she did every visit year after year. The Rogers family seemed to enjoy having her around because they looked forward to her coming. It took some time, but I eventually grew to love this strange, quiet lady and even secretly adopted her as my own grandmother.

One morning during one of her visits, Mrs. Crutcher woke up with extreme pain in her legs and feet. She thought she pushed her body to the limit by cooking too many elaborate meals that called for hours of standing on her feet. Or perhaps it was purely signs of aging. Whatever the cause the discomfort in her legs and feet was unbearable. She found it difficult to walk or stand for very long periods of time without experiencing excruciating pain. Her daughter, Kendra's mom took her to the clinic, the diagnosis was not positive, diabetic nerve pain. She was immediately hospitalized, and the doctors were contemplating amputating her leg. This news upset the entire Rogers' household, especially Kendra who was very fond of her grandmother and didn't want to see her in pain or lose one of her legs. Neither Kendra or I had any idea that this summer and her grandmother's illness would be the spark of a new era in our lives.

I too had come to love Mrs. Crutcher with her unusually quiet ways. I did not want to see my friend upset, and it hurt to hear her grandmother was in such dire pain. Kendra and I sulked around my house depressed and saddened by the disturbing news. When my father learned why we were so upset, he said to us both, "Why are you girls crying and carrying on when you have the power to help Kendra's grandmother? What's the point of reading about Jesus and not doing what He did? Have you ever thought about that?" He walked away leaving us sitting on the porch pondering over his words. It was a light bulb moment for us both as we realized he was right.

That very day we started studying scriptures like crazy. Fasting and praying for strength and increased faith to put into practice all that we had read in the Bible about healing. Finally, we thought we were ready to visit Mrs. Crutcher in the hospital. I brought along my father's little bottle of blessed oil, my pocket New Testament Bible and a prayer cloth. Kendra and I boldly approached the front desk at the hospital and asked for passes to her grandmother's room and without a second glance or any questions from the hospital administration we took the elevator to her floor. When we arrived, Grandmother Crutcher lay in bed her eyes closed appearing to be asleep. When she heard our voices, her little eyes popped open and a huge smile came across her face as she recognized who we were. We gave her the flowers and a get-well card we had purchased in the gift shop. There was a lot of small talk about hospital food and how much she disliked being in a private room with no one to talk to. After a while, I nudged Kendra to remind her of the reason for our visit.

She took her grandmother by the hand and asked her if she would like for us to pray for her. Mrs. Crutcher clasped her hands together and said she would love to have us offer up prayers on her behalf. She mentioned how kind it was that young people knew how to pray. She then sat up in the bed, fixed her hair and straightened her gown as though she wanted to be dressed appropriately, and look her best while we prayed. I removed the bottle of healing oil from my purse and anointed her head in the name of Jesus just as I had seen my father and other ministers do before praying for people. Kendra and I stood on either side of her bed. Mrs. Crutcher closed her eyes. For a few moments, the room was silent as we waited for each other to begin praying. Mrs. Crutcher opened one eye and said she was ready for us to start.

Soon Kendra began praying. I opened my eyes to see Mrs. Crutcher's reaction to the prayer. Her eyes remained closed, head slightly bowed, and her brow was tightly knit as she concentrated on every word her granddaughter said. I watched as a single tear fell down the left side of her face. At the end of the prayer, Kendra opened her eyes to signal me that it was my turn. A little nervous I decided to read from Mark chapter eleven, around verse twenty-two, this was a perfect chapter of Jesus teaching about faith. As I was about to close the Bible, Mrs. Crutcher asked if I would read the passage where Jesus healed Peter's mother in law. She touched my arm, "Baby," She said quietly, "Read all the way to the part where they brought all the sick folk to Jesus to get healed." Obediently, I read the passage and then we began to pray.

Kendra and I placed one hand on her grandmother's shoulder. "Do you want to be healed of diabetes?" I asked. She said of course she did. I closed my eyes again and this time I heard the words of Jesus "….. *you can have what you say.*" Placing my hands on her head and said. "Be healed in Jesus' name." Nothing happened so I repeated the words again. The same result, nothing, no sign of change. After the second time, she opened her eyes and said, "Why don't you try it again dearie? Ask again, it can't hurt to ask once more. I don't want surgery, and I certainly don't want to have my leg amputated. So, let's ask again." She was very serious. I saw in her eyes a look of hopeless and despair that I will never forgot. To this day, I do not know why, but I leaned close to Mrs. Crutcher, placed my hand on the back of her head, and I whispered in her ear, "I command you in the name of Jesus be healed!" Suddenly she began praising God, tears falling from her eyes. "Thank you, Lord! Thank you, Lord!

My leg feels better, the pain is gone." She threw back the blanket and lifted her leg in the air, twisting her foot around for us to see. Then she jumped out of bed and started running around the room. "I'm not going to lose my leg. Thank you, Lord! God, You're so good, so merciful to me." She hugged us both and said, "I'm so glad you girls came and prayed for me."

Days later when Mrs. Crutcher was scheduled for a routine exam, the doctors were shocked to find her blood pressure at a healthy rate and her leg and feet returned to their regular color and size. That was all that Kendra, and I needed to hear, a favorable outcome. Even though we were teenagers at the time, we had faith to believe that every word of the Bible was true. The incident with Kendra's grandmother catapulted Kendra and me into a prayer and healing ministry. If we heard of anyone with the slightest illness, we prayed for them either in their presence or during our private prayer time.

Our prayers for Mrs. Crutcher's healing seemed like eons ago when we were unexpectedly launched into ministry together. Now, decades later standing on my front porch looking at two of my favorite people in the world, Kendra and my sister Karen, along with Karen's friend Tara. As I moved to the porch steps they yelled in unison, "Hey Vanessa" as if on cue. I quickly tried to quiet them down, I was sure they would disturb our neighbors with their boisterous behavior.

Kendra was the first to speak, "I told them you would be awake--- hope we didn't interrupt your quiet time." She said mockingly.

"You did," I laughed "But its ok, come on in."

"We're not going to stay long---- just dropped by for a minute or two," My sister Karen said.

"Morning Vanessa," Tara said loud enough for the entire neighborhood to hear.

"Vanessa, you're the only person I know who has devotions on Saturday morning, everybody else just sleeps in." Karen joked.

I walked further down the steps to the car before we would wake the neighborhood yelling back and forth.

"Where are you going, or coming from?" I asked them.

"Lawrence didn't give you my message?" Karen asked.

"Karen, you know better than to trust a teenager to pass on a message," I said.

"I told him to tell you we're driving out to Summerville and to see if you wanted to ride with us," Karen answered.

"I wished you had sent me a text message. What's going on in Summerville? I asked.

"Tara's dragging us to an art auction, and then we're taking miss Zoe to the mall. It's her birthday next week. I think she wants a bicycle." Karen said.

"Or a puppy," Zoe shouted from the front lawn. She and Brownie were running around in circles.

Remembering I was holding the garment bag I asked. "Karen, what is this?" I held the bag up in the air like a prized trophy.

"Open it and see. Just something I thought you could use." She said leaning on the top of her car. "I've been working on it for a while, finished it last night. Try it on we'll talk later." My sister was an excellent seamstress. She saved us lots of money by sewing clothes for our kids, never once needing a pattern as a guide. All she needed was a picture or a description of the item.

"We came by to drop off that package and to see if you want to meet us at Juno's later on," Karen said.

Juno's was a little café we liked to frequent to enjoy a cup of coffee or a meal and a little girl talk.

"I might be able to do that. What time are you thinking?" I asked. "Around two o'clock or three o'clock is that too early?"

"Don't forget about Audrey," Tara said. "The clinic doesn't close until 4 pm." Audrey was another mutual friend from our church.

"Well--- what about five or six ---is that too late?" Karen said

"I don't have any pressing plans, so five or six is good. Just don't make it too late, you know I have to -- ---'".

Karen interrupted me. "Yea, yea, we know, get ready for church in the morning." Then she laughed.

"At least somebody is trying to be saved…." Kendra said mockingly.

Tapping her watch, Tara reminded them, "The auction starts in forty-five minutes. I don't want somebody to snap up my paintings. My husband would have a fit if I didn't come back with at least two good acquisitions."

We agreed that six o'clock would be a perfect time to meet and give Audrey our other friend, time to get home from the clinic where she worked.

"Don't spend too much money at the auction," I said as they prepared to get back in the car.

"Don't worry we won't," Karen said. "Zoe, step away from the dog."

"Ok Mom, I'm coming. Bye Brownie." Zoe said. Giving the dog one last hug and a pat on the head. He let out a single bark as if to say goodbye.

"Come on little girl we got a lot of running around to do today. Let's go." Karen said opening the car door.

Zoe obediently stopped chasing Brownie. She hugged me around the waist. "I hope you like it." I looked down at her sweet little face. "What are you two up to?" I asked. She smiled as Brownie rubbed against her legs.

"Ok, call me." Karen hollered backing out of the driveway.

"See you later." Kendra and Tara said waving.

Brownie and I stood in the driveway watching Karen's SUV speed down the street. As I held the garment bag, I had to admit I had an idea of what it contained because I knew my sister. And she knew me. "Come on Brownie, let's get inside so I can start breakfast."

The garment bag was rather heavy. How in the world did Zoe manage to hold it for so long? I unzipped it about a third of the way, and a draft of men's cologne hit me in the face. The aroma brought back a flood of memories. I changed my mind and quickly zipped it up and hung the bag in the front closet and closed the closet door. "Out of sight out of mind." I thought.

Weather-wise it was a perfect day to dine on the patio. The sun was beaming brightly not a cloud in the clear blue sky. Every so often, an occasional breeze stirred the branches of our neighbor's weeping willow tree over our fence. Each time the branches would sway in the wind, I imagined they were bowing to the King. The aroma of the red rose trees and Jasmine flowers filled our yard with a sweet floral fragrance and provided a colorful view. Yes, by all appearances I presumed this could be a potentially near perfect day. The weather was cooperative, and the view was spectacular. What could be better than having breakfast with my family under the sun, while taking in such a gorgeous day? Calvin and I along with our children, Melanie and Lawrence, enjoyed late Saturday morning breakfasts. Where we would leisurely enjoy our meals, converse and then order the children to clean the kitchen.

I decided to prepare my family's favorite breakfast of French toast, scrambled egg casserole and crispy bacon along with a fruit salad I had purchased earlier. The aroma of coffee brewing, bacon frying and the casserole baking in the oven would arouse them from their sleep. Especially Calvin, just a hint coffee brewing would stir him from the deepest sleep. Midway through preparing the food Melanie our oldest child, stumbled into the kitchen to give me a hand completing the meal. Since it was such a lovely day, I thought it a good idea to have our breakfast under the pergola. We carried the food to the tables outside. Melanie snapped a few pictures of the table and the pergola for her blog. I had to agree it would make a lovely photograph. Everything was quite charming. It all looked so picture-perfect....I wondered why had such an unsettling feeling in the pit of my stomach. "Are You trying to tell me something?" I muttered under my breath. I ignored the disquieting sensation and joined my family for what I hoped would be a pleasant morning together.

After devouring our meal, we lingered at the table, food long disappeared from our plates and our bellies full, we began discussing our plans for the day. I had kicked off my sandals to relax my bare feet on the wicker ottoman. Lawrence was playing fetch with Brownie throwing a tennis ball, each time he threw the ball, it landed closer and closer to the swimming pool. Calvin was glancing at his newspaper trying to participate in the conversation. Melanie was planning as, usual, to spend our hard-earned money at her favorite stores at the mall.

"Vanessa, honey," Calvin said refilling his coffee cup. "You have whipped up another fantastic meal. Absolutely delicious."

"Yea Mom, I have to say that's the best French toast I've ever had," Lawrence said. "If no one wants the last piece I think I'll take it." He looked around the table before grabbing the toast from the platter.

"Go ahead greedy," Melanie said.

"I'm not greedy. I'm a growing boy," Lawrence replied.

"Emphasis on the word boy," Melanie joked.

"I remember when I could eat four slices of French toast and not regret it," Calvin chuckled patting his stomach. "Not anymore if I want to maintain my svelte figure." He smiled at me.

"Mel, leave Lawrence alone," I passed him the butter and syrup. "Help yourself, honey. You *are* a growing boy, and growing boys need to eat to become young men."

"Mom, the meal was delicious, but, *I* really loved the table setting-----it was so exquisite," Mel said. "I love it when we eat out here."

As in the past, the men of the family would focus on the delectable meal that filled their bellies and my daughter voiced her appreciation for the appealing atmosphere I attempted to create...just as long as everybody was satisfied I was happy.

"Nothing but the best for my family," I said. "Since I cooked, Mel and Lawrence, you two have the honor of doing the dishes."

"I'm glad I got some pictures of the table before we messed it all up," Mel continued. "They are gonna look pretty good on my blog."

"You mean the blog that nobody reads?" Calvin teased her. Melanie playfully threw a napkin at her father.

"That's not true Daddy, the other day I got a few hits, and two people actually commented on my latest article."

Calvin patted my feet. "Honey, what are your plans for today? Thinking about maybe a little reading or studying?" He raised his eyebrows as he spoke. Before I could answer him, Lawrence jumped in.

"Some of my friends are going to the park to work on some new skateboard maneuvers. I was hoping I could meet them if that's ok?" He asked stuffing the last bit of French toast in his mouth.

"Only if all your chores are done," Calvin warned.

"And if the both of you have your clothes ready for church tomorrow," I said to both Mel and Lawrence. "You know how it is around here on Sunday mornings. Make sure everything is clean, ironed, and ready for the morning. So, no skateboarding, blogging or anything else until you're prepared for Sunday morning."

"I'll get my things together right after we finish the dishes," Mel promised.

"Me too, then after the kitchen is clean. I'm looking forward to a free Saturday in the park," Lawrence said tossing the tennis ball in the air.

"I want you home before it gets dark and remember to take your phone," I cautioned him.

"I always have my phone Mom, cause you never know who might call….." he said playfully.

"Might as well leave it at home cause nobody's calling you, but Mom or Dad and maybe me," Melanie said with a sarcastic laugh.

Calvin and I laughed as she kidded her brother. "Whatever---." was Lawrence's weak reply.

"I hope nobody comes by today. I just want to hang around the house and chill," Calvin said. "Depending on how I feel later, I might cut the grass when the sun goes down, and it cools off a bit."

"Well, I'm going to take a hot shower, maybe read for a while. Karen wants me to meet her and the gang at Juno's this evening."

Mel turned to me, "Hey Mom, I thought I heard the doorbell earlier? Was I dreaming?" She asked chewing a bit of bacon from her plate.

"Yes, you did hear the doorbell," I said without looking in her direction.

"The only people I know who rings your doorbell on Saturday mornings, are those people trying to sell their books," Lawrence said

I smiled without any verbal comment. They were waiting for me to add more to the conversation. I deliberately held my tongue.

"Well Mom," Melanie asked. "Who was it? Was it the booksellers or what?" She asked sounding a bit impatient.

"No, it wasn't," I answered. By now it was noticeable that I was trying to avoid answering their questions. Just when I was about to change the subject, Calvin decided he would join the inquiry.

He laid his paper on his lap, a faint smile on his face. "Hon, why are you so vague? You don't want us to know who was at the door?" He asked. "If it wasn't the booksellers hawking their pamphlets then who was it?" I could tell he was becoming a little annoyed at my brief responses.

I knew if I told them it wouldn't go away, they would begin to ask other questions and one thing would lead to another, so I had no choice than to get it over with. I let out a loud sigh. "It was Karen and Zoe, Tara and Kendra," I answered.

"Was that so difficult?" Calvin said almost laughing. "Why were they here so early on Saturday morning? Is everything ok?"

"Yep, everything's fine," I replied.

He wasn't satisfied with my short answers "Well, what did they want, just stopped by to say hello at nine o'clock in the morning?"

I had to decide how deep I wanted to get into this conversation. "Yes, Aunt Karen and Zoe and my friends stopped by to see if I wanted to go out with them later this evening."

"Oh yeah, I forgot to tell you Aunt Karen called the other day," Lawrence suddenly remembered. "Sorry about that mom."

"That's all they wanted? Karen could have called you to ask you that," Calvin said thinking out loud.

I silently allowed him to wonder aloud. "Surely they had another reason for stopping by. What is it that you're not telling us?" Calvin asked. "Come on spill it," He said prompting me to speak.

"Truthfully, it wasn't just a visit. You could say it was more of an errand. Karen dropped off a package." I knew by providing this bit of information I would get a barrage of questions that would lead to even more conversation.

"What kind of package was it?" Calvin inquired.

"I didn't open it." It *was* the truth I told myself, although I did unzip it a little, but had not *opened* it completely.

By now Lawrence and Melanie were curious about the mysterious package.

"Where is it?" Melanie asked. "Why didn't you open it?"

"I didn't want to open it right now. I put it in the front closet and …."

"You want me to get it for you?" Lawrence interrupted.

Before I could answer, Lawrence was running into the house with Brownie barking at his heels. A few minutes later he appeared with the garment bag. "Is this it?" He asked. I shook my head yes and stood to collect the empty dishes and silverware for the dishwasher.

"Is it ok if I open it?" He asked starting to unzip the zipper.

"Wait a minute son," Calvin motioned for Lawrence to give him the garment bag. "I think I know what this is." He sat the bag in his lap a sly little smile on his face.

"Vanessa sit," he ordered. "You can clean the table off later. It's time we told the kids about your, umm..." He was searching for the right word. "...your new responsibility."

Melanie and Lawrence looked at each wondering exactly what their father was talking about.

"Alright, time for an impromptu family meeting," He said

He was right I had been avoiding this long enough. Perhaps talking to the kids would help me in moving forward, a step in the right direction. Calvin and I had discussed it, now it was time to include the rest of the family. They had a right to know because it would significantly affect them as well.

Calvin started first, "Your mother and I have been talking about this for a while and I guess now is a good time to let you two in on the discussion. You're a part of this family, and we want to hear your thoughts."

"Oh no," Melanie said. "Mom, are you sick?"

"I hope it's not cancer," Lawrence said sitting up in his chair.

"No, no," Calvin waved his hands moving the bag from his lap to the table. "Your mother does not have cancer. She is not sick."

"Ohhh, then she must be pregnant," Melanie shrieked. "Mom that's great! I hope it's a girl, I would love to have a little sister ...."

Calvin quickly cut her off. "She's not pregnant either. Thank God."

I decided it was time for me to speak. "Mel. Lawrence, please listen. Let me explain what your father is trying to say. I'm not pregnant and thank God I am not suffering from any illness. I didn't tell you all the complete truth. I did unzip the garment bag earlier, but not all the way, just enough to confirm my suspicions. Your Aunt Karen and I are very different. She likes to face things head on, while I'm a little more hesitant. That's why I stuck the bag in the closet. I didn't want to face this thing just yet. But, this morning I dreamed of your grandfather and then woke up thinking about Elijah and ----then Karen stopping by with this bag------Calvin show them what is inside the garment bag."

Calvin stretched out the garment bag across an empty chair. Brownie hopped on my lap so he wouldn't be left out. Melanie and Lawrence leaned on the table for a better view. As Calvin began unzipping the bag a whiff of my father's Musk cologne filled the air around us. Slowly Calvin lifted the garment out of the bag and held it in the air for everyone to see.

Lawrence was the first to speak. "What is it …a long dress? Is it for you Mom?"

"No. I think it's called a clergy robe," Melanie chimed in. "In fact, it looks like one of Grandpa's robes."

Melanie was right. Calvin carefully laid the robe on top of the garment bag while folding the sleeves across the shoulders. He looked up at me an obvious glow of pride on his face. I reached across the table to touch my father's old robe. I slowly ran my fingers along the smooth, silky material and the gold piping along the sleeves. The memories of Daddy in his robe stirred my mind. I traced the flared crosses embroidered over the breastplate. *"My father, my father……passing the mantle.".* Just seeing my father's robe provoked an abundance of memories. It didn't take much to picture daddy in that very robe as he stood before the congregation delivering the preached Word of God.

"It *is* Grandpa's old robe," Lawrence said "His initials are on the collar. "C.P.W....Charles Preston Woods."

"And there's another set of initials," Lawrence continued. "V.E.C." Lawrence gave me a perplexed look as he figured out the second set of initials. "Vanessa Elaine Collins? Is that you Mom?" he asked in amazement.

I leaned in closer to read the monogrammed label Karen had stitched below the original. She had personalized the robe by sewing my initials right below Daddy's original engraving.

"It's Grandpa's robe alright," Calvin said proudly. "This was one of his favorites, he wore it often." As if reading my mind Calvin began reminiscing about some of Daddy's sermons. "Your grandfather was an excellent preacher, second to none in his day. God used him in such a mighty way. There were times that man could preach the rafters off of the building. When he got started everything in the sanctuary sat up and took notice. Remember the sermon "Jonah's last stand" or "Jesus moves mountains? Those were some of my favorites."

I could see Daddy with the microphone in one hand and the other pointing to the sky, as he proclaimed the good news of Jesus Christ.

Calvin continued, "Those were some of your grandfather's finest moments. Now it's time for the next generation to step up to the plate. And your Aunt Karen had the foresight to repurpose grandpa's robe. I think she has done a fine job. She not only altered the robe to fit your mother, but she has also added some very nice details to it as well. Notice the gold stitching around the hem. She embroidered the words *"for glory and for beauty"* in the pleats of each sleeve and the iconic dove symbolizing the Holy Spirit on the shoulders." He touched each item gently as he spoke. It was a beautiful robe. He was right Karen had done a masterful job on the robe. Adding pleats to the sleeves and the gold trim around the hem made the royal blue look so vibrant and majestic.

"What does... for glory and for beauty mean?" Lawrence asked hesitantly.

"I think it's from the Bible," Melanie responded.

"Yes, it's from the Bible," Calvin said. "It's in the Old Testament, from the book of Exodus." He looked up at the children, "You two should know that maybe we need some more family Bible studies."

Lawrence was still a bit confused. "But what does it *mean*? I know the glory belongs to God...but the beauty part, is that mom?" He asked innocently.

"She's a beauty to me," Calvin laughed. "But, I don't think that's what God had in mind when He wrote these words. The beauty refers to ministry. The beauty of the garment is the honor to serve in God's glorious kingdom. That's the beautiful part. God choosing lowly men and women to serve a holy and righteous God, that's the beauty of holiness. You'll understand when you get older."

"Stand up Vanessa," he said, draping the garment over my shoulders. As the material caressed my shoulders, the feel of it was cold against my skin, and it seemed to be a perfect fit.

"Why on earth would you need Grandpa's clergy robe? Are *you* going to be like a preacher or something?" Lawrence asked.

"Of course, she is dummy," Melanie answered him in a matter of fact tone before Calvin or I could say a word.

"Hey, no name calling," I said.

"Why do you say that Mel?" Calvin asked her.

"Well because..." Melanie began slowly easing to her seat. "Doesn't Mom remind you of Grandpa sometimes? Like I mean, especially when she's teaching or we're talking about the Bible. I know Grandpa and Grandma really wanted Uncle Russ to step in after he died, cause he's their only son..... I never said anything cause I was a kid and no one asked, but Uncle Russ just you know ---he's a great guy and a pretty good preacher, but he never seemed right, I mean he's ok, but I don't know what it is about him... "

I admit I was a bit astonished at her insight, adults are often unaware of what children notice or how carefully they observe people and the way situations evolve in our lives. We think they are oblivious to things going on around them, but their watchful little eyes see more than we give them credit. Melanie was right on many levels, Russell was the oldest child and my father's only son so it was *expected* that he would succeed as the pastor of our growing congregation. It seemed he had everything going for him. For several years, Russ served as my father's assistant at First Deliverance. He was a tall, handsome man who resembled our father in many ways. Like my father, Russell's hair began graying as a young man giving him a distinguished appearance. He inherited the same gap-toothed smile, light greenish-grey eyes and some of daddy's charismatic charm that was especially appealing to the female members of our congregation.

Russ had worked hard to earn his bachelor's degree in psychology. After he married, he went back to school to earn his Ph.D. in Theology. By his education alone, he met all the requirements; he was educated, had the look of a preacher and he was my father's choice. On occasional Sundays, my father allowed Russell to fill in for him from time to time. In the beginning, he struggled to learn how to connect with the people from the pulpit. After extensive coaching from Dad and studying his preaching style along with other prominent ministers who Dad respected. Russ became a capable speaker. Not great, but he learned how to speak well and get the job done.

Although he never quite perfected Dad's moaning and sing-song style of preaching, he discovered how to hold his own. Dad warned him against using too many ten syllable words and complex illustrations that went over the people's heads. He instructed him to keep his sermons at a certain theological level so the people could follow along and not get lost in what dad called his "long lectures."

"...Keep them rejoicing in the aisles they will always come back for more." That was Daddy's way to motivate Russell. For a while it worked, they did come back for more on the rare moments when Daddy would relinquish his pulpit on a Sunday morning. Russell's fan base would be there anxiously awaiting to hear him speak. But soon his admirers began to dwindle, as they realized he was unable to measure up to the usual level of preaching they had become accustomed to hearing.

After Mom and Dad's fatal accident, the board of director's submitted Russell's name to the congregation for consideration as Senior Pastor. Much to his chagrin, he was not elected. Weeks later they began interviewing potential candidates for a fulltime pastorate position. Of course, Russell was hurt and upset by the outcome of the election. He let them know in no uncertain terms that he was offended and threatened to take them to court because by rights he was expected to succeed my father as the pastor. To my knowledge, my father had left no will or anything in writing stating his wishes about the leadership of the church if something were to happen to him. After some time went by Russell realized it was a battle he could not win. We heard nothing more from him about the matter. I often wondered if it finally occurred to Russell that perhaps this was God's doing and not man's.

It was hard for Karen and me to watch our brother go through this difficulty. We said nothing to him about it. Although I'm sure, there were no words we could have said that would comfort him, especially when we agreed with the congregation's decision. Don't misunderstand me I love my brother and will do anything to support him in any way possible. But when it comes to God's business, I believe in doing the will of the Lord. Besides, it seemed that Russ was more enamored with the position and the fringe benefits than he was with serving God and ministering to the people. It appeared that he did not care for souls, for the people. Although he never said it to me, I always suspected that deep down Russ knew it was not in God's plan for him to serve as pastor of First Deliverance.

"I don't know about this Mom," Lawrence said shaking his head. "You're a good teacher and all… but preaching ………." He wisely left the sentence unfinished. "I'm just saying Mom, I mean if Uncle Russ wasn't able to win over the congregation----"

Calvin finished his sentence for him. "You're saying if your Uncle Russ couldn't lead First Deliverance, then your mother doesn't stand a chance either?"

"Think before you answer," Melanie advised him.

"Lawrence, Uncle Russ and your mother are two extremely different people," Calvin said.

"Yea, they're different alright. He's a man and mom is *just* a woman," Lawrence said.

"I'm warning you," Calvin said sternly.

"What do you mean *just* a woman? Her gender has nothing to do with it," Melanie said. "God uses men and women, you moron."

"It's got a lot to do with it," Lawrence answered.

"Son, be careful before you say something you regret, "Calvin warned a second time.

Lawrence ignored his father's warning. He was determined to speak his mind. "That's why Grandpa moved Uncle Russ in as his assistant. He told me he didn't want a female pastoring his church. He said women should never rule over men. He even showed me scripture where God wrote that men are not to be ruled by women."

I decided I should say something since I was the topic of discussion. "Melanie, Lawrence, you're both right. I have a great love for the church and for your Grandparents and the others who helped make it such a thriving congregation. What your Dad and I are trying to say is that God has not just called me to minister but to carry on the church in Grandpa's place." I paused for their reactions.

"You mean as the pastor? Really?" Melanie questioned. "Mom, that's great!" She threw her arms around my neck hugging me as tears formed in her little brown eyes. "It's like you're carrying on Grandpa's legacy. I love it, my mom the pastor," She turned to Calvin…. "What does that make you Dad, her assistant?"

The three of us laughed. Lawrence sat there quietly. The grim look on his face said that he was not too keen on the idea.

"When did they vote you in?" Melanie asked.

"Well, that part hasn't happened. I'm not even sure if the board of directors or Deacon Taylor is aware," I said "Everything is still up in the air. The Lord has spoken to your father and me, now we wait until He opens the door. I suspect it could be very soon. But, whenever it happens, I hope to be ready."

"You'll be ready," Calvin said emphatically.

"Wow, that'll be something seeing you preaching like Grandpa, shaking the microphone and moaning----actually mom I'm not sure I can imagine that," Melanie said wistfully.

"Neither can I," Calvin added. "I think your mother may have a different style of ministry, right hon?"

I didn't respond right away, because I wasn't exactly sure myself. "I really don't know yet," I answered. "I really don't know. But, I plan to be myself, I'm not going to try an imitate anyone, I'll allow God to use my unique personality and gifts."

That was the truth. Like Calvin, I could not see myself preaching in the style of most contemporary preachers. The call and response style, or the moaning and singing in between words ---it was just not me. I loved to hear those who had that gift, and it was my father's style of preaching he perfected it to an art form. He could moan and groan with the best of them, especially when the organist accompanied him he took it to another level. He knew exactly when to pause so the congregation could respond. He knew the right phrases and rhythms to get an emotional reaction from his listening audience. As a young girl, I loved hearing him tell the Bible stories of the creation or recounting the lives of biblical characters. He could tell a Bible story like no one else I knew. My style was entirely different. I knew technique and method were minor things. The most important thing was getting the message across to change lives.

"Mom," Lawrence said sitting with his arms folded and a look of complete disgust on his face. "I just can't get with this, I don't think you're equipped to do something like this."

"I'm not *equipped*?" I repeated. "Just what do you think I'm missing?"

"Well, let's see… first of all, you don't have the time. You're a mother and a wife, you don't have extra time to pastor hundreds of people. It's a lot of responsibility. Why not just concentrate on being a Mom?"

"You mean focus on doing things like making sure your clothes are clean and cooking your meals?" I said sarcastically.

"Exactly!" he said, "I think you should stick to things you're good at."

Calvin and I looked at each other in unbelief. Just when did our son develop these chauvinistic ideas?

"He's afraid he's gonna lose his mommy." Melanie teased in an attempt to lighten the moment.

Lawrence did not try to hide that he was not on board with the idea of his mother becoming involved in the ministry. The day was moving on, and I knew I had much to do so I started giving out orders to clean the breakfast table and clear the pavilion area, hoping to end this conversation and that Lawrence would calm down.

"Come on you two let's clear the table. Lawrence put the dishes in the dishwasher." "Honey?" I said to Calvin, "Will you hang the robe in the closet for me?"

Mel and I began collecting glasses and coffee cups. Lawrence was stacking the empty plates when he started laughing and shaking his head.

"What's so funny?" Calvin asked.

"It's so amazing. I mean it's unbelievable how funny this whole thing is," Lawrence said. "It's funny because it's exactly what Grandpa said you would do."

That explained the chauvinist attitude. "Just what did your grandfather say to you?" I asked him.

"He said that he would barely be in the ground when you would try to move Uncle Russ out of the way and take over his church because of what some phony prophet said."

I was stunned when he mentioned the prophet. No one was supposed to know about that but me and my mother. We had made a pact long ago not to tell anyone about the prophet, including my father. Now Lawrence was saying he heard about the prophet from my father, the very person, I was warned not to tell. All these years I thought it was a secret that no one knew but my mother and me.

"Your grandfather *knew* about the prophet?" I asked wondering why my father would unwisely share this information with a child. So, mom had told him after all. All this time I had kept it to myself. I wondered what else Grandpa had told Lawrence.

"What prophet?" Melanie asked.

This kind of took the wind out of my sails, I had no idea my father was aware of our prophetic encounter at the grocery store. How long did he know? And why did he not say anything to me about it? I gave Melanie the short version of how Mom and I met the homeless looking man at the grocery store who turned out to be a messenger from God. I also explained how the prophet proved he had been sent by God, by prophesying that my mom's sister, Aunt

Laura would be healed of her illness. I hoped that would be the end and they would forget about it or start on another conversation that was totally unrelated. But my young son wasn't through with this discussion.

"Mom," Lawrence said. "Can you explain why Grandpa never saw this so-called prophet? Why didn't God tell *him* about your great calling? Why would God tell you and Grandma?" He asked not attempting to hide the contempt in his voice.

I was trying my best to control my emotions and speak in a steady and calm voice. I am generally patient and longsuffering, but Lawrence's disrespectful behavior was starting to have an effect. "Son," I said picking up glasses and cups, "I can't answer that why don't you ask God to explain His decisions."

"Lawrence, obviously, the prophecy wasn't *for* your grandfather --- he wouldn't have believed it if he heard. Besides, God is not in the business of wasting His prophetic words on unbelieving ears," Calvin said.

"Let me see if I understand," Melanie jumped in the conversation. "Grandpa thought if he made Uncle Russ his assistant pastor, he would be a shoo-in to take over as pastor and this would prevent God from putting someone else to take his place? Boy, that sure backfired on him. He didn't really think that through, did he?"

"It hasn't backfired yet. You'll see Uncle Russ is the *real* pastor," Lawrence retorted angrily. "Because that's what grandpa wanted. He's supposed to be in grandpa's office."

"You're so immature, you don't even know how ridiculous you sound," Melanie said. "It doesn't matter what Grandpa *wanted*. It only matters what God wants. Don't you know anything?"

"Besides, Lawrence I heard that Uncle Russ started his own church a few months ago," Calvin said quietly.

"That makes sense if he wasn't wanted at First Deliverance... he may as well...." Melanie said

"My guess is that he'll be back at First Deliverance one day," Calvin said.

"You're right Dad, he will be back, and when he returns, he can put our church in order. Grandpa said nobody wants a woman preacher. Dad, can't you do something to stop this?' He pleaded with his father.

"Stop it?" Calvin asked. "This is God's doing. It would be foolish to try and interfere with God's plan. Besides, I don't *want* to stop it. I agree with your sister. The legacy has been passed down to your mother. Who knows someday the legacy might be passed to you or Mel or your children. I'm so proud of your mother. I'm glad she's my wife and will one day be my pastor. Very few men can say that and mean it. She will serve as the spiritual leader of our congregation, but I remain the spiritual leader of this house. Maybe you're too young or too spiritually immature to realize the honor it is to be used of God to lead His people----she has my support one hundred percent, and I think your grandfather would be proud of her too----."

Lawrence interrupted. "That's where you're wrong Dad. I know for a fact that Grandpa would *not* be proud of this----" he pointed to the robe laying on the chair. "He wouldn't want a woman wearing his robe, preaching in his pulpit and taking over his church...it wasn't what he wanted for *his* church."

Lawrence's face was red with anger, his eyes watery he was on the verge of crying, and his voice trembled as he spoke. I still could not believe my eyes and ears. I had never seen this emotional side, it caused me to wonder where he was going with this. I passed some water glasses to Melanie but kept my eye on Lawrence to see what he would say next.

"Never mind him, Mom he's just talking out of his head," Melanie said.

I overlooked Melanie's attempt to sweep this under the rug. Calvin was standing behind me with his hands on my shoulders. I presume he thought I might lose my temper and strike the boy. Truthfully, I was glad Calvin was nearby because the more Lawrence talked, the angrier I became.

His tirade continued. "Grandpa said you were insanely jealous of Uncle Russ and that you're not fit to pastor his church. He hated your ideas about running a church., especially how you wanted to add a Bible school, he said people don't want that kind of church. And Grandpa didn't believe that phony story Grandma made up about a prophet at a grocery store. But Grandpa didn't believe it he said it was silly. People would leave First Deliverance in droves if a woman ever pastored his church."

The contempt and anger in his voice made me shudder. Could this be *my* son talking to me like this? Where did this rage come from? It was definitely more than narrow-minded, male chauvinism and teenage angst. He was intentionally cruel. His mind was set to discourage me or perhaps make me even more hesitant about this venture. It was not difficult to see that a demonic spirit was using my son.

"I told you to keep that stuff to yourself. You had to repeat it, didn't you? Sometimes you are just so stupid… " Melanie said to her brother.

MY FATHER'S SHADOW

I was in stark disbelief. How could my father say these horrible things to my own son? "Your grandfather told you this?" I asked quietly.

I turned to my daughter. "Mel, you knew about it too?" I sat down in the nearest chair. Upset with my father for badmouthing me to my own children and upset with Lawrence for believing and repeating my father's unfounded words.

"Mom, don't listen to him he's such a child---- and I'm sure Grandpa didn't mean what he said. I know he didn't," Melanie tried her best to soothe my bruised ego and hurt feelings. It was too late, I felt lower than low.

I knew what he said was true, about my father not wanting me or any woman, for that matter to succeed him as pastor. I gathered from our many conversations that he had little respect for women in authority over men in any capacity. So, it came as no surprise that he was against a female pastoring *his* church. I was furious with my father. Why would a grown man discuss such a mature and sensitive subject with a child, especially when the topic of conversation was the child's mother?

"Lawrence is right when he said Grandpa *would not* be proud of me—" I said fighting back the tears and straining to control my voice.

Calvin was stunned. "Come on Vanessa, how can you say that? You know your father loved you."

"Yes, he did love me. He loved all of us. But, Calvin you know Dad, and I did not see eye to eye on certain things, mainly when it came to First Deliverance. And, it's true he would not have loved the idea of me, a woman standing in his place. This whole thing was not Daddy's wishes, and to a point it saddens me because I loved my father but on the other hand," I turned to look at Lawrence "What your grandfather thought of me and what you or Russ or anyone else thinks of me, good, bad or indifferent will never, ever prevent me from doing God's will."

"I never told anyone this, not even you Cal. But the night my father died. Russ, Karen and I were at his bedside. He was so weak, barely hanging on. It took all the strength he had just to speak. But with his last bit of strength, he called Russell to come closer to the bed. Russell leaned over and put his ear close to Daddy's mouth. His intentions may have been to whisper quietly, but Karen and I heard every word he said to Russell; *'Son, be strong and carry on the church I started* .....Daddy could barely sit up and point his finger in Russell's chest. I always thought he said those words just so I could hear him. He wanted me to know how he felt. Those were the last words I heard my father say."

"In a way, I understand how Daddy felt. Russell was his firstborn child and his only son. It makes perfect sense for his son to inherit the leadership over the church. Corporations do it all the time, Junior is groomed to take over father's company. But in God's kingdom, there's one teeny, tiny little glitch, Grandpa *does not own* the church. The church *belongs* to God, and since we're God's people and its God's church, that means *He* calls the shots. He decides who's in and who's out, not me, your grandfather or Uncle Russell."

"You're my son Lawrence, and I love you. I really do. But I don't love you so much that I'm willing to forfeit God's will for my life just to please you. I love you but not that much. And quite frankly if you don't like it, that's tough. You'll have to deal with me as your pastor for as long as God allows. I plan to serve His people in His church---not *Grandpa's* church."

As Lawrence stood up the tennis ball rolled off the table to the floor and Brownie went after it assuming they were still playing fetch.

Lawrence stood there glaring at me, I suddenly noticed how tall he had grown

"So, that's it? That's your decision? You're just gonna abandon your family to do what you want to do? Is that how little you care about us?" He said with a tremble in his voice and eyes glistening wet. I attempted to touch his arm to console him, but he jerked his arm away from my hand. Calvin gently pushed me back in the chair.

"Shut up Lawrence!" Melanie yelled. "Nobody's abandoning you."

"Look, Lawrence," Calvin said, "I think you're making too big a deal out of this. It's not like your mother is moving across town or out of the country. She's just taking on a bigger role at the church that's all. She's not abandoning you. We'll both be here for you and your sister."

"Yeah right. That's what you say now," Lawrence stated banging a stack of dishes on the table so hard I was sure he had cracked my fine tableware. "We'll see what happens later when Uncle Russ has to come in and rescue you from the mess you'll make of Grandpa's church."

"Lawrence, I'm doing what God has told me to do. I'm not trying to hurt you or to take anything away from Russell."

"What about us? What about me?" He asked, using his t-shirt to wipe the tears from his face.

"What about *you*?" I replied attempting to understand his concern.

"Does it matter that I don't *want* a mother who's a preacher?" He asked. "Does that matter? Did you ever think about that?"

"No," I answered him. "I never gave that a thought, and no it does not matter what you want or what I want because it's not about you or me. It's about what ..." before I could complete my sentence, he cut me off in mid-sentence.

"We all know what it's about, you're all about you. The great Vanessa Collins," He said mockingly as he reached down to pick up his skateboard and helmet from the ground. "That's all that matters to you. Trying to outdo grandpa and Uncle Russell, that's all you ever cared about."

Up until this point, I was disturbed by Lawrence's accusations, thinking they were based on things my father had said. But this was something, different. I never thought he felt this way about me or my working in the church. As I listened to him speak a rage began building up in me that I found hard to control. He was heading out of the pavilion with his skateboard and helmet in hand. As he turned to look at me, I will never forget the look of disgust on his face. My son, my flesh, and blood had never looked at me this way before. This could not be *my son*, not *my* child spewing such hatred and animosity from his mouth.

"Truth hurts doesn't it Mom? Grandpa said you were always jealous of Uncle Russ cause, Grandpa chose him and not you. You're upset 'cause Grandpa favored his son over his daughter," He kept taunting me. "At least he didn't make up some phony story to deceive his own father." By this time, I had stopped trying to hold back the tears.

"What really hurt was the election when you didn't vote for your own brother. Why didn't you vote for him Mom? You said nothing--- you and Dad sat in your seats and said nothing. I was hoping Grandpa was wrong—that you would support your own brother--- but you did nothing. As usual, you just looked out for yourself. Well, you won't have Daddy to rescue you from the mess you'll make of Grandpa's church, you're gonna have to call Uncle Russ to come and fix ....."

Before he could finish his outburst and before we knew what was happening Calvin had collared Lawrence swung him off his feet and pinned him against the nearest column of the pavilion. As Calvin lifted Lawrence off the ground, his skateboard and helmet flew out of his hands. The whole scene seemed to happen in slow motion. His helmet slowly rolled on the ground past the silver bell trees and landed among the shrubbery. The skateboard fell from his hands and crashed loudly against the bluestone tile, bouncing along the walkway until it rolled onto the grass.

Lawrence was tall for his age, but he was not too big or too old for his father to manhandle him when necessary. "Boy, that's your mother and my wife you're talking to." Calvin had his hands tightly around Lawrence's throat and his head plastered against the pavilion wall. Never had I seen my husband this angry with either of our children.

"Having a mother who preaches is not as bad as you think ------- she could be the kind of mother who abuses her kids just for kicks, or supports her drug habits by selling her kids to sexual perverts. You have no idea what it means to be abandoned. You should thank God, every day that your mother loves God and your puny little behind. If I ever hear you talk like that again --- about your mother or Melanie or anyone else in this family, I promise, you'll regret you ever opened your mouth!"

Calvin released his hold around Lawrence's neck. Lawrence slid to the ground, coughing, trying to catch his breath. His face was red, wet and stained with tears. He was shocked, embarrassed and angry.

"Apologize to your mother!" Calvin ordered. Lawrence slowly straightened out his rumpled shirt, removed the dirt from his jeans and wiped the tears on his face. He was moving much too slow for

Calvin. Calvin grabbed by the arm and yelled in his face. "I said to apologize to your mother!" He pointed in my direction.

Lawrence was fuming, but he quietly walked over to where I was sitting and muttered words of apology in my direction. I could not look at him.

Calvin grabbed Lawrence by the shoulder and spun him around to face him. "When you finish the dishes meet me in the garage so you can get started on the grass." Lawrence walked toward the house with his head down, Brownie trotting along at his feet, he stooped to pick up the skateboard and helmet that had fell during the commotion.

He had barely picked it up from the ground when Calvin demanded: "Give me the skateboard!". Lawrence silently passed him the skateboard. I thought Calvin would hold onto it for a while and return it to Lawrence after his anger had subsided, but I think we were all stunned to see what he did next. Calvin took the skateboard, raised it over his head and broke it across his knee. He threw the broken pieces of the skateboard at Lawrence's feet. We watched in silence as Calvin walked away towards the house. Lawrence followed behind him, Melanie continued cleaning the table, I picked up the pieces of the broken skateboard and placed it in the trash.

What a morning! It had started out so beautifully, so peacefully and now this. I was afraid to see how the rest of the day would turn out.

Hearing the roaring sound of the lawn mower coming from the front yard I assumed Calvin had Lawrence cutting the grass. I continued to sit under the pavilion trying to sort out the events from this morning. I could not understand why my father would bad mouth me to my own child? I had never spoken ill of Russell or my father to anyone, especially to my children. It didn't make sense. I knew we had our disagreements about how our church should operate, but for the most part, I kept those conversations I had with my dad to myself.

Calvin came from the side of the house and sat on the ottoman his face glowing with sweat. While he wiped his face, I poured him a glass of iced tea and watched him swallow it with one long gulp. I promptly poured him another. "Hey babe, you alright?" he asked placing the glass on the table.

"I'm fine, I'm just trying to get it together mentally."

I detected a slight tightness in his voice indicating he was still upset.

"You know you can't let him talk to you like that Vanessa. I kept quiet as long as I could until I couldn't stand it any longer. You can't ignore that kind of stuff. He's not your baby boy anymore, he's almost a young man."

"I didn't ignore it Calvin----what do you want me to do? He's never done anything like that before. Melanie may talk back every now and then. Not Lawrence. It completely caught me off guard. I wasn't expecting it."

"He talked to you like you were one of his little friends. For goodness sake Vanessa, the boy is fourteen years old. I don't understand why you can't see what's wrong with that."

Calvin was wrong I did see it. I understood full well the significance of my child respecting me as an adult and as their parent. But, I could not help but wonder...if there was a respectful way to tell your parent, you think they're a phony and a fraud? Even if they say it nicely, it's still painful. Whatever way you cut it, it still hurts.

"Calvin, I do get it. I understand perfectly what you're saying, Lawrence, must respect us, his parents. You get no argument out of me on that. What's surprising is not only that daddy would discuss such a sensitive subject with a child, but also that my child *believed* what he said about me. Is that how he views me as a phony, jealous of Russ? He believed all that garbage was true ----those awful things Daddy said about me—I'm his mother –isn't he supposed to at least defend me? Or come to me and ask me about it? If it had been someone else, someone not a family member, I would understand and I expect that kind of maliciousness from other people--- not Lawrence, not my flesh and blood."

"Don't be so shocked, doesn't the Bible teach us that, *children will rise up against their parents.*" He was right, but hearing that did not help. "Look Vanessa-- you're focusing on the wrong thing." Calvin stood and drank the remainder of his glass of iced tea. "Forget about whether he *believes* it or not, that doesn't matter ---what matters, what's important is what God said to you. Not what your father said or what Russell said about you. It doesn't matter how you felt about Russ. Did God tell you to pastor or not? If so, then you have nothing to worry about. If God didn't call you, then maybe you should be concerned about what Lawrence thinks. Sometimes it irritates me --- because you care more about what other people think about you than what God thinks...."

"That's easy for you to say, Calvin ----- it's not *your* character being maligned, you're not the one being second-guessed by your own child," I said to him.

He took me by the shoulders, sweat dripping from his face. "For once Vanessa, take your mind off yourself ---- look at the big picture then you'll be able to see what's really going on. I'm going to check on Lawrence." He walked away leaving me wondering what he meant by those words.

He knows how it frustrates me when he makes vague statements and then walks away, expecting me to read between the lines. How could I take my mind off myself, when I'm at the center of the confusion? He was focused on one part of the equation and I on another. Although I must admit, Calvin was usually right when it came to handling the children, especially Lawrence. Our children were far from perfect. Of course, we had to correct them and punish them every now and then. But they were never blatantly disrespectful or the type of children who verbally challenged us. Neither of them ever spoke a cross word to me or said hateful things. This was a first.

I knew my children and how to deal with their individual personalities. The day she was born I could tell Melanie would be an inquisitive child. When we brought her home from the hospital, she tried turning her little head every which way to survey her surroundings. Ever since then Melanie has been an outspoken, curious child. She has always been much more vocal than Lawrence. If there was a comment or a question to be made it came from Mel. As mother and daughter, we have had a good relationship. I must admit she and I also experience the most run-ins, as mothers and daughters are prone to do. Usually, we disagree from time to time, but it has never been over anything major, mostly Melanie trying to assert her independence and me reminding her that I'm the parent and she is the child.

With Lawrence, it was different. He was the youngest and a boy, which sometimes makes a big difference. Believe it or not between the two kids he was the more affectionate one. As a little boy, up until about the age of six or seven, every morning Lawrence would jump out of bed and run into the kitchen in his pajamas and bare feet, hug my legs, and say "Morning mommy I love you." Then he would ask for something to eat. It was a sweet morning ritual I loved and looked forward to every day. As a toddler, he would look at me as though I was the most fabulous person in the world. Until he was four or five years old, he hung on my skirt tails following me around the house, in the store, at church, whenever we visited other people. He was there and believe it or not, his constant presence did not bother me, even though I knew one day I would have to cut the proverbial apron strings. He was not ashamed to tell anyone that he was mama's boy. But he was never one to argue or rebel against anything Calvin, or I instructed him to do.

Now, years later, I can see how all of this may have harmed him mentally, emotionally in some small way. As expected he has outgrown some of those childish behaviors that I thought was so cute and adorable.

I tried to give both of my children the same amount of attention. I was careful not to favor one over the other for any reason. Calvin and Karen warned me that I coddled Lawrence too much when he was little. Maybe I did. Perhaps this was the root cause of his outburst. Maybe he relied on me too much and was threatened by the possibility that I may not be as available as I had been in the past. That seemed too simple a solution and not like Lawrence at all. He was developing into an independent young man. No, it was something else, something more profound than that.

As I entered the kitchen, Melanie was inside stacking the dishwasher. "Hey Mom," she said.

"Are you ok?"

"Yes, honey I'm fine." I placed the glasses in the sink and sat on the stool near the island.

"Don't let Lawrence get to you. I hate to say this, but you know he's still a bit of a *mama's boy,* and he practically worshipped the ground Grandpa walked on."

"Do *you* think I'm abandoning my family?" I asked her.

"Of course, not. If I felt that way, I would have said something. I'm excited about your pastoring. I hated how Grandpa would say *my church and my people, my ushers and my this and my that.* I cannot tell you how much it got on my nerves. I wanted to say to him so many times. Grandpa this is God's church, and we are God's people. But I never had the nerve, and I guess I was a little afraid of him. So, to answer your question, no I do not agree with any of the stuff Lawrence said about you being jealous of Uncle Russell or any of that other stuff."

"You know I had to ask, to see if possibly you felt like your brother."

"No way. I think he made that abandoning stuff up off the top of his head. You've always been here mothering us ever since I can remember. Lawrence spent a lot of time with Grandpa, apparently a little too much time. I was always around Grandma hanging out in the kitchen. When Lawrence told me some of the stuff, Grandpa was saying. I couldn't believe he was telling a kid things like that about his mother. I told him to ignore Grandpa because he didn't know what he was talking about."

"You know Mom, this really shouldn't surprise you, I mean Lawrence's rage and Grandpa's lack of faith in you. Jesus warned us that offenses would come and we should expect them even from our family members. Forget about those male chauvinists, Mom.

P. M. Smith

You can depend on Jesus, Dad and me and one day you'll be able to depend on Lawrence too."

"Your father said the same thing ---" I said rather weakly.

"He's right. When we were little kids Grandpa was great to be around ---we had fun with him and Grandma--- but then things changed, and he began talking too much about family issues. I just couldn't take it."

"He wasn't always like that Mel."

"Whenever you and dad sent us over to their house I hung around Grandma or played with the neighborhood kids, anything but listen to that nonsense. Lawrence just ate it up, to this day I don't understand why."

"Why didn't you tell me what was going on?" I asked her.

"Honestly, I thought you knew. I thought you were aware…"

"What made you think that, how could I have known what was going on if you didn't tell me?"

"Well mom, -- you kept sending us over there –so I thought it was okay."

"I thought you two loved going over there. Your grandmother always said how well behaved you were and how they enjoyed you guys being there so….I assumed everything was going great. I didn't know all of this was going on."

"Mom just put it out of your mind. Can't you see it's just a distraction?"

"You're right Mel that's exactly what it is, a major distraction."

Melanie looked around the kitchen. "Well the kitchen is back to normal, think I'll take a shower. I was thinking about writing an article on family disputes for my blog. Do you mind?"

"No, I don't mind. Don't mention names and do not use what happened at breakfast as an example."

"Oh no, I wouldn't do that. I was thinking of something in general, like misunderstandings that occur in family situations…something like that."

"Ok, but make sure I read it before you publish it," I advised.

"Alright I will," She said and went upstairs to her room.

Melanie was right about the fact that we could expect offenses and that the Bible warned that some of our greatest attacks would come from our home, our own flesh and blood. I anticipated opposition. I even expected distractions to pop up and hostility from others possibly in the same field. Persecution is often hardest to accept or deal with when it comes from family because family knows you so well. They know what buttons to push, your weaknesses. Never in my wildest dreams did I think it would come from my own household. It's not that I think my children are perfect or that we are the model, ideal family, we're far from that. We make mistakes and have disagreements all the time. I was not prepared for that and did not see it coming at all.

Maybe that's what Calvin meant by looking at the big picture, that this was a distraction designed to take my mind off the task that lay ahead. I decided it was best to leave Lawrence in the hands of the Lord. I had no time for his adolescent self-centeredness. I had a huge task ahead of me that I knew was coming to fruition any day. If I was to excel at an optimal level, I had to be mentally, spiritually and physically prepared. I refused to lose sleep or spend precious time stressed out about things I could not control. I prayed God would give me the grace not to physically shake some sense into the child and that he would one day accept the fact that this was the Lord's doing and it was going to happen if it was the plan of God.

After talking with Mel, I showered, changed my clothes and put fresh water in Brownie's water bowl. Calvin was watching a baseball game while Brownie lay on the floor wrestling with his chew toy. I informed Calvin that I was leaving for a drive and then to meet Karen at Juno's. The slight nod of his head let me know he had acknowledged my announcement.

I started driving without any specific destination in mind. Sometimes a long quiet drive alone was just the thing to help me sort through my thoughts. I drove along Lakeshore Drive, looking at the calm St Clair River and admiring the huge mansions. Then I aimed my car toward my old neighborhood. Back then and even now it is a proud community of professional people; doctors, preachers, educators and an occasional lawyer or two. The home I grew up in was a traditional southern style home with an elegant wrap around porch, flower boxes in the front windows and thick green lawns. Most of the houses on the block were similar moderate-sized homes. I still loved that house with its huge wrap around porch and the large backyard where I engaged in many childish games and activities.

The whole block looked clean and safe. There were no vacant homes as I could tell. Signs had been posted of neighborhood watches and crime alerts. I brought my car to a stop in front of our old house. The new owners had maintained the grounds but painted it a pale yellow. Mom always loved it in antique white. She felt the antique white was tasteful and pleasing to the eye. Daddy wanted to add a little color, but Mom would not allow it. One year she did permit him to paint the swing and the porch railing a bright red. Boy, the times we had in that house. If I closed my eyes I could picture Karen, Russ and myself chasing each other around the backyard, racing through the streets on our bikes, starting water balloon fights with neighborhood kids and enjoying occasional backyard picnics with my parents.

I smiled thinking of the countless number of hours I spent swaying in the sun on the porch swing with my little playmates or in the mornings waiting for the school bus to arrive. Sometimes I would sit on the swing all alone or after dinner with Mom and Dad. Whenever Dad and I sat on the swing, he would read his newspaper, and within minutes his head would be bobbing up and down as he tried his best to stay awake. The night air and the gentle rocking of the swing would almost always put him to sleep. I would snuggle up close to him on the swing and pretend to read the paper along with him, or he would read me the comics, and we would laugh together.

It was during my college years that I began to assert some of my beliefs about how the church should function. To say the least, this gave my father a fit. Many of our lively discussions were carried out at the dinner table. There were times when daddy and I did not get along so well. Looking back in retrospect, I must admit that most of our struggles may have been my fault. I was trying to help where my assistance was not needed or wanted. I must have inherited his stubborn ways because I didn't learn this right away. I was convinced that *one day* he would see things my way. One day he would come around. Well, that day never came. It took me a long time, years actually, to finally come to the realization that my father was not interested in my assisting him at First Deliverance in any kind of way.

In fact, I recall the day when Dad made it crystal clear that my assisting him would never happen. I was around nineteen years old at the time. In my second or third year of college. I was so young and immature in many, many ways. While away at school I came across some fascinating brochures from another church on campus offering a variety of Bible study classes. I thought this would be an excellent idea for First Deliverance. I bought some of the brochures home and placed them around the house in strategic areas hoping my father would see them, and take the hint to add some theology classes to our regular Bible class or Christian Education program. He found them alright and during dinner one evening he let me know just what he thought about my brochures………..

"Iris, dear, will you pass me some more of those little brown peas, they are so delicious." Daddy said reaching for the bowl.

"They're called Crowder peas. This is not the first time we've had them for dinner." Mother responded as she passed him the bowl.

"You must have done something different with them this time, cause they sure are good---simply delicious. I think your mother is trying to make me into a vegetarian." Daddy said to me, "She thinks I didn't notice there's no meat on the table. But the meal is so delicious I'm not going to complain that there is no meat on my plate." Daddy laughed and continued dishing more peas and sweet potatoes onto his plate.

"By the way Vanessa," he said turning his attention to me. "I would appreciate it if you would stop leaving those leaflets on my desk and

inserting them in my Bible, and all over this house." I started to speak, but he continued talking.

"Don't deny it, young lady, I know it's you. Your mother would never do anything like that. I haven't gotten so old or become so forgetful that I don't know what I'm reading. Pass the butter, Iris."

While Mother passed him the butter I saw it as my opportunity to defend my actions. "Daddy I wasn't going to deny anything. I was going to say that I---."

He cut me off, "I know exactly what you're doing and I tell you right here, and now it's got to stop." He grabbed a piece of cornbread and slathered it with butter.

"Daddy I was going to ask if you had time to read the pamphlets?"

"No, I did not read them."

"Did you even look at them?"

"Didn't have to. I already know what the pamphlets are and I know what you're trying to do. First Deliverance will not become a seminary. How many times do I have to tell you that?" I could see he really didn't want to discuss it any further, but I pressed the matter.

"But Dad can't you see how we can increase Biblical knowledge if we offer more classes on different subjects and modify the children's ministry. There's this great church near the campus where the children are so well-versed in the scriptures it was amazing to see little kids quoting scripture."

Without even looking up from his plate he said: "Well then, why don't you become a member if you like that church so much."

It was a cruel thing to say. Daddy knew I had no desire to move my membership to another church. "I don't want to change churches, I thought if we add more …." He cut me off in mid-sentence.

"We?" He said. "What do you mean 'we' since when did 'we' start pastoring? The 'we' in the equation happens to be me, your brother Russell and the other ministers of the church. Has God called you to pastor Vanessa?" His hand froze in mid-air holding his water glass as he waited for me to respond to his rhetorical question.

I didn't know what to say, so I shoved more food into my mouth. From the corner of my eye, I could see Mother glaring at me, this as a sign to keep quiet. Daddy presumed my silence as a negative response to his question.

"That's what I thought." He looked at me over the top of his glasses. "God does not, I repeat, He does not use women in these capacities. The Bible says a woman should not usurp authority over a man and I agree with what the Bible says, don't you?" He said emphatically

I knew I should have left it at that, but I couldn't help it I had to respond to that last statement.

"Dad, haven't you read what the Apostle Paul wrote in the book of Galatians that there is no male or female in God. God has no respecter of persons. And what about all those women all over the world who God is using to successfully pastor? You're saying God didn't call them and He's not using them? Come on Dad get out of the dark ages, this is the twenty-first century."

"I'm not in the dark ages Vanessa Elaine, I'm in the Bible. If you want, I'll show you the scripture later on. As for all those women all over the world you're talking about, trying to pastor, they're in sin. They're---"

I dropped my fork on my plate. "Daddy! You've got to be kidding me." I looked at Mom to see if she heard this ridiculous statement from her husband. Even she had a look of unbelief on her face.

Daddy wasn't backing down, "That's right you heard me. They are out of line, and anybody who chooses to follow them is heading for destruction right along with their so-called leader. Show me in the Bible where Paul started a church and left a woman in charge. And don't tell me about Aquilla and Priscilla or Phillip and his five daughters. They were not the head of any work started by the Apostle Paul."

"So, you're saying God does not use women in His church?" I asked.

"I'm saying" Dad placed his butter knife on the side of his plate as he spoke. "God does not approve, endorse or support women pastoring over men, they can barely get away with preaching. Your mother agrees with me isn't that right Iris?" He turned his attention to my mother.

Mother tried her best to avoid being roped into our discussion, mainly when the topic was theology or the church. She would silently listen and let us hash it out together. This time was different I could tell by the look on her face, she felt provoked to speak.

"Charles," she said placing her fork on the side of her plate. "Normally I try to stay out of your theological squabbles. But this time you have forced me to tell your baby girl about the female evangelist from Spring Meadows. Charles, you remember her? I think the name of the church was John 3:16 Church of the Living God. We thought that was an interesting name for a church. Remember? Let's see if I can recall her name." Mother looked toward the ceiling pretending to be deep in thought.

Daddy almost choked on his food. "Look, all I asked you to do was to agree with me or not. A simple yes or no will do. Besides Spring Meadows was different----- that was a lucky guess."

"Lucky guess? Charles!" Mother said pointing her fork at him. "I wasn't going to go into detail because I didn't want to embarrass you in front your child. But if you're going to sit there and lie on how the Lord used that woman --then you leave me no choice----."

"Wait minute honeybun, wait a minute. Don't go pulling things from the past. You don't have to tell everything." Daddy started doing some serious backtracking, he was stuttering and calling Mom by the pet name he used when he needed a favor or when he was in deep trouble. I took great pleasure seeing him on the hot seat as he desperately tried to recover. Beads of sweat were forming on his brow a sure sign he was in way over his head.

Mother folded her napkin and placed it on the table. "Vanessa, back in the early 1980's, several years before you were born, your father suffered from severe back pain. It was so painful he could hardly walk or sit comfortably. We prayed and prayed, asking God to heal his back. The pastor and the whole church prayed for God to have mercy on your father. The doctor said the only solution was to operate on his spine, we really began fasting and praying for another option. One day while we were in prayer God spoke to your father and said to go over to this church in Spring Meadows."

Mother was really into her story, gesturing and becoming dramatic. Daddy kept his eyes on his plate.

"We piled your brother and sister in the car and drove forty-five miles out to this quaint, charming little church out in the country. They were the friendliest, holiest group of people I ever met. And they really loved God, you could tell when you walked in the door... something was different about the atmosphere."

"Well, when your father saw there was a female evangelist he immediately said 'Baby let's go home. I don't want to fool with no woman preacher.' Then out of nowhere--- just like that," Mother clapped her hands together. "A sharp pain hit him in the lower region of his back. The pain was so strong —he doubled over, holding onto me with his right hand and clutching his back with the other. I asked him if he still wanted to go home, but the pain changed his mind. He was limping and could not stand up straight without experiencing excruciating pain. Cousin Earl had to guide him in the building." She began chuckling a little. "It wasn't funny at the time because he was really hurting Vanessa, but your father was walking bent over staring at the ground --- Karen and Russ made a game out of it... they started mocking him-- walking bent over too. I had to scold them for making fun of their father."

I laughed and glanced at daddy to see if he was amused. He pretended to be upset I could tell he was enjoying her story as much as I was. "It's not Christ-like to make fun of people, especially when they're suffering from illnesses." He said sipping his coffee. Daddy had stopped eating and was engrossed in mother's story.

"This is how I know it was God because we weren't in that church five minutes, barely sat down in the pew when the evangelist stopped singing and pinpointed your father. It was as though the Holy Spirit spoke to her the moment we entered the building. The Lord gave her a word of knowledge about your father's back pain. She called him out of the audience, made him come to the front of the church. She prayed for him never laying one finger on the man. Just stood there pointing at him and God was speaking through her. While she prayed, I was praying too. All of a sudden --- I heard this noise, at first it was a low rumble, I opened one eye and saw your father, hands in the air, I was for sure he was going to take off in flight." She stopped talking and laughed at the thought. When she calmed down, she continued. "I have never seen your father praise God like that, he felt so good. He was so happy to be free of pain he started running in place right there in the aisle, hands waving in the air high above his head and he was moving."

Noticing Daddy's coffee cup was getting low Mother grabbed the coffee pot and refilled his cup. She remained by his chair and placed her arm around his shoulder. "I knew it was God because the poor thing could hardly walk and here he was running for Jesus. He rejoiced all over that little church. He was so full of joy he set the whole church on fire. We danced and praised God for a long while." She hugged his neck they both laughed as they reminisced. Daddy even shook his head in agreement several times.

She patted him on the back, "He has not had another problem with his back since. Now tell the truth Charles," Daddy looked up at her. "Are you really going to lie on the Holy Ghost just to win an argument and say that God doesn't use women in His church? You know the Holy Spirit used that woman to pray for you and heal your back pain. Remember we stayed for the whole service and she preached fire from heaven? I think your father even enjoyed her preaching but he will never admit it." She replaced the coffee pot on the stove and returned to her seat at the other end of the table.

Daddy pretended to be unmoved by the story. "Aww," he said waving his hand. "That was just one woman, and besides, I don't recall it happening quite like that." He said. "You're embellishing it a bit. I was rejoicing because I was healed. You would have been rejoicing too if you had felt the pain I was feeling."

"Alright then," Mother said. "If I'm exaggerating things, let's call Earl and Gracie. They were there. I'm sure Earl remembers. He might even be able to contact the Evangelist I think she's still around .... " Mother winked at me knowing she was calling Daddy's bluff.

Daddy quietly sat back in his chair with an embarrassed grin on his face. He knew when he was beaten, and Mom was usually the one who could shut him up. Later that evening while my father was relaxing, mom came into the kitchen as I was putting away the last of the dishes. She walked over to the window, pulled the curtains back and said, "I think it's a nice evening for a walk. Why don't you and I take a stroll and enjoy the night air? Ok?" I had a feeling I had no choice in the matter. She passed me a sweater, and I followed her outdoors. She was right it was a lovely fall *evening. An endless array of stars splashed across the sky. The moon was so huge, it looked like you could stick your hand in the air and grab a piece of it if you wanted to. Our street was quiet except for a few barking dogs, and car alarms sounding in the distance. One of the neighbors was out walking his dogs and another was sitting on his porch smoking a cigar. As we walked, Mother spoke of how the bright stars lit up the night sky and how she hoped for a much-needed rainstorm.*

I love taking walks in the evening with your father, sometimes we play a little game to see who can recite the most verses, he usually wins. His favorite verse is that one about man. You know what I'm talk about Vanessa........" I wasn't sure which verse she was referring to, so I remained quiet.

"Let's see, umm your father quotes it a lot,... Now I remember, When I consider thy heavens, the work of thy fingers, the moon and the stars, which thou hast ordained, What is man, that thou art mindful of him? and the son of man, that thou visit him?" Vanessa, when I look at nature, I'm always reminded of God's greatness and how little we really understand Him. Who else but God would think to create brilliant little lights to illuminate the night sky or one giant ball of fire to heat the entire universe? Who thinks like that? Who is that creative, that intelligent? Nobody but God." She said thoughtfully.

Nearing the end of the block, she put her arm through mine and began to slow her pace. I thought she's about to reveal the real reason she dragged me outside for a walk. I knew we were not walking just to survey the neighborhood or to gaze at the stars. I braced myself for what she was about to say. Mother, unlike Daddy, was a woman of few words, but when she spoke one had no choice but to listen because she spoke in such a way that made one want to strongly consider her words.

She began slowly. "You know Vanessa, there was a time when I might have agreed with your father. When we came into the church, it was *unthinkable for women to hold certain positions of authority. The only ministries women headed were the Missionary or the Women's Guild. For a long time, I believed that's what Paul meant when he wrote; 'women keep silent in the church' or 'I forbid that a woman should not be in authority over a man.' As the years went by I noticed how the Lord began using women in various leadership positions. These women had it together. They were intelligent, eloquent speakers, equipped with strong leadership abilities and some of the greatest theological minds. It was mesmerizing to hear them teach or expound on the Word. After seeing this I became a firm believer if God gives you a gift, He intends for you to use it ---for His glory of course. If he intends for you to use it, He will provide the right set of circumstances for you to utilize whatever dream or desire He has placed in your heart. After I saw God using these women in every area of His church, I came to the conclusion that Paul's teaching on women speaking in the church may have been a tradition for that time period rather than a rule for the church to follow. It's hard for me to fathom God gifting a person and never presenting an opportunity for them to use a talent or skill. Why gift someone with leadership abilities or speaking skills and not allow them the chance to use their God-given gifts or talents? That does not make sense, and it does not sound like the God I serve."*

"I know in my heart of hearts the Lord used that Evangelist to heal your father. And I still believe God sent us to that little church so your father could witness with his own eyes God using someone other than a man working in His kingdom. This lady was fantastic. She had it all, she was pastoring the church, had the gift of healing and she could preach like nobody's business. And to top it all off, God sent us to that little country church as an answer to our prayers."

"I'm afraid after all these years your father still has not learned. His eyes are still blinded to the fact that God uses whomever He chooses. That kind of scares me a little bit---- I often wonder what else is your father missing that God may be trying to show him?"

She stopped walking and turned to look at me, "Sweetie, it's almost too late for your father to change, but you, young lady, I want you to stay focused. Hear me good, Vanessa stay focused, or you will miss your opportunity and the promise that was given to you. I'm sure you don't want to forfeit your opportunity to be used of God. Do you?"

"No, of course, I don't want that to happen," I answered her. Still a little confused, I asked, "Mom, how am I getting off track?"

"Leave your father alone!" She said sharply. "Vanessa let him do his thing, his way...you'll have your time. You and I both know that God never makes a promise He does not keep. I know your father's getting old, slowing down. Poor man thinks I can't see just how tired he is. He doesn't have the same energy he had twenty, thirty years ago. It's natural for people to slow down as they age--- for some reason he's got it in his head that he's supernatural. Besides Vanessa, if God did not intend to use you, He would never have sent that angel, prophet or whatever he was to us when you were a little girl."

"If you had told me that something like that happened to you I might have been a little skeptical, but since we both were there -- I heard what the man said, how he knew our names and even knew my sister's name too--- and then God confirmed it by healing my sister. We know God is not a man that he should lie—and He's not playing games with us. All you have to do is be ready when He provides the perfect time for you to do what He has planned. It's just that simple."

"Your father loves you, but he is not an easy man to change. God did not make him privy to His plan for your life. For some reason, He gave the plan to you and me. Let's use wisdom with your father ok? Please stop leaving pamphlets around the house, seems like he's not interested in them or in taking First Deliverance in a different direction. So please stop arguing with him about his leadership style. It's too late in the game to change him. He's too stubborn and too old," She patted me on the hand. "let your father use your brother, and God will use you."

She took hold of my arm again, and we turned back towards our house. "I have two words for you, Vanessa. I want you to remember: information and inspiration---- never forget that. That's the key to taking First Deliverance a little higher in God. We lack balance right now-----you get my meaning?" *She asked.*

Before I could answer, she kept on talking "If you don't understand now you'll get it later. Your father is doing all he knows to do. This generation needs something more than a whoop and hollering. I can see it and truth be told, I believe he see it too. He refuses to admit to me or anyone else he doesn't have the answer. I'm ready for a change myself. It's getting so every time he steps in the pulpit I can almost predict everything he is going to say and do ---- Don't misunderstand me, he's still my favorite preacher—always will be. However, I think his time is coming to an end. Maybe he could be pastor emeritus or something like that. Whatever he decides I'd like to see him go out with some sense of dignity---but he's a different bird sometimes all we can do is continue to pray. Pray for him and your brother Russell, heaven help him."

"Now Vanessa, promise me you'll leave your father alone, let him run the church as he thinks is best—- whatever you do, do not offer him any advice, suggestions or assistance—he has made it painfully clear that he does not want to hear what you think. Alright?"

"Mother I promise not to bother dad anymore," *I said.*

"Thank you! Hopefully, you staying out of your father's church business will keep some peace in our happy little home."

I squeezed her arm a little tighter and said, "Mother what would I do without you?"

"You'd be fine, you would make it, but don't worry, God willing, I plan on being around here for a long, long time to come."

Without warning, she abruptly changed the conversation to our neighbors who lived down the street. "It's been a while since I've seen Roberta and her husband --- I wonder if they're back from their trip. I want you to check on them for me tomorrow before you go back to school and then I need you to take me downtown to the dress shop so I can return a few things........"

That was the last conversation my mother and I had on the grocery store prophet. It amazes me that we never spoke of it more often. Maybe because I didn't dwell on it and neither did she. I went about my normal everyday life, not knowing all the while God was guiding me in the right direction and aligning me with the right people to prepare me for His work.

That was one of the lighter moments of my discussions with my father at the dinner table. There were times when Dad and I engaged in heated debates and not just about women's roles in the church, but church activities in general. As I sat in my car, remembering the days of my youth, I thought of how being in a place can trigger certain emotions, thoughts and old feelings that you thought were gone or had forgotten about.

When I promised mother that I would not interfere with Dad operating his church, I really meant what I said. But my stubborn ways got the better of me, and I could not leave well enough alone. For a while, I was faithful to my promise to my mother, until a few years later, during my senior year of college. I was home on semester break Daddy, and I were talking in his office, I had just finished trimming his hair.......

Dad was sitting in his chair, explaining how he was physically drained and ready to step down as pastor. I had finished trimming his neckline and was brushing stray hairs from his shoulders when he revealed to me that he was considering turning the church over to my brother Russell........ .....

"Baby girl, don't tell your mother this, I don't think she knows yet --- but it seems that I don't have any more to give. I have literally given my all. Time, energy, strength, finances --- yep gave it all to the church." He looked up at me, and it was clear how tired he was. I tried to find some comforting words, but as I looked at his slumped shoulders and the fatigue on his face. I could only agree with him. At one time, he had been a robust, healthy man brimming with energy. But now he had become frail and slow. He was no longer the towering, muscular man I used to admire as a young girl. I still respected and adored him despite our sometimes, rocky relationship. But I was becoming concerned about his health. I removed the towel from his shoulders and passed him a mirror for him to inspect his hair-cut.

"Come on Daddy. Don't talk like that." Was my very feeble attempt to encourage him as I shook the stray hairs from the towel into the trashcan.

"No, no Vanessa, its sweet of you to try and encourage your father. That's what a good daughter should do. However, the old man is just exhausted, worn-out ---seems, I've lost some of my zeal…"

"Your zeal for God?" I asked in disbelief.

"No. That's not what I mean. I don't know why I'm telling you this. Suppose I need someone to confide in. I know I can trust you." He leaned back in his chair and crossed his long legs. *"Don't misunderstand me, Vanessa. I still love the church and the people, that will always be. And my love for God will never fade. The desire to lead has lost its appeal. When I look at all there is still to be done, it's mentally draining. God has allowed me to realize much of my original vision for First Deliverance. We have accomplished a lot of things that he put into my heart. But there remains a lot that has yet to be fulfilled. The Lord always sent help. We have many capable assistants and now that your brother is on board on the ministerial staff that's a great relief to me. You don't know how overjoyed*

I am to have him working right beside me." He clasped his large hands in mine and smiled.

"What concerns me, Vanessa is that it's not just my desire to lead that is fading--- but my desire to preach is decreasing, I didn't know that was possible. It's scary because preaching was my forte. That was all I wanted to do, tell the world about Jesus! I preach now because I have to, it's expected of me. Most of the times once I get into the sermon the tiredness decreases. When I was a young man, I couldn't wait for my turn to share the Gospel, and that wasn't too often back then. But when I got a chance, I tried to put everything I knew into one sermon. I ran the aisles, stood on top of benches, I shook the microphone, whooped, hollered, --- used every illustration that came to mind for one passage of scripture. Sometimes I put too much into one sermon. It's a wonder anybody ever got anything out of it." He laughed shaking his head. *"I was so young back then, so inexperienced--- I didn't know any better, young, brash, foolish."*

He removed his glasses took a handkerchief from his shirt pocket and cleaned his eyeglasses. Without his glasses, the tiredness around his eyes and the heavy bags underneath was quite evident making him look so much older and fatigued. The truth was the man I admired for so long and once thought was invincible was showing signs of aging. Somehow along the way he had gotten old on me. I had never heard him talk of giving up the church. It was no secret that it was his desire for Russell to replace him as the next pastor, but I didn't think he was ready to retire or to give up without a fight. This was not like my father. I set the hair clippers and brushes aside and sat on the edge of his desk. I watched as he struggled to get out of the chair and walk over to the window.

"But Dad you enjoyed serving God and serving the people too. I mean, building the church, the congregation, all the souls you evangelized, marriages you saved. You don't have any regrets, do you?"

"Of course, I loved serving and building God's church. I sure did. As for regrets, well yes, I have plenty of regrets. I could have been a better father and husband, I could have been a better son to my parents. But that's water under the bridge, can't do much about that now. But I'm still working on my fatherhood and husband relationship."

"I didn't always do everything right. I tried to do everything the Lord told me to do, even things that made me look foolish. I did it because I knew He had a purpose in it. It was hard sometimes, enduring the ridicule. People laughed at us when we bought the church in that neighborhood. Said it was a wasteland and that we would starve. But I knew the Lord's voice. He said to purchase that building and that's what we did. You should have seen us fifteen people sitting in that humongous sanctuary. Three or four singers in the choir box. Deacon Taylor tried to make me preach in the small chapel, but I would not do it. Whenever we worshipped in the large sanctuary, I saw visions of faces in the pews. All over the sanctuary. While I was ministering the Word to those fifteen people, supernaturally God showed me hundreds of people sitting around in the pews. Families, children, mothers and fathers. In the spirit, I saw a full congregation long before it materialized. I held onto that vision and never let it go. And I refused to use that small chapel, that would mean giving up on God's vision to grow the church. Sure enough the Lord sent people from all over Michigan. I don't even know where most of them came from. But God sent them and I was more than happy to lead them. I knew the Lord did not call me to preach to no empty pews."

"That was then, I was much younger, much more energetic. Now, I'm not as energetic as I once was. He chuckled to himself, "Long before you were born, Vanessa, there wasn't no better preacher than your father. Got my start reading the scriptures on the street corner, did I ever tell you about that?" He turned around to look at me.

I walked over to the window where he stood. Put my arm around his waist and laid my head on his shoulder. He pulled me close and lightly kissed me on the forehead. "Yes Dad, I remember, but tell me again." It was no secret how much he enjoyed reminiscing about the early days of his ministry. I loved watching his eyes and face light up as he recounted all over again how God used him to win souls. I had heard this story so many times I could tell it in my sleep. Because I knew how much he loved talking about it, I patiently I listened as he began re-telling how God gave him the thought to take the Bible to the people since they refused to come to church. How God led him to read various passages to the pedestrians on Saturday afternoons. I could listen to him tell it a million times because I loved hearing how he came to know and love God.

"Yep," He continued. "Your father went from the street corner to the pulpit, I didn't need to attend seminary or Bible college. My preparation came from the Lord Himself. He taught me, He guided me and put in me everything I needed to know about Him and His Word."

I had to interrupt him, "That's a good thing Dad, there's nothing wrong with acquiring knowledge through your own initiative, but a formal education —like Bible college or a seminary is not a bad idea either --- God works through Bible college teachers too."

"I know that Vanessa. But, you don't have to have that kind of training to be used of God. My point is that I didn't have formal instruction as you call it. I had divine training from on high. People would come from all over Michigan to hear the little preacher from the south. I would make it worth their while too. People used to say that boy came out of the womb preaching. When I finished preaching my clothes would be drenched, my voice so hoarse I could hardly talk and my feet aching from running all over the pulpit ---- some say it shouldn't take all of that, but they don't understand that's how God spoke through me and I loved every minute of it. I loved seeing people rejoice and come to their senses and give up their sinful ways. I didn't desire to travel and evangelize, there were too many in my own neighborhood, in this city, who had strayed away from the church and needed God. Evangelizing in the field wasn't my calling. I aimed to build up the people right here in Macklin County."

P. M. Smith

"I still love seeing people give up their life of sin and come to the Lord. I'll never lose my passion for God, I might grow old and gray, but I will always love the Lord. Passion I got, but energy and drive ------" His voice trailed off as he couldn't bring himself to finish the sentence. My heart went out to him.

"It happens to us all, doesn't it?" He grinned a little as he came to terms with the fact that he was getting older and slowing down. *"Yes, it happens to us all. Aging ballplayers can't run like they used to, singers strain to hit those high notes, and preachers can't preach as hard or as long. Something about aging that takes away your get-up-and-go. You lose motivation. All you do is dream about what was and what could have been."*

It was hard to see how he not only was slowing down but that he failed to understand there were other ways to get the job done. Somehow along the way he believed or was taught that ministry meant one had to exert a great deal of physical energy to preach the Gospel. I believed that ministering the gospel was never intended to be strenuous work. Yes, it was expected that we labor in the Word to hone and perfect our skills. Yes, people should be enlightened and inspired whenever a minister spoke. I wanted to say this to him, but I feared he wouldn't understand or presume, as usual, that I was trying to tell him how to run "his church" when I only desired to see him strengthen First Deliverance and continue his ministry.

"Daddy, you will always be my favorite preacher. It's true, ever since I was a little girl I loved sitting on the front row right next to mom hanging onto your every word. I may not always have understood everything that was going on, but I loved it mostly because you were my daddy and I knew you were preaching the truth about Jesus."

He squeezed my shoulder. *"Little Vanessa Elaine--Daddy's little girl, next to your mother, you were my biggest fan. Karen had her mind on other things and Russ, he was either sleeping or grinning at those little girls. But you, little Vanessa---you were so much like your daddy when it came to having a love for the Word. Hey, do you remember that little white desk, your mother bought for you and we sat in the corner?"*

"How could I forget that? That desk was one of my favorite toys. In fact, I still have it. I will never ever get rid of it."

"Baby girl that was our thing, studying the Bible together. Even when you were a little child. I was always amazed at how much you wanted to study the Bible even as a small child---sure wish I could get your brother to be like that. But oh well—in time, in time."

He patted me on the shoulder and returned to his desk. I stayed at the window looking out into the street. "Russ is alright. He's doing a pretty good job. He'll get better you'll see."

He handed me the clippers, the brush and the other tools used to trim his hair.

"You're absolutely right he will get better because I'll see to it that he learns. My days of being the man in charge are gradually coming to an end. It's getting harder and harder to come up with a fresh sermon, they're all starting to sound alike. Or sometimes the words just don't come, I find myself staring at a blank page for what seems like hours."

"How often does this happen?"

"Oh, I don't know....every once in a while, not every week. Sometimes I preach a rerun hoping no one notices, I try to add a little twist here or there. Some days Vanessa, I am at a loss, and it scares me. It's terrifying that I have no new revelation or the subjects I've preached in the past are becoming stale and warmed over. When I was a young man, I dreamt of preaching, and the Lord put sermons in my mind while I was sleeping or brushing my teeth. But lately, it's a struggle, and sometimes I don't know what to do."

P. M. Smith

I have never viewed my father as a quitter. He was not someone who gave up quickly, primarily when it was something he was determined to accomplish. I put my arm around him as he wiped his face and blew his nose.

"Daddy, have you prayed about this?"

"Of course, I've prayed, fasted and almost pleaded with the Lord....but things remain the same. Don't you worry about me. I'll be alright ---it's just a dry spell or a test of some sort."

"Maybe you're still trying to preach like when you were a young man," I said carefully. "Maybe you should adjust your preaching style to your age. If you slowed down a little or used the other ministers to -----"

"Vanessa?" My father interrupted. "What do you know about preaching? Never preached a day in your life. How can you have the nerve to advise me on something you know nothing about?"

I had offended him with my suggestions, he moved onto another subject before I could respond.

"Hey Vanessa, come over here let me show you something I've been thinking about buying for your mother and me." He pulled a glossy magazine from his desk drawer, a boating magazine. "This little beauty right here, isn't she something?" He pointed to a picture of a sleek white boat. I looked at it smiled and murmured something about it being okay.

"It's been my dream to move back home. I've been thinking of buying a few acres of land in Oakdale City, Alabama for me and your mother. I would love to build a small four-bedroom home with a little lake in the back. I can just picture it----a nice little gazebo where me and your mother sip iced tea and put our feet up in the shade. Maybe have a small vegetable garden, a few chickens, a dog or two. Why I might even buy me a horse. What do you think about that?"

"A horse? Daddy what on earth would you do with a horse?

"I would learn how to ride it of course." He laughed at the absurdity of his statement.

"Vanessa, look at this motorboat, isn't it a beauty? I love how sleek it is, I can see myself at the helm. We'll get us a little boat, take it out on the river, your mother will drive while I fish and nap in the sun. Think she'll like that?" He asked.

"I think she would love a little place in Oakdale, but fishing --- I'm not so sure. I think you're being premature about retiring. You're giving up too soon. Russell doesn't appear to be ready to take your place just yet."

"I'm not saying six months from now or even next year---, I'm thinking maybe five or six years. By then you'll be on your own or married with other things on your mind." He leaned back in the chair spreading the magazine on the desk. "Just give your brother another five years or so, and he'll be well trained and ready to step into the position."

"Dad you don't have to quit preaching altogether, why not just teach more? You have a lot of wisdom you can impart just as well without doing spiritual calisthenics. A lot of that is just tradition. The Word is the Word, no matter how it's delivered. Everybody will understand ----- you're aging, it's a natural part of life."

"You really think it's that's easy, that simple? Girl, you got a lot to learn. Why do you think people come to First Deliverance, to see me sit at a desk and lecture? Walk around with a clipboard and a laser pointing at a blackboard? Those folks would laugh me out of the building, and we would lose all our members to that church down the street. No, baby girl, I think your brother will be just fine. He has to learn some things, but he's smart, and I taught him well."

P. M. Smith

"You should really consider teaching before you just give up Dad."

"Teaching?" He waved his hand in the air. "People like to hear good old-fashioned, preaching-- the kind of preaching they can feel."

"I'm not denying Russell's intelligence or your teaching ability. I'm just saying there are other ways to …."

"Vanessa!" He said slamming his fist on the desk so hard that I jumped in my seat. "When will you learn?"

He walked over to the chair where I sat. He leaned over putting his face so close to mine I could smell the coffee on his breath.

"How many times do I have to tell you First Deliverance is not a Bible college. I have told you time, and time again that will never happen while I'm here on this earth. A bunch of dried up people trying to be deep and talking theology they barely understand. If God wanted us to know Greek, we would have been born speaking Greek and Hebrew. Not at my church. Russ knows exactly what to do, just like I taught him. You just stay out of the way. Keep on teaching your little Sunday school classes, and your Friday night women's services or whatever it is you women do out there. Russ and I got it all under control."

"But Daddy I only want to help you, the people want to learn more. I know they do."

"You're a smart girl, I don't understand why you can't see Vanessa that your help is not needed or wanted! You keep on doing what you're supposed to do, what women are supposed to do--- follow the men. Learn how to follow the men---- the true leaders of the church."

"When you learn how to do that you'll be doing just fine. Now if you don't mind….."He walked to the door and held it open indicating it was time for me to leave. Without another word, I left his office.

"Thank you for trimming my hair." He said as I exited his office.

I had almost reached my room door when he called me from the hallway. "Vanessa?" he said, "Before you go to your room pour me a fresh cup of coffee and cut a slice of that pound cake your mama made if there's some left. Leave it on my desk I'm going to the restroom."

As I started down the stairs, he stopped midway down the hall. "Vanessa?" I stopped on the landing, my back to him. "Turn around and look at me. Cause I want to make sure you understand what I'm about to say."

Reluctantly I turned and looked at him. "I'm tired of talking about this with you. I'm tired of telling you the same thing over and over again. I can't understand why you don't get it. I hope you get it today because we will never have this conversation again, not about the church, your brother's preaching or how I'm leading my church. Russ and I got everything under control. Do you understand?"

"Yes, sir," I responded quietly. "I understand."

He cupped his hand behind his ear, "I didn't hear you."

I repeated that I understood in a louder voice.

"Good! I hope so. Now don't forget my coffee." He went into the bathroom and slammed the door.

He and Russ had it under control? Where was God? Wasn't the body of Christ God's church? I was seething with anger and embarrassed that he would talk to me as though I was a child. The ignorance of that man and his narrow-minded, antiquated thinking was unbelievable. Men, the only real leaders of the church! "Yea right" I trudged into the kitchen slamming cabinets and muttering under my breath. Couldn't he see First Deliverance was dying right before his eyes? Couldn't he see that the congregation wanted more and that there are more ways to deliver the Word than screaming and hollering at the people?

Mother startled me when she came up from the basement with a basket of clean towels. She placed the clothes-basket on a stool near the kitchen island and stood by the counter. She was not pleased.

Before she could utter one word, I started. "Daddy doesn't get it, I tried telling him what needs to be done, but he won't listen to me, he refuses to --."

I expected her to hug me and comfort me the way mothers do when their child is in distress. I hoped she would offer some consoling words to make me feel better. Tell me that I had done the right thing. Silently, she listened to me whine, complain, cry. She let me go on for quite a while until I had my say.

Finally, she spoke, "I suppose you want me to say poor Vanessa? Or belittle your father because he refused to take your advice? You expect me to take your side don't you Vanessa? Quite obviously, you're the one who doesn't get it." Her voice was at a reasonable volume, but the seriousness of the sound of her voice revealed she meant business, and the look in her eyes a combination of disappointment and anger.

"Do you think everybody is going to move over and make way for Vanessa Woods because you've been called to do a work for God? Not even your own father will do that! We've talked about this before, I meant it when I said to leave your father alone. He's not supposed to see what you see! He doesn't want your suggestions! For goodness sake, stop making a fool of yourself and wake up!" She picked up her clothes-basket and left the kitchen.

I poured my father a fresh cup of coffee, removed the cover from the cake stand to reveal a single slice of pound cake. As I placed the slice of cake on a saucer, I contemplated stuffing the entire piece of cake in my mouth.

I knew it would be cruel and mean---but it would feel so good to deprive my father of something he wanted...besides he would never know......I didn't really want cake, I left the slice of cake and a fresh cup of coffee on my father's desk.

That is a night I will always remember, it was my last conversation with daddy about running his church. Soon after we had that unforgettable talk, my father started using Russell more and more on Sunday mornings, even though there were rumblings of displeasure from the congregation. He insisted that this was God's plan for First Deliverance. Years later my parents had their fatal accident. I never disclosed my father's struggle of maintaining his desire to preach or his inability to complete his sermons. Although I think the congregation could tell something was not quite right with him.

We certainly had our differences, but I still loved the man, he was my father. When I was younger, we were the best of friends. In my eyes, he could do no wrong, and there was no one better, stronger or smarter than my Daddy. My father knew everything about everything and could always make me laugh when I was down, help me solve a problem or find a way to lift my spirits whenever I was experiencing disappointment. In many ways, he was my inspiration. I'm not sure he knew how much I looked up to him and sought his approval in almost everything I did.

"Daddy you were something else," I said out loud. "I miss you and mom so much." I continued to look at our old house and reminisce about the good and the not so good times. That *was* the absolute last time mom and I had that conversation. I went on to get married, start a career and have kids of my own. I got so busy in my own life I forgot about my father's ways until Lawrence brought it up at breakfast this morning.

P. M. Smith

I wiped my eyes, blew my nose and slowly moved the car down the street. Lingering at the homes of various neighbors that I remembered from childhood days; like the Harpers who lived next door and across from them were the Pritchard family, who had a house full of unruly children and of course the Rogers a few doors down from us where Kendra lived.

Directly across the street from the Rogers lived Dr. and Mrs. Solomon. Dr. and Mrs. Solomon was an older, somewhat quiet couple who carried themselves in a dignified manner. The husband, Dr. Eason Solomon, taught at one of the universities. He enjoyed sitting on the front porch smoking his pipe, blowing smoke rings in the air as his wife, who was a gardener of sorts cultivated her flower gardens. They never seemed to talk much, he silently sat on the porch, gazing into the sky and puffing on his pipe. Mrs. Roberta Solomon always had a small radio playing music beside her. She and her husband were one of the last original families who continued to live in the neighborhood. Everyone else had either, moved away, died or retired to live out their final days in nursing homes.

During my childhood, Mrs. Solomon *was* our neighborhood watch. Nothing occurred on our block without her knowing it, especially with us kids. She would not hesitate to inform our parents if we were disrespectful, rude or involved in something she knew was against their wishes. As a child, I perceived Mrs. Solomon to be a mean and cruel woman. The kids on my block were always at odds with her, trying to damage her flower gardens or ruin the thick grass that she was so proud of. Whenever she caught us messing with her flowers, she would chase us out of her yard screaming and calling us names. Sometimes we intentionally rode our bikes over her lawn or ran on her grass to retrieve our balls because we knew it irked her so. Behind her back and out of our parent's earshot we called her the "old bat lady," mainly to be spiteful and because she used her son's baseball bat to chase us from her house.

Despite our foolishness with Mrs. Solomon, she and my Mom developed a friendship over the years. Many days I would come home from school to find them in our kitchen talking, laughing, sharing recipes, drinking coffee or reading the scriptures. Once or twice I walked into the house and Mrs. Solomon would be crying into her handkerchief and mother would be attempting to comfort her. Of course, I never knew what made her so upset because my mother made me leave the room or sent me outside. I guess my Mom was the only person Mrs. Solomon had to talk to about her troubles.

It wasn't until I became a teenager that I discovered the main thing that caused much stress in Mrs. Solomon's life was her husband, Dr. Eason Solomon. Dr. Solomon was a well-respected mathematics professor. He was an intelligent, quiet man but his one vice was that he loved to drink. When I was growing up, it was a disgrace to be an alcoholic or to be seen as a sloppy drunk. It was one of those things people swept under the proverbial rug, everyone knew about it but never dared to bring it up in everyday conversation. I always believed it was out of respect for the Solomon's reputation in our community or because I was a child at the time and that wasn't the kind of conversations a young child should overhear.

As a young girl, I witnessed firsthand the effects a drinking problem could have on a marriage, a family and even a community. When I was a teenager, an incident occurred in our home that is forever imprinted in my memory. It was the day we saw another side of who we thought was the mild-mannered, Dr. Eason Solomon our next-door neighbor ....

It was the last weekend of our summer vacation. Kendra and I were thrilled about starting the new school year because we were starting junior high school. Mom and Dad allowed Kendra and I one last sleepover before beginning the new school year. It was a Friday night, Kendra and I were in the family room watching movies, eating pizza, popcorn, drinking sodas and acting as young teenage girls are prone to behave. Daddy had fallen asleep in his recliner with the newspaper over his face. Mother was in her and daddy's bedroom talking on the telephone, every now and then we could hear her laughing and talking.

We were in the middle of our second movie when suddenly we heard footsteps running onto our porch. Then a loud knock on the front door, a frantic, consistent banging as though someone desperately needed help. We could hear a woman's voice yelling "Help me, somebody please, help me." The sudden noise woke my father. Kendra and I ran to the window to see who was beating down our front door. Daddy shooed us away from the window and cautiously opened the front door. It was our neighbor, Mrs. Solomon. She was in her night clothes, her hair tied up in a scarf, she had a bloody lip, and her clothes were ripped. She was sobbing and talking so fast it was hard to understand what she was saying. I immediately ran to get my mother. I was gone only a few minutes, when I returned, Dr. Solomon had followed his wife to our house. He was sloppy drunk, and it was not too difficult to determine they had been fighting. Dr. Solomon was wearing slacks, a brown tie and a white shirt stained with what looked like spaghetti sauce and noodles, there were even a few noodles caught in his hair. He was a wild man. He stood at the threshold of the door waving a wooden meat mallet, taunting his wife, yelling, "Roberta, come back here! I'm gonna get you, Roberta." He was wildly waving the mallet from side to side.

Daddy stood between them as they traded insults. Dr. Solomon called his wife some of the most awful names I had ever heard. Mrs. Solomon kept a safe distance from her husband as she stood behind my father continuing to return the verbal insults at her husband.

Mother tried to calm Mrs. Solomon, but she kept at her husband. It was getting harder and harder for daddy to keep Dr. Solomon away from his wife. He was inching closer and closer to his wife. He was an arm's length away, when Mother yelled at Kendra and me to go into the kitchen, then she grabbed Mrs. Solomon by the shoulders and forcibly drug her into the kitchen and sat her at the kitchen table. Kendra and I obediently ran in behind them but peeked around the corner to see what would happen next.

Once we were out of the room, my father and Dr. Solomon began to physically struggle. Dr, Solomon was a little older than daddy, but he was a strong old man. He was so drunk he could barely keep his balance, but he fought my father as though he had the strength of ten men. Daddy and Dr. Solomon were tussling, knocking over lamps and flower vases. Dr. Solomon was wildly swinging the meat mallet, coming close to daddy's head. He kept calling for Roberta, to come out and face him, waving the wooden meat mallet. He knocked daddy to the floor and got close to entering the kitchen when my father tackled him to the ground and threw him back onto the dining room table. Dr. Solomon swung the mallet with all of his might and the blow caught daddy on the side of his forehead. He winced in pain as blood trickled down the side of his face. Kendra let out a little scream, my mother called on the Lord, and I sunk to my knees and prayed for God to send help.

Mom pulled Mrs. Solomon from the kitchen table to the basement steps. Mrs. Solomon was so frightened she was shaking, mother held her tightly and continued to pray. They sat on the steps watching the scuffle, then my mother closed the basement door shut to hide Mrs. Solomon from her husband. Suddenly a thought came to me to call Kendra's father. I grabbed the phone from the wall and told Kendra to call her father to help my Dad. Hearing the panic and fear in his daughter's voice, Mr. Rogers was at our house before Kendra could hang up the phone, his wife along with him. I breathed a sigh of relief when Mr. Rogers, who was much younger than daddy and in much better shape wasted no time, taking hold of Dr. Solomon around the waist and lifting him in the air. Dr. Solomon somehow gained even more strength, as he freed himself from Mr. Rogers' stronghold and threw Kendra's dad to the floor. Dr. Solomon kept inching towards the kitchen, but dad and Mr. Rogers held him in the living room area. The brawl continued until Mr. Rogers, and my father wore out Dr. Solomon and pinned him to the living room floor where he eventually passed out.

My father slumped to his knees for a moment to catch his breath, then he walked into the kitchen, leaning on the sink he grabbed some paper towel to wipe the sweat and blood from his face. Realizing mother and Mrs. Solomon was still hiding on the basement steps he opened the door and held out his hands to Mrs. Solomon she fell into his arms sobbing. Daddy asked her if she was injured in any way. She shook her head no. He tried to convince her to call the police and report her husband's behavior. She was emphatic about not making a report to the police.

Daddy warned her that next time could be fatal if her husband did not get some help. Mrs. Solomon kept repeating that she did not want to damage her husband's reputation.

"I just want to go home," Mrs. Solomon said sadly. "Just let me go home." Stepping over her husband.

Daddy and Mr. Rogers carried Dr. Solomon's limp body back to his house. Mother tried to persuade Mrs. Solomon to stay with us until the morning, but Mrs. Solomon refused. She pulled herself together told Mother she felt it best to be at home with her husband. Kendra and I stood on the sidewalk watching my Mom and Mrs. Rogers escort Mrs. Solomon all the way to her house. Kendra's parents decided she should be at home with them sleeping in her own bed.

I remember being both embarrassed and terrified for Mrs. Solomon. Embarrassed for obvious reasons. The shame and humiliation she felt. No one else on our block witnessed the incident, but because we saw it that was enough to cause disgrace and embarrassment to a proud woman like Mrs. Solomon. I was terrified for her because this wild, abusive, name-calling side of Dr. Solomon was a great mystery to me. I was shocked to see him behave in that way, he never, ever raised his voice, always had *a smile on his face and appeared to be a kind man who, I thought really loved his wife. Apparently, things were very different when Mr. & Mrs. Solomon were alone, and he had one too many. It baffled me how such a mild-mannered person could become so violent. I could not imagine what it was like to live in a house with someone like that—quiet, reserved one moment and a few drinks later would transform into a raging bull ready to slay everything in sight.*

Later that night as my parents cleaned up the broken glass and returned our living room back to normal. I laid in bed looking at the ceiling thinking about Dr. Solomon behaving like a madman, my father exerting superhuman strength to pin him to the floor and Mrs. Solomon screaming profanities at her husband. I feared Dr. Solomon would badly injure either my father or his wife. That was something I did not want to witness, and I didn't know what I would do had he severely harmed my father in any way. What a terrifying night it had been. I remember having a difficult time falling to sleep that night. As I lay in bed thinking I could hear my parent's voices getting louder and louder. I jumped out of bed, ran to the hallway, to listen to what was being said.

Daddy was talking about Mrs. Solomon, "I have told you time, and again that lady and her husband are nothing but trouble. I don't like her being in this house."

"She's my friend Charles, I can't just abruptly end our friendship, that would be rude and obvious."

"She's crazy, and her husband is an alcoholic who needs psychiatric help. Did you see the look in his eyes? He looked like a maniac. Thank God it was only a meat mallet, if he had had a hatchet, we may all be dead."

"You're right they do have some problems, -- I've been trying to help her, talk with her---- but to just drop our friendship, so unexpectedly would be cruel and besides we have a responsibility to help people, don't we?" Mother asked.

"We do, but I can't endanger you and Vanessa. I have a responsibility to protect my family. Iris what if something had happened to Vanessa or her little friend? What if that deranged man was waving a gun instead of a meat mallet? How could you explain that to the Rogers if something terrible had happened to their child?" Daddy was talking loud—almost yelling I no longer had to strain to hear what they were saying.

"Not so loud Charles, you're going to wake Vanessa."

"It could have been a gun he was threatening to use on his wife -----how would we explain that to the Rogers? I couldn't live with myself if you or Vanessa ----"

Mother remained quiet.

Daddy lowered his voice, "I understand she's your friend, but if something were to happen---- I could never forgive myself or I might have to hurt that man ..... Yes, I'm a man of God, it's true, but I'm also a father and a husband, and that makes me the protector of our home."

"Roberta needs someone to talk to I feel God is slowly drawing her, just a little more time and she'll come around---"

"Not here Iris. I mean it, not in our home. Find another place to have your heart to heart talks—meet her at the church or a coffee shop or the library anywhere but here ---- do not endanger the life of my child or yourself. I know it sounds harsh, but I don't care. What would you do if her crazy husband comes around and I'm at the church-----what on earth would you do? I'm sorry, but it ends tonight, this is the last time she steps foot into this house. Understand?"

Mother was quiet, so I presumed she nodded or silently agreed.

"I'll finish cleaning up this mess. Go on to bed and get some rest." Daddy said. I heard mother coming towards the stairs I ran into my room and quietly closed the door.

My father was right. I had not thought about any of those scenarios. If Dr. Solomon had come into our house waving a gun or a butcher knife, it could have been an entirely different night. I wondered if Kendra was sleeping. I knew it was too late for me to be on the phone but I decided to take the risk and call her anyway.

She answered on the first ring. "Vanessa, what's up?"

"Hey, I couldn't sleep, I was just thinking about tonight, that was unbelievable, wasn't it?"

"I have never been so afraid in all my life. Especially when he struck your father in the head ---is your Dad alright?"

"Yea, he's ok. My mom cleaned the wound and put a bandage on him. He's downstairs cleaning up the mess they made during the fight."

"I feel a little sorry for Mrs. Solomon, don't you?"

"Yeah me too, I'm looking at their house right now, it looks dark, quiet. Think she'll stay with him?"

"Probably, they've been together all this time, and I'm sure this isn't the first time he's gone loco on her. Hey, my parents said they're gonna to talk to your mom and dad."

"About what? What happened tonight at our house? About the Solomons?"

"Yea, they want to try and help them."

"You mean like marriage counseling?"

"I guess so, they didn't say exactly what kind of help--- but that's what they need before he hurts somebody. Vanessa that's not all, I think my parents are going to stop me from coming over to your house."

"Because of what happened tonight? It wasn't our fault, maybe I could come over there?"

"I'll have to talk to them."

"Yea we'll see. I better get in the bed. I'll see you tomorrow."

"OK, see you later."

I lingered at the window looking at the Solomon's now quiet household. There were no signs of life anywhere. I wondered if Mrs. Solomon was hiding from her husband. Had Dr. Solomon woken from his drunken stupor if so, did he have any recollection of his wild actions? Before I got back into bed, I knelt and said a prayer for the Solomon household. Even years later I can recall the prayer I prayed that night. I remember thanking God for my parents, who I never witnessed physically fighting one another. Then I asked God to forgive me for all the times I made fun of Mrs. Solomon and deliberately rode my bike over her lawn and pulled the heads off her flowers and called her mean names. Finally, I asked God to help Dr. Solomon to stop drinking and to learn how to truly love his wife.

Days later when we went back to school, Kendra and I were standing at the bus stop with the other kids waiting for the school bus. We saw Dr. Solomon getting in his car to go to work. He was dressed in a suit, carrying his briefcase, looking like a regular, everyday guy. Not the kind of person who would chase his wife waving a meat mallet like a wild man. I would have never known he was such a terror if I had not witnessed it with my own eyes. As he pulled out of the driveway he waved and smiled at us as if he had no recollection of that night whatsoever.

MY FATHER'S SHADOW

After the incident, I began to see Mrs. Solomon's life from a different perspective. Before the disturbance I saw her as an arrogant and spiteful woman. But, As I watched Dr. Solomon drive away, recalling his psychotic behavior. I realized how unhappy and miserable she must be. Perhaps that's why she spent so much time outside digging in the dirt.

Almost overnight, after the fight at our house, Mrs. Solomon became another person. Not quite an entirely different person, she maintained her dignified manner. But, Mrs. Solomon lost that spring in her step, her nose was not as high in the air as in the past, and we no longer had to endure her bragging about Dr. Solomon being a university professor. She was outside more than usual, not just gardening but occasionally she would take walks along the block, or stop by to visit with neighbors. The night at our house revealed a little bit more about her life and possibly her actions. Perhaps her constant gardening wasn't a fascination with flowers, but a way of escape from an abusive situation.

My friends never knew why, but after that night I stopped teasing Mrs. Solomon. I no longer joined in their cruel jokes about her looks or her obsession with flowers. Instead, I tried my best to defend her and did everything in my power to prevent them from destroying her flowerbeds. Of course, my friends misunderstood my behavior. They never knew the reason why I suddenly became an advocate for Mrs. Solomon. The unfortunate events of that night helped me to develop a sensitivity for Mrs. Solomon, and I began to understand a little more of what life was all about.

That was an unforgettable night, Kendra and I spoke of it many, many times. We still found it hard to believe we could have witnessed someone losing their life. Through the eyes of a young teenaged girl, I recalled her as an unpleasant, grumpy old woman. Now a woman myself, much older, more mature I certainly saw her as another person. I stopped my car in front of Mrs. Solomon's house and observed her from afar in her usual place on the front lawn. Sitting on a plastic stool weeding her flowers. She had not changed much at all, the same bifocal glasses hanging around her neck, her familiar flashy jewelry sparkling in the sunlight, and that same silver-haired wig peeking through her big floppy sun hat and the cotton long- sleeved, florally patterned house-dress, exactly like the ones she wore when we were kids. The only difference about her was the earphones stuck in ears. I watched as she sat on her green plastic stool patting her feet and shaking her head along with the beat of the music. What kind of music could be on her playlist I wondered?

Slowly she moved from shrub to shrub, pulling weeds, pouring water when needed and digging around the plants. She was so engrossed in weeding her flowers and the music playing in her ears that she didn't notice my car driving down the street.

I slowly edged my car a little closer until it sat directly in front of her house. The sound of the engine finally got her attention she turned towards the street squinting in the sun. She pulled off her sunglasses and yanked the earphones from her ears. Not wanting to frighten her I got out of the car so she could recognize me and not think I was some nut job stalking her.

I removed my sunglasses and waved at her, "Hello Mrs. Solomon, it's me, Vanessa Woods." I used my maiden name hoping to jog her memory. I wasn't sure if she recognized me or not. I was careful to avoid stepping on her lawn. I ran up the walkway and got as close as possible, I smiled and called her name once more.

"I'm trying to make sure I'm not having a mirage or seeing things." Looking up at me and using her hand to block out the sun. As she struggled to stand, I reached out my hand for support. She grabbed me and hugged me tightly. I inhaled an intense fragrance of medicinal ointment mixed with eau de toilette from her clothes.

The big smile on her face and warm bear hug let me know she was as glad to see me, as I was to see her. It had been almost two years since I saw her at my parent's funeral. She seemed to have aged quite a bit and even shrunken. She held my hand tight and looked up at me still using her other hand to shield the sun out of her face.

"My, goodness ---- look who it is—Vanessa Woods. What are you doing around here?" She asked.

"I was out for a drive, and my car somehow led me back to the old neighborhood."

"Well good. I'm glad you didn't forget the old lady. I think about you, Karen and Russell often. I most certainly do. Come on round back and help me carry my container of tools if you don't mind."

She motioned for me to pick up her basket of gardening equipment, her gloves, and water bottle. She retrieved a walking stick I had not noticed laying in the grass and her miniature plastic chair and led the way to the backyard. Not only had she shrunk, but she was also walking slower, and I noticed a slight limp as she relied heavily on the cane.

"I have a few little plants round back that need my attention and then I'll be done. And we can sit down and talk, have a nice friendly visit."

Her backyard was stunning. The grass was the greenest, thickest lawn I have ever seen. Colorful flowerbeds were perfectly arranged around the perimeter of her backyard. Multi-colored rosebushes climbed all along the wooden fence. Fresh water flowed from a white small-tiered fountain set in the center of the yard. Mrs. Solomon stood to the side and announced, "Welcome to Roberta's botanical garden." She was glowing with pride. From the looks of her garden, she had every reason to be proud of the work of art that she called her backyard. The yard was a veritable display of exotic flowers, bonsai trees, unusual plants and even a small vegetable garden. The lovely fountain added the soothing sound of cascading water making it seem like one had stepped into another world.

"My husband gave it that name, he said I put so much work into this place and spent so much of his money, it may as well have a fancy name. He even had a sign made and posted it on the fence. Right here." She pushed aside some greenery growing along the fence to reveal a brown wooden sign that read "ROBERTA'S BOTANICAL GARDEN" in white lettering. I didn't know quite what to say. The sign was fitting because her yard was unlike any backyard I had ever seen. It was like a miniature forest complete with almost every kind of plant, flower, and shrubbery you could name and some you probably didn't know existed.

"Mrs. Solomon, you have put your heart and soul into this backyard. I wouldn't call it a backyard. It's beyond a flower garden --- I am completely lost for words at how to describe this. Do you mind if I take some pictures I would love to show this to my husband?"

"Thank you, Vanessa. Of course, take as many pictures as you like." She said gleaming.

I took pictures of the entire yard from various angles planning to show them to my husband, Kendra, and Karen.

Mrs. Solomon, I don't recall your backyard being like this. Has it always been this exotic, did you have this many plants?" I asked her.

"No, no, it wasn't nearly like this. This is years and years of planting, watering. It is hard work, it looks easy, but pulling these weeds and watering them is hard on my back and my knees, but I have to keep an eye on them. Besides I love gardening. It's peaceful, and I like to see things grow, flourish. I always say flowers are like children, you gotta watch 'em or else they will grow wild before you know it."

"Come here Vanessa," she beckoned for me to come closer. I stooped down to get a closer look.

"These are some of my finest plants, right here is a row of impatiens. I got peonies in the back, in front of the rose bushes are my four o'clocks. I just planted a couple beds of four o'clocks in the front yard I just love the way they bloom. But this one here is my newest flowerbed, planted them just last year. Do you recognize them?" I looked carefully at the colorful plant but had to admit that I had no idea what kind they were.

"Ohhh and I thought you were a gardener." She laughed a bit. "I'm just fooling you. These flowers are named after one of my dearest friends, they're Irises." She said looking up at me.

She had planted a special plot of flowers named after my mother. "That is such a sweet way to remember my mom. It seems like you and mom were friends forever."

"Oh boy, Vanessa, for many, many years I have called her my friend. We were here when your mother and father moved across the street with your brother and sister--- I don't think you were born yet. Did your mother ever tell you how we met?"

"No, ma'am she did not," I said eager to hear this story.

"Oh well, it was a long time ago, years and years before you were born. My husband, Dr. Solomon had a cute, mid-sized dog named

P. M. Smith

Mr. Dobbs—Lord knows where he got such a name for a dog. Anyway, when my kids were little, they loved that dog so much. He was a good little dog, friendly, didn't mess up too much. My husband loved that dog a lot-- in fact, he loved that dog so much he would call home almost every day on his lunch break to make sure I took Mr. Dobbs out for an afternoon walk. Mind you, he didn't telephone to talk to me or to see how I was doing ---he was more concerned about a four-legged animal getting his exercise.

Anyway, one day I'm walking Mr. Dobbs along the sidewalk and something catches that little rascal's eye, he took off so fast that his leash slipped out of my hand and he scatted across the street. He stopped by a tree in your parent's front yard. Of course, I chased him, I was afraid he would get hit by a car, and Dr. Solomon would surely blame me. Well, he didn't get hit, but he ran straight to this tree chasing after a butterfly. I pulled and pulled at his leash, telling him to come on, but he was mesmerized with this butterfly. I let him stand there for a few moments watching the butterfly flit around the tree.

As I was watching the dog, an unusual flower in the grass caught my attention, so I stooped down to get a closer look at the flower. As I'm trying to figure out what kind of flower it is, all of a sudden, I hear somebody singing. I looked around to see where it was coming from and sure enough it was coming from your parent's house. I listened to the sound a little closer. I didn't know it then, but I learned later it was your mother---just singing away. At first, I thought it was a little strange--- then when I made out the words she was saying --- who she was singing to --- that made the difference. Vanessa, your mother, was praising God. I took a few minutes to listen to her singing and praying. I really don't think she knew the window was open."

So, every day around that time, I would take Mr. Dobbs for a walk, and I would time our walk when I thought your mother would be saying her afternoon prayers. This went on for quite some time, probably weeks until I got the nerve to put a little note in her mailbox asking her to pray for my family and me. I figured anybody who prayed that regularly must have a close connection to God. So, I put a note in the mailbox, and I signed it "lover of God." I didn't want her to know who I was.

Every day I heard her praying and singing to God. It was music to my ears. Gave me peace of mind just to take in her sweet voice singing the praises of God. Made me want to pray too. Back then I wasn't praying much, didn't really know how. But I loved to hear Iris call on the Lord. I don't know if anyone else ever heard her. Didn't matter, I always believed that God made that little dog run across the street at the exact time she was on her knees in prayer just for me.

"I have to say I have never heard that story, Mrs. Solomon, how did she find out it was you?"

"Vanessa, they say your sins will find you out. One evening just as I was placing another prayer request inside your parent's mailbox, Iris and Reverend Woods pulled up in the driveway. Caught me red handed. It was hilarious, their headlights shining on me as my hand was stuck in their mailbox. I had to come clean. She was so sweet about it we laughed about my little notes. Said she kept every one of my prayer requests, put a date on them and placed them in her Bible. She looked forward to going to the mailbox to see what my next request would be. She said she hoped that one day we would meet. From then on, we became the best of friends and the rest as they say, is history."

"Vanessa, I loved that woman, she was like a sister. Although she was a little younger than me, I never met a wiser person who knew so much about life and about the Words of Life. I loved that the most about her, her love for God and His Word. I would come by the house every once in a while to talk with your mother, then after the incident---you might have been too young to remember—but one night my husband had a bit too much to drink and like a fool almost tore up your parent's beautiful home--- after that unfortunate evening --- seemed like your father banned me from your house. Your mother was too polite to come out and say it, but I knew your father didn't want me over there anymore. Who could blame him, I probably would have done the same thing if the situation was reversed. Before the incident, Iris and I would sit at your kitchen table drinking coffee, eat coffee cake or whatever was available and talk for hours, trade stories about our lives, our families, the goodness of the Lord and she would help me with my problems. After the incident things changed drastically --- we started meeting outside sometimes we would sit in the garden and talk."

I had no idea Mrs. Solomon was such a talker. It seemed that she wanted to talk and since I was in no hurry, I patiently listened to her reminisce about the past. It was clear she really loved my mother, and they had a close friendship.

"Sometimes I'll come out here, and talk to my little patch of Irises, just like I used to confide in your mother." She began pulling stray weeds and pouring a little water on the plot of Irises. "They're not growing …. not budding like they should. I must be using the wrong fertilizer or too much water. Something I'm doing wrong. I'm gonna have to refer to my plant books and see what they recommend." Giving up on them she placed her tools in the basket and reached her hand towards me to help her up from her chair. She headed to the rear of the backyard towards the vegetable garden. I picked up her little plastic stool and followed.

"Most of the vegetables, they did really good this year. The tomatoes are growing all over the place as they always do. I'm really pleased with the whole garden, it's not often that happens. Look how green the greens are and the squash so bright yellow and those rutabagas—everything, well almost everything grew so well this time." She picked a few tomatoes and leaves from the greens and passed them to me to inspect.

"You're right Mrs. Solomon these tomatoes are very plump and red…." I didn't know what else to say about them.

"I'll get a bag, and we can pick some nice vegetables for your family before you leave. These old turnips never did do right, an awful batch." She pulled a stalk from the ground and shook the dirt off. "Feel how dry they are, and the color is so odd. They usually do better than that. I wonder if some kind of earthworm got in there and chewed at em." She continued to pull weeds and dig around the plants. She moved from plant to plant either exclaiming how well it was growing or her disappointment in the plant's failure to bud or grow as expected.

"Over here in the corner is a row of green beans and cabbage patch. I planted these for your mom. She told me how much your father enjoyed cabbage. I like cabbage too, but I'm not crazy about it. Now I have all these cabbages, I'll have to find somebody to give them to." She pulled the withered leaves from the patch and threw them aside.

"Be a dear and hold this for me." She handed me several large heads of cabbage and stacked a bunch of carrots on top. I obediently held the vegetables and continued to listen as she surveyed her garden.

"By the way how are things at the church? I'm sure your brother is doing a fine job since he took over for your father."

"Things are going well," I said slowly. "But ----uh we don't a have permanent pastor yet."

She looked up at me. "Oh? He must be temporary until they decide?"

"Well, no, not really," I said hesitantly, not really wanting to get into a discussion about First Deliverance.

I tried to change the subject several times asking about her husband, their kids and grandchildren, but she always brought the conversation back to First Deliverance.

"Well, I thought your brother was going to take over, at least that's what Iris said to me."

Now she had my attention. "What exactly did my mother say to you?" I asked her.

She pulled more vegetables from the ground and stacked them in my arms, several cucumbers, two eggplants and several very large red onions. I did not have the heart to tell her it was more than enough.

"Your mother told me Reverend Woods was planning to make your brother the Senior Pastor and he would become Pastor Emeritus. He had papers drawn up made it legal so no one could change it." She struggled to stand up, I hugged the vegetables close to my body with one hand and with my other hand I took her hand to help up from the stool. She wiped the sweat from her face reached into the pocket of her house dress and pulled out a small bottle of water.

"Your father never told you or made it known to the church members?" she asked me. She tilted her head back and drank the entire bottle of water.

I shook my head no. "No ma'am I never heard anything about that."

"Now that's interesting cause your mother said he was planning to publicize it ---must have been few months before the accident. Their car accident was in April right?"

"Yes," I replied. "Two years ago."

"Iris and I talked earlier that year—I remember it was cold out but no snow on the ground--- so must have been somewhere around the last of January. When the accident happened, I remember thinking it was a good thing your father had the mind to set up Russell to take his place---but you say he's *not* the pastor? ----Well tell me --Vanessa, what happened?" she asked. "Did he go to another church or something?" She stacked more vegetables in my arms.

I explained to her about the election process and how the congregation decided they wanted to continue looking for someone else to pastor First Deliverance.

"Well how do you like that?" she said shaking her head.

"I'm sorry Mrs. Solomon, what do you mean?" I must have missed something.

"Your mother wasn't pleased with your father's decision--- the announcement he was going to make about your brother becoming the pastor. But there was nothing she could do about it ----- other than pray."

She looked around her yard making sure each plant received some attention. "I think I'm done with gardening for today-- can't do too much more. I'm tired, and it's hot out here. Come on inside, I got a pot on the stove I need to check. We can have a glass of sweet tea and some of my home-made butter cookies."

P. M. Smith

My entire childhood years, I had ridden my bike by her house hundreds of time and occasionally waved hello at her, but I had never seen the inside of Mrs. Solomon's home. It was just as I expected, neat as a pin and squeaky-clean. The décor was like I had stepped back in time. The furniture was outdated, but in perfect condition as though it was brand new. There was a sweet aroma of collard greens wafting in the air. She placed her gardening tools in the sunroom, removed her straw hat and we washed our hands at the kitchen sink. As she washed her hands I noticed scars and scratches on both of her arms. When she removed her jacket on her shoulder was a scar about two inches long shaped like the state of Florida. I wondered if the marks were results of her scrapes with her husband. She moved quickly around the kitchen, talking about this and that. She was so excited to have a visitor at her house, I wondered if she had many friends.

Underneath her cabinet sink, she found two large paper bags for my vegetables and then she turned to the pot on the stove. As soon as she removed the lid from the container, the delicious smell of collards filled the kitchen and stirred my taste buds.

"I'm cooking collard greens for dinner. The man loves collards so much till I believe he could eat them every day."

She began stirring the pot, she went to the cabinet and retrieved a small bowl and put a few of the greens in it for me to taste. I could feel her watching me as I ate.

"What do you think? Need more seasoning?"

She *knew* her greens were good. I told her they were as delicious as they smelled. In fact, they were so good I politely asked for a second helping. As I sat at the table enjoying my bowl of collard greens, Mrs. Solomon poured two glasses of iced tea and set a little saucer of cookies on the kitchen table. She looked out the backyard window in silence. When I finished, she took the bowl rinsed it out and placed it in the dishwasher.

"Your home is lovely, clean and neat, just as I imagined. You know, I've never been inside your house before. You seem to be an excellent housekeeper."

"Thank you, since it's just my husband and me it's much easier to keep clean. No toys and books and things scattered all over. It's not so hard to keep it neat and tidy just like we like it."

"If it had not been for your mother Vanessa, I don't know if Eason and I would have made it. I knew what she was trying to do, get me to give my life to the Lord—I wasn't ready, not until that night when he almost took my life. I thought I was a dead woman. Somehow your mama convinced the Reverend to counsel my husband and me, it did a lot of good, got us on the right track, kept our marriage strong and helped us get right with the Lord. Best decision I ever made in my life."

She stared out the window as if in deep thought. I wondered if she was reliving that fateful night.

"Do you remember what happened that night? I know you were kind of young back then, but not too young to understand what was going on."

I didn't say it to Mrs. Solomon, but I knew I would remember that night for the rest of my life. "Yes ma'am," I said, "I remember."

"One of the worse nights of my life! I have done some foolish things in my life, some things so foolish it's a wonder I'm still alive. But that night I thought for sure would be my last ------" I thought she was about to cry then a smile come across her face. "And you know what, it was also the best night of my life."

She began smoothing out imaginary wrinkles on the plastic table-cloth.

"Vanessa that was the night I stared death in the face, and that was a frightening thing. Right then and there I knew I needed to make a choice real fast. Not so much a choice about living but a choice about *how* I was going to live. I could live the rest of my life in fear or I could have peace and joy unspeakable. Eason would have killed me or injured me real bad if I hadn't got out of this house. Earlier that evening he came home sloppy drunk. I hated him like that ----such a foul disposition, just horrible and it always brought out the worse in me."

"I was trying to stay out of his way, hoping he would pass out and leave me alone. But he found me in the sun-room and started his ranting and raving, next thing I know we're arguing then we started tussling. Somehow we ended up in the kitchen, and he had my back against the wall." She pointed to the corner of the wall near the stove.

"His hands were wrapped around my throat, as he was choking me I stumbled to the floor, knocked over a pot of spaghetti noodles I had cooking on the stove. The water was hot, not scalding, but hot enough to burn him and cause him to release the hold he had on my neck -- while he was on the floor screaming I ran like the wind."

She laughed a little bit. "It wasn't funny then—not at all. I was scared to death and embarrassed by it all. I didn't want your family to see us acting like hooligans. I was so sure Eason was going to kill me or hurt your father. It was that incident that brought the Reverend and Eason together. I don't know if Iris talked to your father or what but --- somehow he got that stubborn old man to give up drinking— no Alcoholic Anonymous or nothing like that. I suspect they spent a lot of time praying with him. One day he came home and threw away every bottle of alcohol in this house. Gave it up just like that."

"Do you know what good came out of that horrendous night Vanessa?" She placed her hand on mine.

"I have an idea …"

"That night while looking death right in the eye, I decided I wasn't ready to die no sir, not the raggedy life I was living---half in the church and half out. So, I made the decision I wanted to live not just exist. I decided I wanted to live for God. While I was crouched in the corner of your kitchen hugging your mother I promised God if He got me out of that house alive---He could have my life and do with it as He pleased. I would do anything He asked of me."

"After your mom and Carla Rogers made sure I was safely in the house. Eason was passed out on the couch, I went straight into my bedroom, got down on my knees and asked God's forgiveness for every foolish thing I had ever done in my life. I cried and pleaded with God to save my wretched soul. It wasn't all Eason's fault. Sometimes I intentionally provoked him. I knew just what buttons to push, and I did it sometimes just to be mean and spiteful. You may find this hard to believe, Vanessa but I had some nasty, unpleasant ways about me and a proud heart. I asked God to change my heart. He did, and I'm grateful for it every day."

"That was over twenty years ago, I haven't talked about that night in a long time. And I didn't expect to be talking about it with you. But every now and then it runs through my mind. I don't look back in regret, I'm thankful for the life we have together, it's so much better now. We swore we would never go back to the way we used to be arguing, fussing and fighting—never again and we haven't. That's not to say Eason still doesn't get on my nerves every now and then...." We both laughed.

Mrs. Solomon went to the refrigerator and removed a pitcher of iced tea which she sat in the middle of the table. This was not the Mrs. Solomon I knew as a teenager. This Mrs. Solomon was a much more pleasant person to be around. She was a true testament of what God could do in our lives when we yield ourselves to Him. Salvation had transformed her into a peaceful, sweet and gentle woman.

"I used to be so proud to be the wife of Dr. Eason Solomon, a college professor. That pride wore off real soon---the first time he came home so drunk he didn't know his name. Things got worse when he started using my face as a punching bag. I was too proud to ask for help, too proud to leave him. I didn't want anyone to know what kind of man I had married and what kind of man he really was. A prominent man in the community. A well-known college professor. Upstanding citizen during the day but at night when he came home, it was a different story. That night when we ended up at your house, I knew the cat was out of the bag. I'll never forget the terrible part of that night, but what I'm most grateful for is how God exposed our secret...that allowed me and Eason to find salvation. Yes, it was embarrassing for Iris and your father to see us acting like that, but it took me down a peg or two and saved me from the pit of hell and that I will never forget."

She slid the saucer of butter cookies to the center of the table. "Enough about me. I want to hear all about your family, the kids, your husband I forget his name....."

"Calvin."

"That's right, Calvin! Such a nice man I remember him well," She said, "Now tell me about the kids and Russell and Karen how are they doing?"

We conversed a while about my family and Russell's and Karen's families as well. Mrs. Solomon turned the conversation back to my parent's fatal car accident.

"Vanessa, now that I think about it your mother may not have been the only one who wasn't pleased with your father's decision----I used to think it was strange how God took your parents like that. So suddenly, --- it's always been a little bizarre to me---- but now it's becoming a little clearer. Remember I said your mother could do nothing but pray? Well, your mama must have prayed day and night for God to move in some way. She must have prayed real hard."

She touched me on the hand. "You know what they say about prayer?" I looked at her with raised eyebrows unsure what reference to prayer she was thinking of.

"Be careful what you pray for—cause you just might get it." She took a sip of the iced tea. "God will give us just what you ask for, but often not in the way you expect it. He answered your mother's prayers, just not *how* she expected, -----if your father never got a chance to make his big announcement and your brother was *not* elected or installed as pastor...seems to me that your father's plan was *not* God's plan----so He moved your father out of the way permanently."

She took a bite out of a cookie and waved it at me as she spoke. "Vanessa, I guess all things, even the most dreadful things in life *really do* work together for good ---don't they?"

"Yes ma'am," I said. "They most certainly do."

After my drive through the old neighborhood and my visit with Mrs. Solomon, I was tired and really wanted to go home, but I had promised Karen and my friends I would meet them at Juno's Coffee House.

Our busy lifestyles didn't afford us the time to have these outings very often. With our personality differences, some older, some younger, most of us married and being at various stages in life, we all had one thing in common, our love for God. Our faith was first and foremost in our lives. Church, God, the Bible or biblical issues or just plain old life was something that always surfaced in our conversations. There was never a shortage of topics for us to discuss. Knowing each other for so long we were comfortable sharing our stories. No issue or personal problem was off limits.

Being the first to arrive gave me a few moments to rest my eyes and reflect a little on my conversation with Mrs. Solomon. I made a mental note to keep in touch with her. I thoroughly enjoyed our talk. Her comment about how God answered my mother's prayers at first seemed a little insensitive, but I wondered was that how God worked? I know that God's ways and thoughts are not like ours and she was undoubtedly right God had some creative ways of answering prayers. I wish my mother had spoken to me about her concerns. I'm not sure what I would have done or said, but maybe she and daddy would still be alive. I knew that was wishful thinking on my part because there was no way I could change God's will if it were meant for them to have a fatal accident. I sat in the car watching the people who passed by. It was a struggle to keep my eyes open. It wasn't long afterward that Karen's SUV pulled up behind me.

After locating a table by the window large enough for five, we sat down and the waitress took our orders. Someone said that Audrey would be there a little later. I asked how it went at the auction and they began telling me about the pieces Tara purchased. Several art acquisitions by young new artists her and her husband had been hoping for. I listened as they chatted away about family, work, children, the usual topics. I was mentally and physically drained. I was in no mood to be sociable. I was beginning to think I had made the wrong decision, I knew should have gone home. Suddenly, my phone started vibrating. It was a text from Karen that read: "SNAP OUT OF IT! JOIN THE CONVERSATION....we'll talk about Lawrence later!!!!"

Lawrence? How did she know about Lawrence? Calvin! He must have told her. I gave Karen a little smile and forced myself to join the conversation.

Audrey joined us in the coffee house about an hour later, dressed in her hospital uniform of scrubs and clogs. The waitress took her order of iced green tea and a Caesar salad. Audrey, a general practitioner, was a friend we met through Tara. She was an avid health nut, always offering unsolicited advice about our mental and physical well-being. She ate only organic food, swearing off any chemicals in her diet, her body, and her home.

When she spoke, she was out of breath, "I'm so sorry, tried to get here sooner, but it's been a crazy day." She hugged us all and took a seat near the window. "I brought something for us to snack on." She sat a bag of almonds and trail mix on the table. "Go ahead dig in, they're good for you."

We exchanged looks around the table. "Uh, Audrey we kind of prefer salsa and chips. " Karen quipped.

"Or chocolate chip cookies" Tara joined in. "That would go perfectly with my iced coffee." She held up her coffee cup.

Audrey poured some almonds into her hands. "Cookies and chips may taste good, but they are fattening and not very healthy.

Almonds on the other hand not only taste good, but they also have fiber and eating almonds has been known to aid in losing weight."

Hearing that last bit of information made us all stick our hands out for some of her almonds.

"Why are you wearing your hospital garb?" Tara asked. "Going back to work?"

"Yeah," She sighed. "We're leaving for the Philippines in a few weeks ---so we're still packing stuff and receiving supplies. Kelli, my assistant, was supposed to finish up, but her mother had health issues, so the responsibility falls on Dr. Irvin and me."

Karen took notice "You mean that good-looking Dr. Irvin?"

"Yes," She laughed. "That's the one...good-looking Dr. Irvin."

"When will you invite him to church so he can make one of our sisters, like Kendra, a good Christian husband?" Karen asked.

"I have invited him, but he has his own church. So, I don't pressure him about it." She replied.

"Excuse me Karen, but I can find my own husband. "Kendra said teasingly.

"You wouldn't be saying that if you saw Dr. Irvin," Karen said. "You would be thanking me."

"I've seen him," Kendra said. "He's alright. There's more to a man than looks. He's got to have more to offer than that." She said dismissively.

Audrey continued telling us their plans for their mission trip, "After we finish packing supplies at the clinic, we're going to Mercy General they're donating the bulk of the medical supplies. Thanks to them and Tara's gallery we are going to have more than we need."

"I'm really hoping that our new pastor will include missions and outreach in the budget. I can't tell you how many times I asked Pastor Woods for outreach funds, but he never gave me any response. There was so much I wanted to do for the outreach ministry. But he would not allow us to move forward." She said sipping her tea.

"Audrey," Karen said abruptly. "We all had something we wanted my father to implement or to change, but Daddy was old school all the way."

"All the way," Tara agreed. "Remember that laundry list of rules –of things we could and could not do or could and could not wear," Tara said.

"And he loved the old hymns, sung one every Sunday," Kendra said. "And Sister Woods would be the first person on her feet, singing away, supporting her husband. Sometimes I miss that about them."

Karen said wistfully. "They were a one of a kind couple."

"Maybe our next pastor will be more missions-minded," Kendra said.

"Yes, somebody who'll reach beyond the pulpit --- outside the four walls of the church," Tara added.

They began rattling off a list of qualities they wanted in a pastor. "He's gotta love people," Audrey said. "Nothing worse than a pastor who does not like people. I never could understand that, I mean why become a pastor if you don't like people? Doesn't make sense to me."

"Please him let him have some preaching skills," Tara said.

Audrey laughed. "Not too long winded though, but have some substance. Sometimes you need something a little deep, to make you think or go home and research what you've heard."

I took mental notes of their requests, *a preacher who loved God- check, was on fire for the Lord, check --- knew how to preach…..well two out of three wasn't bad.*

"Must be a good dresser too," Tara said. "There's nothing worse than a badly dressed pastor."

"A good dresser----what does that have to do with pastoring?" Audrey asked.

"Well he doesn't have to be on the cover of Vogue, ---- but have some idea of how to put his clothes together nicely," Tara replied.

"Girl that's silly," Audrey said.

"Not to mention superficial." Kendra agreed.

"Maybe if you started praying a little harder, then God would send him or her," Karen said.

"I hope the Lord sends a him," Audrey responded.

"What's wrong with a woman pastor?" Tara asked.

"There's nothing *wrong* with a female pastor. I don't think I would want a female pastor," Kendra said. "Some positions of leadership I think are more fitting for a man."

I felt Karen's eyes on me.

"My Aunt Florine in Atlanta has a female pastor," Tara said. "Actually, they're a husband and wife co-pastoring team. We visited their church while we were there on vacation and that lady is a baaaad preacher. The way she teaches the Word it was amazing---we loved it! Her husband preached for the evening service, and he was just as good. They were a great team. Now if we get one like that -- we'll be alright. I checked out their website, and it appears she has the more public ministry. I don't have a problem with a female pastor as long as she can take care of business in the pulpit and is a good leader."

"I hate to burst your bubbles ladies," Karen interjected. "... but it really doesn't matter what *we* want. Remember whose church it is? Whoever God sends, male or female will be equipped to do the job."

"Sounds like you know something we don't," Audrey said.

"All I know is that in His own time, God will send the right person," Karen responded.

Tara turned to me, "Vanessa, what do you think? Would you prefer a female minister?"

I was trying not to say anything at all. "Sure, I wouldn't mind that at all, if that's God's choice. Just as long as they love God and the people .... gender is unimportant. If they happen to be female, it's alright, if it's a male that's fine too."

"Do you think you would make a good pastor?" Audrey asked me.

Now, why would she ask me that? What in the world is wrong with her?

"I think she would be a good pastor," Kendra said before I could respond to Audrey's question.

"You do? I thought you just said you didn't care for women---" Audrey asked.

"Let me finish please…" Kendra continued---- "She would make a good pastor if the senior pastor is a man. I can't explain why, I'm just used to men leading…not saying it's right or wrong, just how I see it."

"Kendra, women, are leading in all capacities, and almost every pastor makes his wife the co-pastor. It's the latest trend, and it seems to be working." Audrey replied.

"I'm not saying women should *not* lead in churches, I don't think *I* would want to be part of a congregation who is pastored by a female," Kendra said.

Karen felt like playing devil's advocate. "Tell the truth now, would any of you consider leaving First Deliverance if the next Senior Pastor was female?" she asked.

Kendra was the first to answer, "I would seriously consider leaving. If God said to stay, then I would give her my utmost respect as the leader of God's church. But if the Lord gave me the go ahead, I think I would have to change my membership."

"Then maybe you could find a husband," Tara said jokingly. We all laughed including Kendra. "But seriously you would leave just because of her gender? What if she's a great leader, can preach the

Word and knows how to reach people? I think your reason for leaving is rather trivial." Tara said.

I was stunned by Kendra's comment. *Would she really leave First Deliverance if a woman became the pastor?*

Tara and Audrey said they would not leave First Deliverance, but it would take some adjusting to the new leadership.

"We'll have to adjust anyway," Karen said. "Whether it is male or female because everybody has a different style of leadership. So, everybody will be forced to adjust to a certain extent."

"You're right to a point," Tara said. "We're used to seeing men at the helm, not a woman. There's a big difference between adjusting to different personalities rather than different sexes. Men and women do things much differently."

"A woman can be just as strong a leader as a man, it's been proven time and time again they are just as capable," Audrey said. "I could get used to a female pastor. I wouldn't want to leave First Deliverance I love my church."

"You're implying that I don't love my church too?" Kendra said pretending to be offended.

"No, I wasn't even thinking of you, simply voicing my opinion."

"Ladies, ladies," Karen said. "What does the Bible say about women pastoring? Paul said for women to keep silent in the church, right? Now that was eons ago, and churches, synagogues, whatever they were back then were structured differently. The men sat on the floor and women were in the balcony, so that rule made sense for that time period."

"So, you're saying it's more of a Jewish tradition--- not a standard for us modern day church folk to practice? "Tara asked.

Audrey commented, "Isn't there like a list of things that will not be permitted in heaven---I've never seen women preachers on that list. Where is it? Ephesians or Corinthians?"

"There's a lot of things *not* listed in the Bible that will send you straight to the lake of fire," Kendra stated emphatically.

"I can't believe we're having this conversation in the year 2017. Gender in this day and age, in certain positions, remains to be an issue with a lot of people, especially women…unbelievable." Tara said.

"I think women don't want to be led by other women because we are emotional creatures and sometimes we do some immature things to each other for the silliest reasons," Kendra remarked.

"Maybe that's why God put a man in charge," I said. "Since the fall of Adam and Eve men have dominated in all areas, the family, business and church world. They lead on all fronts because God designed it that way and it was part of God's judgment."

"Emotions aren't all bad," Audrey said. "Don't you think the people are moved when the leader expresses some kind of emotion when he or she is touched by God—that has a great effect on the congregation. On the other hand, it's not good when our emotions rule us, and we make decisions based on how we feel."

"Ninety-nine percent of the female gender are emotional creatures," Karen said.

MY FATHER'S SHADOW

We continued discussing the men versus women predicament. The conversation turned to other things, and we talked for another hour or so. I looked at my watch it was almost nine pm. Calvin was probably wondering where I was. I checked my phone for any missed calls or messages. Zero. He hadn't even called to check on me that was slightly disappointing.

I placed my car keys on the table, knowing my friends would get the meaning. Audrey agreed it was late. She still had to get her kids ready for Sunday morning service. The laughter and conversation continued out the door till we got to our cars. We exchanged hugs. Kendra asked if I would take her home since her apartment was on my way. Tara pulled Audrey off to the side for a private conversation. Karen ran to my car and knocked on the window.

I rolled down the window. "Hey, what's up?" I asked her. She reminded me not to forget to straighten things out with Lawrence. She promised to call next week to check on me. I appreciated her concern, I really did, but sometimes my older sister tended to act like my mother even though I was a grown woman with two teenage children. I knew she would not leave me alone until I talked to him.

"Don't let it linger too long Vanessa," she warned. "If you do you'll regret it. You two have a good night and drive carefully."

On the drive home I told Kendra that I saw our old friend Mrs. Solomon. We began talking about the old neighborhood and recalling the night she and her husband had the fight in our home. Just as we turned the corner to Kendra's apartment, she said.

"Hey, I don't mean to be nosey or anything, but are you and Calvin having trouble with Lawrence?"

"Sort of," I replied.

"What do you mean sort of?"

"He and I had an argument. He said some things, I said some things and one thing led to another...."

I knew I could trust her, so I explained to her about the accusations Lawrence made but chose to leave out the possibility of becoming the next pastor.

"That's interesting, that he would make those accusations... ... cause I kind of thought there was a problem between you and Russell." she said.

"You did? ----what kind of problem are you talking about?"

"The green-eyed monster type----."

"What!? Me jealous of Russell or the other way around?"

"I always suspected *you* had a problem with *him*."

I couldn't believe she was accusing me of being jealous of my brother. "Are you kidding me, Kendra?"

"No, I'm not joking." She said matter-of-factly.

"Where did this come from? All these years I've known you, you've never said anything."

"Just something I've noticed --- but I think it's something you never dealt with. Truthfully, I thought you would have grown out of it or whatever ..."

"Grown out of it? You know me better than most people, Kendra I can't believe what you're saying there's nothing to get over. Kendra, I'm not jealous of Russell, not now nor have I ever been." I could feel myself becoming upset. "I don't know where you get that from you have never heard me say anything bad about my brother or mistreat him --- I've always been complimentary."

"You're right, I've never seen you belittle him or anything, but----I did notice whenever your father commended Russ or praised him for his work at the church. The disappointment on your face, at least to me, was extremely obvious. You were respectful and all, but I knew something was going on with you. That was your main insecurity, and to me, it stuck out like a sore thumb."

If anybody knew me well, it was Kendra. I quietly listened to her and allowed her to make her point.

"Vanessa, I could see how disturbed you were and how it affected you, it made you do things just to impress your father. Some of the things you did, I thought were out of character for you. I could never figure out if you were trying to get attention *away* from Russ or trying to get the same kind of attention Russ was getting from your father."

I thought for a moment about what she said---insecure and uncertain about my father's confidence in me. At least that part was right, especially about my feelings concerning Daddy and Russell's relationship.

"But Kendra, I may not have agreed with everything Russ did or said over the pulpit, but I have never said or did anything to Russ that was insulting in any way."

"No, you didn't, but you worked overtime to get Reverend Woods' attention. I used to wonder why he praised Russ so much----whatever Russ did Pastor Woods was supportive, praising him for the smallest things. Then I figured it out----your father knew most of the congregation didn't really appreciate Russ' ministry. You remember how I always said you had your father's skills when it came to the Word----but Russ, even though he started ministering years before you even knew what Sunday school was. Articulating his thoughts in front of a crowd of people was a struggle for Russ. So, praising his every effort was your father's way of boosting his self-confidence. Frankly, Vanessa, I don't know how you lasted all these years with that stuff in your heart. How you managed ..."

"What you do mean managed---- I'm not a basket case or mental..." I said incredulously.

"No," she laughed dryly. "You're not crazy, and I wasn't implying that. You must have the favor of God or something, all this time you've thrived wonderfully ------*without* your father's approval, support or endorsement. You couldn't see that his approval was not n*eeded* for you to be successful in ministry. To be honest, I would rather have God's approval than men. Wouldn't you?"

I pulled the car in front of her house and applied the brake. "Kendra, my father didn't care for women in ministry."

"That may be true, but that doesn't matter. One minor thing I think you missed Vanessa – your motive. Ministry is not about impressing people. It's to edify people and to glorify God. But I don't need to tell you that—you know that already. Right?"

I turned off the car and continued to listen to her talk.

"You spent too much time, seeking daddy's approval and forgot about God--seems like it's still a problem, at least the denial part. Lawrence may have been wrong for *how* he talked to you----but is there a chance God used your child, someone very close to you--- to reveal that the problem you thought you had overcome is still troubling you? I'm just a little puzzled why now after all these years? Why would God have it resurface at this point in your life? What your father did was inexcusable—but think about Russell for a moment. It's possible that encouragement from your father *helped* him."

"Helped him….to become more arrogant?"

"You already had the encouragement you needed from the congregation. But Russ *needed* it too, and he wasn't really getting it from the congregation other than the young girls who were more impressed with his looks than his preaching."

It was hard to admit, but I knew she was right. "Kendra, I never thought about Russ *needing* Daddy's approval. His self-confidence was already through the roof. Daddy was there, patting him on the back, applauding his every move, no matter what he did, whenever Russ took the pulpit, every time and not once, not once did he ever ……."

It seemed I could not escape this thing, first Lawrence and now Kendra…. I guess God *is* trying to tell me something. Kendra and I sat in silence. After a while, she spoke breaking the silence.

"Vanessa, I wish we had had this conversation years ago when I first noticed something wasn't quite right between you two. Yea, Russ was pretty cocky for a while— but have you ever considered that maybe it was an act—that he was trying to *appear* confident and self-assured? Russ didn't win over the congregation as your father hoped and planned. The important thing is that you figure out why after all this time God brings this back into your life? Do you have any idea why?" She looked at me for an answer.

"Yep, I sure do, and I know exactly what I need to do," I answered her.

"Good. Just as long as you know why and how you should handle it. Look, it's getting late, I better get inside." She hugged me before exiting the car. "Thanks again for the ride, --love you, Vanessa," She said. "Now get your act together."

"Yea, yea I will," I said. "….love you too." I watched her go into her apartment. I started for home. On the radio, someone was singing "All to Jesus I Surrender."

It hurt to hear her say those words, but it helped me see how wrong I was and that God was sending me notice that it was time to face some of the demons that had been tormenting my life. Jealousy lurking in my heart----- all this time? How could I have not known this? The idea that my father was attempting to uplift Russell's confidence, something I had never considered. The more I thought about it, the more I realized Kendra could be onto something. It was hard to admit, but I recall some moments of jealousy because of the attention daddy gave Russell. He did it all the time, and it seemed that anything I did went unnoticed or any advice I offered was not appreciated. Maybe that's why Lawrence's words stung more so than his blatant disrespect--- because there was an element of truth in them.

When I unlocked the front door to the house, I almost tripped over Brownie who was sprawled out on the floor near the entrance way. I think he was waiting for me to come home because as soon as he heard the door open and saw me entering the house, he jumped up and began barking and jumping on my legs, as I walked through the house. He was excited that I was home. I patted him on the head. It gave me some satisfaction to know that someone was glad to see me, even if it was my pet dog. Melanie and Calvin were less than excited about my arriving home. They were glued to the television in the family room.

"Looks like Brownie is the only one glad to see me," I said playfully. I kissed Calvin and pecked Melanie on the cheek."

I picked up the mail and began thumbing through the envelopes.

"Where's Lawrence?" I asked them. Calvin said that he had worked him so hard, cutting the grass, washing the car and all the windows on the house that he was tired, sore and probably still angry. After he finished his chores, he went to his room and had been there all day.

"Where have you been?" Calvin asked me.

"Went for a drive and then met Karen and the girls at Juno's--- had an exciting afternoon."

"Must have been, you've been gone for hours," Calvin remarked.

I suddenly remembered the vegetables from Mrs. Solomon, "Cal there are some bags of vegetables in my car can you bring them in and Mel can you put them away for me please?"

"Sure mom, are you hungry? I made some chicken enchiladas." She said. "There's plenty left since Lawrence didn't have anything to eat."

"No sweetie I'm not hungry, I'm a little tired, think I'm going to get ready for bed."

I excused myself and made a comment about needing to get my things ready for church in the morning. I don't think they heard a word I said. I left them enjoying whatever show they were too fascinated with to notice I had left the room.

Brownie followed me upstairs. I stopped by Lawrence's room because I heard music playing. I was going to say hello, but he was fast asleep. A book he had been reading and his glasses lay on his chest. I placed the book and eye-glasses on the nightstand. He was sleeping as though he didn't have a care in the world. I kissed him lightly on the forehead, "God loves you Lawrence, and I do too," I whispered. I covered him with the blanket, turned off his CD player and softly closed his bedroom door.

I took a shower and prepared for bed. Laying my Bible on the bed, I knelt at my bedside to pray. Everything Kendra said going through my mind. I was aware of why the subject of Russell and my father had suddenly reemerged —it was time for me to confront some things that had been troubling me and eradicate them from my life once and for all. I closed my Bible and cried out to God to heal my sin-sick soul.

Because First Deliverance was still searching for someone to fill the pastoral position, the ministers and teachers were required to serve the congregation by taking turns teaching the weekly Bible study sessions. Two days before our weekly Bible class the teacher who was scheduled to teach became ill. I was asked by the chairman of the minister's council to fill in for the sick teacher.

With all the chaos and confusion going on in my life, specifically, the accusations levied by my father and his questionable ways of managing God's church and even my selfish reasons for coveting my father's approval. All of this led me to think about God's ultimate purpose for creating man and adopting us into His family; to glorify Him. Glorifying God should be the one motivating factor in every Christian's life for everything that we do, not to please others, not to gain people's attention or approval and certainly not to make a name one's self. I began searching the scriptures to put together a class to explore the glory of God.

The following evening, I arrived at church ready to teach. It could have been my imagination but it seemed the moment I stepped into the church doors I felt a chill in the air that was not coming from the air conditioners. As my foot crossed the threshold of the doors conversations appeared to cease and heads covertly turned in my direction. Outbursts of barely concealed laughter occurred with every step I took as I made my way through the foyer. *"It's all in your mind,"* I told myself .."*you're being overly sensitive."* "Praise the Lord," I said with a forced smile. A few of the people returned the greeting, and those who normally greeted me seemed to be standoffish. Their greetings were curt, or they spoke warmly to my family and ignored me altogether. Real or imagined there was something unpleasant brewing in the air, and I had no idea why. Mother's words came strongly to mind " *…..you can't do anything for God without expecting some pain."*

I shook it off and headed for the ladies' restroom. As the restroom door swung open, several familiar ladies were standing at the mirror chatting and combing their hair. I approached the mirror to make sure I looked presentable. I politely spoke, and one or two of the ladies smiled in my direction, but the others either did not hear me or just chose to ignore me. *What is going on? Why am I getting the cold shoulder?* I was still checking my appearance when Kendra entered the restroom.

"Hey Vanessa," she said standing next to me at the mirror. "I hear you're teaching tonight?"

I nodded yes. A lady standing next to me overheard our conversation, she asked, "You're teaching tonight?" pointing her hairbrush in my direction. I replied that I was. She began stuffing her things in her purse. "Now I know I'm going home," she said to the lady beside her, but loud enough for me to hear. "Wait for me." Her friend replied, and they both exited the restroom.

I looked in the mirror at Kendra hoping she could help me understand what that was all about. She was as much in the dark as I was. She smiled weakly, "I don't know what that was all about, but I'd better go. I'll talk to you later." And she left me staring in the mirror too dumbfounded to say anything. I started to search my mind to recall if I had said anything or done anything offensive to anyone. I wondered if this had something to do with Russell? Or was it a test of some sort? Whatever was going on I didn't have time to concentrate on that now, I put on my best face and headed toward the sanctuary, I sat next to Calvin and waited for the service to begin. After being introduced I went through the proper preliminaries; acknowledging God and all the leaders in their perspective positions, I turned to the scripture for the Bible lesson. At first, it was hard to focus on what I was supposed to be teaching with too many thoughts crowding my head, especially when I perused the audience. The faces looking back at me seemed apathetic, unmoved ----- *It's all in your mind Vanessa, all in your mind. Just do what you were asked to do......*

The silence in the room made me nervous and uncertain and I wasn't sure if they were listening to the lesson or too polite to get up and leave --- I hoped the silence was an indication they were listening attentively. After a while, I forgot about the coldness of the room and got into the lesson. Midway through Bible study, I forgot about the crowd and concentrated on teaching the lesson, hoping that someone would be blessed.

At the end of every service, First Deliverance has a tradition of the congregation shaking hands with the person who has taught or delivered the message. Whether we have a guest speaker or the speaker is a member of the congregation. The one who has ministered receives their blessings, in appreciation for teaching the Word. After the invitation to join the church was over I stood in the aisle, as a few members of the congregation came forward to show their appreciation. Afterwards I made a quick exit out the side door for the ladies' room.

Thankfully the restroom was empty. I splashed some cold water on my face. As I looked in the mirror Mother's words came to my mind.... *it's not easy to minister when you're being talked about...Vanessa, can you wholeheartedly teach the very people who appear to despise your very presence?* Was this one of those times I thought as I wiped my face? Maybe, I was not ready to step into a position of leadership, if I could not handle the cold shoulder treatment from a few people. The Apostle Paul's words to his protégé Timothy came to mind, "………..be instant in season and out of season"

I will be the first to admit that lesson needed some tweaking—it definitely wasn't my best effort. I had to hurry before the minister received the offering and gave the dismissal prayer. I was hoping to avoid as many people as possible. I was still mentally beating myself up over the outcome of the Bible class when the bathroom door opened.

"Sister Collins? Sister Collins?" It was Sister Marian Westbrook our head usher, "There you are, I thought I saw you come in here dearie. Deacon Taylor wants to speak with you before you leave." She said.

Deacon Horace Taylor was our head deacon. Since the church began, he had been father's right-hand man, and after my father died, he took charge of maintaining the church and spearheading the search for a new pastor.

"Alright," I said. "I'll be out in a moment. Thank you." *What could he want?* "Is it something that could wait until tomorrow or Sunday?" I asked Sister Westbrook.

"Oh no, Sister Collins," said very sternly. "He wants to see you tonight. He's waiting for you in the conference room."

"The conference room?" I repeated to make sure I heard her correctly.

"Yes. The conference room," She said smiling.

Why the conference room and not his office? "Alright, thank you Sister Westbrook, I'll be out in a minute." I returned to the mirror assuming she would leave the restroom and trust that I would find Deacon Taylor when I was done. But she remained in the doorway holding the restroom door open making sure I would not escape the building. I checked my hair once more, washed my hands and exited the restroom.

The vestibule area was strangely quiet. Typically, once our Bible study were over we filed out of the sanctuary hurrying to get home to prepare for work and children for school. But the hall area was strangely bare. Not a deacon or an usher was visible. Everyone was still inside the sanctuary. I checked my watch it said 9:05 pm. That was quite odd. It appeared the congregation was having a discussion. I could hear voices coming from inside the sanctuary that sounded as though they were arguing or someone was very passionately making a point. I strained to understand what they were saying, but Sister Westbrook was walking so briskly that I almost had to run to keep up with her.

Sister Westbrook led me all the way to the conference room as though I was unaware of its location. When she opened the door inside were: Calvin, Deacon Taylor, and several leaders of the church Dr. Lewis McClellan and Sister Claire Robbins. Also, sitting at the table were several faces who looked familiar but names I could not recall. Dr. McClellan was an elderly gentleman who serves as the Director of Christian Education. By profession, he is a teacher of biblical theology. He has always been a very kind man who was easy to talk to and extremely friendly, he possessed an excellent mind for teaching and studying the Bible.

Sister Robbins is a friendly and intelligent woman in her late fifties. She's a short, plump woman who loves to dress in bright colors and wear large fancy hats. Her affable personality and active mind make her one of our most valued leaders in the church and a person of influence among the congregation.

I greeted everyone and searched each of their faces, hoping to find a meaning for this spur of the moment meeting. Deacon Taylor wore his usual stern, hard to read facial expression. Calvin's stone-faced appearance gave me no clue either. Dr. McClellan and Sister Robbins seemed to look at me with blank expressions.

Deacon Taylor motioned for me to sit down. When about to broach a serious subject, or try to find the right words to say Deacon Taylor had a habit of rubbing the patch of gray on his beard or removing his glasses to rub his eyes. If Deacon Taylor made either of those gestures, I knew for sure something important was about to go down.

"Alright, Sister Collins come on in, have a seat. I think that you know everyone here. I don't know if you had any other plans or meetings tonight?"

He paused waiting for me to reply.

"No, Deacon Taylor I don't have any plans other than to go home," I said searching the faces staring back at me for a clue of what was going on.

"Good, good, this should not take too long. Here's what we want to do…" He started flipping through papers in a folder. Cleaning his glasses with his handkerchief. He placed his eye- glasses on the table and rubbed his beard as though he was in deep thought. I was getting older by the minute. I wanted to yell at him to get to the point.

"I know this is a little unorthodox, not our usual method…… however when God gives you a directive and tells you to act right away--- then you have no recourse but to act immediately. Would you agree with me, Sister Collins?"

"If the Holy Spirit is leading, then yes I would agree," I answered. *Directive? What kind of directive?*

He continued, "I've already spoken to your husband, Deacon Collins and he has given his consent in this matter. While you were teaching, the Lord spoke to myself and Dr. McClellan. Then we met with Sister Robbins, and after a brief but thorough discussion it turned out we were all on the same page. So, we called in Deacon Collins, and now we are meeting with you."

Again, I nodded, silently waiting for him to continue. *This impromptu meeting must have something to do with all the dirty looks I've been getting lately. But what on earth have I done?*

"The congregation of First Deliverance Christian Church and the pastoral search committee have been divinely led to ask you to become our interim pastor. At the command of the Holy Spirit, we held a spontaneous election while you were out of the sanctuary and a decision was reached to ask you to consider accepting this position."

What? Are you serious? I knew it was coming, but tonight? Just like that? I tried to look more pleasant than surprised. I was speechless. Deacon Taylor continued talking.

"You probably think this is last minute and why the rush? You're right it is last minute, but sometimes God works this way. He sets the rules and has the option of changing them when He pleases. We, Dr. McClellan, Sister Robbins and I all believe we are following the leading of the Holy Spirit."

"I must warn you of what to expect before we enter the sanctuary. As always there will be challenges and oppositions. Everybody is not on board with having a female pastor. A lot of the brothers and surprisingly even some of the sisters do not want a female as their spiritual leader or senior pastor. You do understand that?"

"Yes, I understand," I responded.

"We are mature enough to know that in God it's not so much about male or female as it is about carrying out the Lord's commands and instructions. We feel, or rather believe that the Spirit of God is leading us. Well, how about it Sister Collins, are you up to the challenge?" Deacon Taylor said peering at me over his eyeglasses.

For reasons unknown I suddenly felt the burden of this task ---- overseeing souls, leading God's people. The weight of my mother's words hit me like a ton of bricks--- *"Don't toy with God's people ---there is a heavy toll for those who lead deceptively----remember your purpose is to help people get to heaven.* I don't know why, but suddenly I found it difficult to make my mouth move. My hands started to sweat, and my throat became parched.

Calvin leaned across the table. "Vanessa," he whispered, "They're waiting for an answer---- say something."

"We must hear your verbal consent before we can proceed." Deacon Taylor said looking at me very intently.

I cleared my throat. "Yes. Yes, I accept....I would love to lead this congregation," I said

Calvin sat back in his chair and breathed a sigh of relief. Deacon Taylor stood and shook my hand. The others in the room did the same. Sister Robbins hugged me tightly and said: "God is going to do some great things."

Sister Robbins with a business-like air took the floor. "We understand the vote from the congregation was not unanimous. However, it was enough to ask you to become our next interim pastor. Before we go into the sanctuary, there are a few issues we must discuss, and afterwards, Deacon Taylor will explain your job requirements."

Deacon Taylor explained the terms of the interim pastor. "Since we've never had an interim pastor the board and I sat down and wrote a list of your expected duties, the salary and general expectations. I won't go into everything tonight--- let's see here…"

He opened a manila folder and began flipping through several pages. "For time sake, I'll just cover some of the main topics, Sister Collins and I will cover the minute details later."

"Alright, the board agreed on a six-month probationary period where all facets of your leadership style and the effectiveness of your leading will be evaluated. For example, we'll monitor how well you motivate the congregation, counseling members, the ministry leaders, how well you execute your God-given vision, and also your ability to give directions as well as interact with the board, etc, etc,. For the next six months, you'll serve as our Senior Pastor. This includes the teaching and preaching portions of all major worship services. You will be expected to work with all the leaders and ministry personnel of the church. Since you are already familiar with everyone this should not be a difficult adjustment."

He looked down at his file folder of papers. "At the end of six months, we will return to the congregation for their approval to determine if you should be retained or dismissed. Our determination will be based solely on your performance as a leader of the people. If elected as our new Senior Pastor you may choose your staff for various positions as the Lord leads you. However, during the six-month probationary period, you are required to work with those assigned to you or already in position."

He closed the folder and placed it on the table. A serious look came over his face. "Sister Collins, there is one more thing— I may be redundant in saying this but I'll take the risk anyway. An exemplary lifestyle is expected, and should be especially seen in the pastor. I think you know what I'm saying, but I'll spell it out so there won't be any misunderstanding. I'm talking about living a sinless life to the best of your ability. You are expected to be an example before and to the people. We know you can't be perfect…we, this board and your congregation expect you to come as close to perfect as you can possibly get. Any kind of disgrace, even just a whisper or a hint of your involvement in any reprehensible activities that tarnishes the name of God's church will result in immediate dismissal. This is not my rule or our rule, this is God's rule and commands according to His law."

Again, he peered at me over his glasses, "Am I making myself clear?"

"Yes sir, perfectly."

"Good. Now, Sister Collins, do you have any questions about the trial period or your duties or anything that I have covered tonight?"

I thought for a moment. "No, I don't have any questions at this moment, I'm sure later on I may have plenty of questions and concerns."

"Great! Nothing like getting a good understanding." He gathered his papers and closed his folder.

Sister Robbins passed Deacon Taylor another folder from which he pulled two sheets of paper. "Alright, these are the letters of agreement. If you will sign both copies of this letter of agreement, the business portion of this procedure is complete." I quickly read the letters and signed my name. Dr. McClellan gave a copy to Sister Robbins and the other copy he put in an envelope and passed it to Calvin.

"Alright, are we all on the same page?" he asked. No one said anything "Your silence means consent. Let's take this to the congregation." He stood, grabbed me by the shoulders hugged me and gave Calvin a hearty handshake.

Deacon Taylor called for the usher, and we quietly exited the room. Calvin held my hand tightly as Deacon Taylor, and Sister Robbins led the way. I was glad we entered the sanctuary through the side door rather than parade down the center aisle. My first thought was to sit in the pew with the congregants, but Sister Westbrook gently but firmly took me by the arm and led me to the front of the pulpit area and motioned Calvin and me to face the congregation. As soon as we took our places the people began applauding. I scanned the audience until I found Melanie and Lawrence. Melanie was clapping her hands wildly and beaming from ear-to-ear. It came as no surprise that Lawrence was neither applauding nor smiling. He stood with his hands stuffed into his pockets, his eyes glued to the floor, a sour expression on his face.

As I continued to search the audience, I noticed that most of their responses were favorable. Many did not try to hide their feelings of indifference or disappointment. I forced myself to focus on the approving faces and choose to enjoy the moment.

As the applause died down Deacon Taylor took the podium. "I am pleased to announce that Sister Collins has been selected as our new interim pastor." Once again, the assembly of people stood and applauded, and I think I even heard a few cheers.

Deacon Taylor continued. "First Deliverance did you enjoy that lesson tonight?" Again, the audience applauded. "I love to hear teaching on the glory of the Lord. I think we need more of that and I think that Sister Vanessa may be a chip off the old block. She teaches as well as her father. I've known this young lady since she was a babe in her mother's arms. It's obvious how much she has grown in the Lord. Her parents, if they were with us would be godly proud of their daughter. I thank God for the blessing they've been to this church."

"How many know that this is God's church and because it's His church, He can do as He pleases? Well it has pleased the Lord to make a shift in the leadership of this congregation. The first shift came, of course when we tragically lost Pastor Woods and his wife in the horrendous car accident. Some of you may be aware there was something in the works before the Lord called Pastor Woods home, to move certain people into specific positions. But apparently, that was not the Lord's will. Tonight, God has instituted a move, that neither I nor Dr. McClellan realized until this very evening. Sister Collins was not on our short list of candidates. As it turned out she was on God's list, the only list that really matters."

He removed the microphone from its cradle and moved to the side of the podium. "Let me say, that for those of you who think Sister Collins campaigned for this position or heard rumors of Sister Collins belittling others so she might be the front-runner-----and you know who the others are. Let's just put things out in the open. You all know who they are and what was said----Sister Collins did nothing of the sort." Looking intently out into the audience, he pointed his finger at me as he spoke. "Sister Collins and I never spoke of this matter until tonight. She and I never discussed any of the other candidates, because she did not know who they were. Sister Robbins and her committee were the only ones aware of those in consideration."

"There is a myriad of rumors circulating about Sister Collins and others who were supposedly fighting for the leadership of this church---others may have been clamoring for this position ---- but not Sister Collins. Not a word of it is true. I want to get that out in the open. Because this is the Lord's doing...."

"Saints, tonight is a night of destiny. In the by-laws of First Deliverance Christian Church section five, article seven, third paragraph, states that we may hold a spontaneous election if we are so led by divine counsel. We were divinely led during Bible class when the Holy Ghost spoke to Dr. McClellan and myself, we had words in the hallway and agreed God was saying do it tonight."

The people applauded. He turned to look at me. "Sister Collins, tonight you are stepping into your destiny."

"Yes!" Shouted Dr. McClellan. "Glory to God!"

"Church, I believe God has a special work for this great body of believers. We've endured many hirelings in the past year or so---- those who cared more about the position than they did the people. And even some who just wasn't right. But I'm so glad that God had someone waiting right here in our midst that He wants to use. Someone we never considered, but that is unimportant. Most of all I'm so glad that she is the daughter of our founder and first pastor of this assembly. First Deliverance Christian Church I introduce to you for the first time, your newly elected Interim Pastor, Pastor Vanessa Elaine Collins."

The people stood and applauded. Several people from various areas of the room left the sanctuary.

"The scripture in First Timothy commands that we pray for all those in authority. The ministers will come and anoint Interim Pastor Collins and her family. We're going to petition God's very best blessings for this congregation and the new leadership He has given to us." Melanie and Lawrence came forward. We stood in a circle as the ministers laid their hands on our heads Deacon Taylor lead the congregation in a fiery and sincere prayer.

After the prayer, Calvin, Melanie and Lawrence took their seats. I was asked to say a few words to the congregation. As I looked over the many faces in the room, I was both nervous and excited. I couldn't believe that this moment was finally here, I did not have time to prepare a speech or any kind of words. I knew that whatever I said would be short and to the point.

"On many occasions I have stood behind this podium, as teacher, sometimes as a soloist and in my younger days when I recited scripture as a young child. Never have I stood before you in this role as a leader of God's people. I know it sounds cliché, but I am honored and humbled, and I mean that from the bottom of my heart. I feel very privileged that God would choose me to serve in His Kingdom and that you would allow me to serve you in this capacity. One of the greatest blessings we can receive in this life is not material things, it's not houses or land, but to be used of God----to be a willing vessel in His Kingdom.

"It goes without saying that I wish it could have happened under different circumstances. It has been almost three years since my parent's death but like you, I continue to miss them both very much. Although, it was not God's will for them to be with us tonight, I believe it is His will for us to continue the work that was begun by my father Pastor Charles P. Woods." The entire congregation erupted in applause. I paused as the audience celebrated his memory.

"With the help of the Lord, we will work diligently not only to continue his work, but also to expand the ministry he started. I believe he would want us to go higher and deeper in God and ministry. He gave us a strong foundation built on the Word and faith in God. It's time that we leave the elementary things and go onto perfection. I am incapable of doing this great work alone. I need your help. We must work together to fulfill the destiny placed on our lives. You have my word that I will do my level best to lead this congregation as God leads me. I will continue to pray God's best for each one of you and please keep my family and me in your prayers." I returned the podium to Deacon Taylor.

Deacon Taylor pointed out, "As we have already scheduled an evangelist for this Sunday. Pastor Collins will deliver her inaugural sermon the following Sunday. That will give her a little more time to prepare." He chuckled. "Let's remember the Collins family in our prayers they will certainly need it."

Deacon Taylor looked around the room and out at the congregation. "Well," he began. "It has been a glorious evening, now it's time to go home. Before we leave, there's a song that's been in the back of my mind, I hear the words and the tune ringing in my head. How many sense the presence of the sweet Holy Spirit? I certainly do. Before we exit the building, let's sing a little bit of the glory song. Let's see if you remember how it goes." He retrieved the hymnal from the shelf on the podium and located the page of the song. I don't know why he picked up the hymnal, he knew the entire song by heart. Deacon Taylor did not have the best singing voice, but what he lacked in melodiousness, he made up in the lively way he could lead a song.

You know how certain odors or songs can evoke a specific image from the past? Or prompt you to recall a memory of something or someone that you have long forgotten? I had not thought of this song in years, it didn't have the prettiest melody or the catchiest tune, but it aroused in my mind memories from a long time ago. Good, sweet memories. The moment Deacon Taylor began to sing, it took me back, way back to when I was a little girl, and my Daddy would be puttering around the house, whistling and singing this very same tune. I could hear his deep baritone voice:

> *My soul has a story one I love to tell.*
> *Of my precious Savior, whose love I know full well.*
> *Glorious righteous savior, trusted Friend is He,*
> *Sacrificed His life for me by hanging on a tree*

I closed my eyes, and in my mind's eye, I saw my father in the bathroom, a towel on his shoulder, shaving cream on his face, whistling and shaving. Or he would be in the garage working on his car and singing at the top of his lungs, or standing behind his podium, as he called it, in the sanctuary, singing his heart out. Or on occasion during our family prayer time, he would lead out with this song, sometimes tears streaming down his face. Every verse, every word, every phrase conjured up more and more memories of my father glorifying His God in song.

> *I'm giving God the glory, I'm giving God the praise.*
> *He's worthy of the glory, forever and always.*
> *Every day its glory and every day its praise.*
> *I love to give Him glory, I love to give Him praise*

As I sung the words of the song, I began to understand why it was one of Daddy's favorite hymns. The lyrics tell the story of someone determined to give God the glory, and that, I believe was my father's greatest desire; for God to get the glory out of his life. Without a doubt, my father made many, many mistakes, as we all do. However, I believe he loved God and desired to give Him his best and his all. Daddy's favorite verse told the story of Moses on Mount Caramel, I hoped Deacon Taylor would sing that line, sure enough he did:

> *Moses saw His glory up in the mountain high*
> *In His glorious presence, his face began to shine*

> *Amazed by His beauty, engulfed in His love*
> *Covered in God's glory shining brightly from above*

With our hands lifted high in the air, the entire congregation sang loud, energetic, sounding like one voice ringing throughout the sanctuary. We praised our great God for His glorious presence that permeated our place of worship and our everyday lives. It wasn't long before the glory of the Lord filled the entire room as we sung each chorus. What started as a quiet flow of worship gradually transformed into a rousing song of praise, as the lyrics reminded us of why God is so deserving of glory and praise.

> *The angels up in heaven worship around the throne*
> *Singing holy, holy, holy, is God and God alone*
> *They never cease to praise God and His only Son*
> *Worshipping the Father is all they've ever done*

Soon very few were singing, they were caught up in the spirit of worship and enjoying the presence of the sweet Holy Spirit. Only the soft dulcet sounds of the organist playing could be heard as the praises of God resounded across the room. I fell to my knees in worship. I tried to subdue the feelings, soon I gave in to the promptings of the Holy Spirit. We continued to worship until the spirit lifted. Before leading us in a dismissal prayer, Deacon Taylor sung the chorus a few more times:

> *I'm giving God the glory, I'm giving God the praise.*
> *He's worthy of the glory, forever and always.*
> *Every day its glory and every day its praise.*
> *I love to give Him glory, I love to give Him praise*

Calvin and I greeted the members of the congregation. We were overwhelmed by their congratulations, hearty handshakes, warm embraces of hugs, kisses, and promises of prayers and cooperation.

Other disheartened members very boldly stated their feelings of disappointment and their plan to move their membership to another church since I was not their choice. Others walked by without saying a word. For the most part, most of the members offered words of support. With a smile plastered on my face, I pleasantly acknowledged and thanked all those who supported me and sincerely wished all the others God's blessings.

Audrey and Tara ran towards me with their arms extended. "Why didn't you tell us? I knew something was up with you." Audrey said. "Congratulations Vanessa."

"Wow congratulations," Tara said hugging me. "I hope you remember everything we talked about at Juno's?"

We laughed. "Believe me I remember exactly what was said."

"Ohhhh Vanessa," It was Karen and Zoe.

"Did you know it was going to be tonight? You looked like you were in complete shock."

"I had no idea."

"Congratulations Pastor Vanessa...." She laughed and hugged me tightly. "Hey did you take care of what we talked about?"

"Not yet," I said while hugging little Zoe.

"Have you tried on the robe Aunt Vanessa?" Zoe asked. "You should wear it for your first sermon."

"Yes, sweetie I did try it on, and I promise I will wear it."

I turned to Karen. "I never thanked you for the robe, did I?'

"No, you did not," She said smartly.

"You know I appreciate you," I said. When I looked at her she had tears in her eyes. Karen was not one to easily to cry.

She grabbed my hands, "I love you too. I just wish Dad was here to see his baby girl. I know you're going to be such a blessing to this church."

"I hope so Karen," I whispered in her ear.

Just about when everyone had left, and I was gathering my purse and notebooks together I felt a hand on my shoulder, I spun around to see Kendra's smiling face.

"Vanessa, I didn't see this coming—at all," She said with a wry smile. "Congratulations Pastor Collins." She gave me a hug. "Guess I have to get used to saying that."

Remembering the conversation from the other night, I asked her, "Does this mean you won't be sticking around?"

"I'm not sure what I'm going to do…we'll talk about that later. I'm more interested in your new responsibility--- I never imagined— why didn't you tell me?"

"Well, it's not the kind of thing you go around telling people…."

'I'm not just *people*, I thought we were friends--."

"We *are* friends Kendra. I wanted to tell you, I really did, especially the other night when we were talking in the car …but it wasn't the time…. " I didn't know what else to say to her.

"I'm happy for you, really I am. And if I know you, you're going to do a fantastic job."

"Thank you, Kendra, I hope so, hey, I'll call you tomorrow, and we'll talk – I promise."

"Vanessa, you'll be pretty busy getting things together and organizing stuff so…. if you have time I'd love to talk…if not I understand…I'm sure we'll talk when you get a free moment." She hugged me again and left the building. I had a feeling she was not going to be with us long. The possibility of losing my dearest friend in the whole world, kind of put a damper on the entire evening.

Calvin, Melanie and I were so overcome with the excitement of everything that had occurred in the last few hours that we completely forgot about Lawrence's sullen attitude. The three of us talked excitedly about the evening's events as Lawrence sat in silence the whole ride home.

Have you ever felt an unbelievable feeling of joy that you just can't describe? Or fell asleep grinning from ear-to-ear and woke up the next morning with the same smile on your face? Or just had a feeling in your heart of high expectations? That's how I felt tonight and to think earlier that evening the weight of the world was on my shoulders. And I felt like all hope was lost. I only had to wait on God. Allow God to fight my battles, and soon enough He would come through for me. I felt a little like Joseph whose life was changed overnight. One moment he was locked up in Pharaoh's prison, and the next day he became second in command in Egypt. I'm not saying my circumstances was that dramatic, but I think you get my point. The sovereign God is capable of literally changing your situation overnight. All those years Joseph held his dream in his heart until God made good on His promise. He also made good on His promises to me. He alone had opened a door that no one could close. Not my brother, my deceased father, even my own son. I understood now, what the older saints meant when they said: "If God has something for you can't nobody keep it from you but you." I always knew He had something great in store for me but never knew when it would be revealed. Now was the time for celebration and unbridled rejoicing, in a few days I would have to roll up my sleeves and get to work leading God's people.

Before going to bed, I made a list of things I had to do within the next week:

-Ask Calvin to fast with me,

-Write sermon—(one week to complete)

- Meet with Deacon Taylor and First deliverance leadership

-Visit my brother Russell

-Shop for a new outfit for inaugural sermon

While Calvin was brushing his teeth, I closed my journal, and slipped to my knees to pray before laying down for the night. Soon I felt Calvin beside me. He clasped his hands in mine and together we worshipped God. The presence of the Lord filled the room as we rejoiced in Him. I thanked God for His goodness towards me. I thanked Him for a praying husband who loved God and was secure enough to support me in the work God had given me for His glory. My heart felt so full of love and joy and at the same time so undeserving of God's blessings.

As we lay down for the night, I said to Calvin: "I think I'm going to talk to Russell."

"You are?" He said sitting up in the bed to look at me in the dark.

"Yes, I've got to. It's important and necessary that we talk."

"I still say he's the one who needs to apologize to you, let him come to you. Russ is a grown man. He's more than capable of handling his business."

"That may be true…..but I have a feeling he'll never come around. I'll call Karen, see if she'll go with me. You want to tag along?"

"No thank you, I'll let you and Karen deal with that mess."

"Ok, then good night."

"Good night."

"Mom? Mom where are you?"

Melanie was calling me from the bottom of the stairs. I was in my bedroom, on my hands and knees searching for a missing high heel that somehow mysteriously ended up underneath the bed.

"Aunt Karen is here," She yelled up the stairs.

"Alright, tell her I'm coming," I called to her from the bedroom. I put on a light jacket, grabbed my purse from the dresser and headed downstairs to meet my sister. Zoe and Melanie were sitting on the bottom stair blocking my path.

"Excuse me, girls if you don't mind I'd like to get by please."

"Hi, Aunt Vanessa" Zoe said, "My mom is waiting for you in the car."

"Hello, Zoe. I know, I'm running a little late." Turning to Mel, I said. "I expect you to handle things until your father and Lawrence comes home. You know the rules. Don't let a soul into this house, I don't care who it is, and you two do not leave this house. You know what to do if an emergency occurs. We may be gone a couple of hours, so don't expect us back too soon."

"Ok Mom I've done this many times before, don't worry," Melanie replied.

"Yea, Aunt Vanessa," Zoe said, "We got this." Zoe, Karen's youngest child, was all of nine years old, barely four feet tall, she didn't know how ridiculous she sounded.

"Me and the little squirt will be just fine." Melanie and Zoe laughed. "She wants to help me work on my blog. So, we'll do that and then maybe we'll find something to watch on TV."

"Always working on that blog, aren't you? Alright, well you and the little squirt behave. Call me, your Dad or Aunt Karen if anything comes up, alright?" I gave them both a kiss and left the house.

Karen was waiting patiently in the car. I apologized for being so late, and we drove off to meet Russell at his church, St. Aubin's Christian Community Church in North Commons Park. It had not been too hard to get Karen to agree to go with me. Unlike Calvin, she thought it a good idea for us to talk to Russell. There was a possibility he was still upset by the results of the election and we agreed he may want an explanation as to why neither of us voted for him.

"We gotta hurry," Karen said soon as I entered the car. "Their Bible class starts at 7:30, and it's already after 5:00."

"I know. I know," I said getting into the car.

"You're sure he'll have time for us?" She asked.

I had already spoken with Myra his wife, and she said he would have ample time to talk with us.

"I think so. Myra said he has a few hours before Bible class begins, that should be enough time I hope."

"Don't take all day. Just say what you gotta say to smooth things out between you two and let's get out of there." She said.

"Karen, I'm not going to rush in there and rush out. I'm going to take my time and make sure we're ok. You're just worried that something will happen to your precious car."

"That's right I sure am. If we were driving your car, you would be concerned too."

She had a valid point. I would not only be concerned about the security of my car but more concerned about my life. North Commons Park was not an area you would want to be in at night or maybe even during the day.

"How do you think Russ ended up at St. Aubin's?" I asked.

"That's a good question. I'm not sure." She replied. "He has worked with substance abusers in the past, so maybe he's lending his services to this community Lord knows they need it."

She was right again. North Commons Park was a neighborhood that sorely needed much attention in almost every way one could imagine. Each block we passed crawled with those considered to be the lowest in society; ladies of the night stationed on virtually every street corner. Men and women wandering the streets wasting their existence on drugs, alcohol and any substance that would provide a temporary high. Local police and government pooled their efforts to clean the area by removing the unwanted characters and working to make this part of the city more family oriented and safe.

City reformers fought to repair the historic buildings in the area rather than destroy them. The best part of the project was the need to reform lives rather than repair houses and office buildings. They offered temporary shelters for the homeless, counseling for the troubled teenagers, assistance for those who abused drugs and alcohol. The police department along with the city's crime commission swept the streets clean of unwanted corruption. A great revitalizing was slowly taking place.

Karen and I both knew it was unlike Russ to rub shoulders with those who did not come from a certain level of society. I would have expected him to associate with a more intellectual, high society type congregation. Perhaps he had changed in ways we did yet not understand. We would soon find out exactly what was going on in his life.

"Maybe we really don't know Russell like we think," I said partly thinking out loud.

"That's possible," Karen said. "You think you know your family and then they do something totally uncharacteristic."

"Here he is attaching himself to a church, in what most people would call the sleaziest part of town. I thought he was the type to run with the well-to-do-intellectual-type crowd."

"Maybe this was all he could get, you can't just waltz in and start pastoring the church of your choice. That's kind of difficult to do. ...."

"What is St. Aubin's doctrine? What kind of church are they and what do they believe?" I asked.

"I can't say for sure, ...but I believe they're a conservative church... not as charismatic as we are." Karen said thoughtfully.

"Oh, you mean, no hand clapping or foot stomping?"

"Exactly!" She said "You think he wants to pastor that bad? That he'll join up with just anybody?"

"I don't know Karen, not really...maybe he wanted to get as far away from First Deliverance as possible. I think he's still a little embarrassed by the outcome of the election. That's why I wanted to talk to him. Hopefully, he'll be receptive."

"Any idea what you're going to say?" She asked.

"Haven't given it much thought--- I'll apologize, ask for his forgiveness, blah, blah blah----you know how it goes."

"Apologize for what Vanessa, you haven't done anything wrong. You voted your conscience and what you knew to be right."

I didn't reply to her last statement. I knew I had done nothing wrong. But I also knew Russ, and I needed to clear the air. Sometimes the best way to get someone to open up is to ask for forgiveness even if you have not wronged them in any way.

"Say what you want, I'm here for moral support…. his beef is with you. I'm not in this at all." Karen said.

"You didn't vote for him either Karen, so there is a chance he may be upset with you too."

"By the way, Pastor-elect Collins, as Deacon Taylor likes to call you. Have you been getting a lot of suggestions from people about how to run the church?"

"Oh, my goodness, Karen, you wouldn't believe how many, calls, texts, emails…. even Audrey called the other day with some ideas. Actually, some of her suggestions are worth considering. But a lot of them I just ignore."

"You should have expected that. Maybe it'll die down after a while, you think?"

"Hope so or I'll just re-direct them to you."

"No thank you ma'am….no thank you." She said laughing. "Vanessa, what about Kendra?" She glanced over at me. "Have you heard anything from her?"

"We haven't had a chance to sit down and talk since the announcement was made."

"Think she'll move her membership from First Deliverance? You're not just *some* woman off the street. She knows you. You two been friends since you were little girls…."

"I would hate to see her go. On the other hand, she has the right to go to the church of her choosing. Truthfully, it would be painful to lose her. But if that happens, I'll learn to live with it, and life will go on."

"Vanessa, it's not that simple, I mean she's one of your closet friends---."

She was right we had known each other since grade school and developed a closeness over the years. I also understood it wasn't about me or friendships or being close to people. What mattered most was her soul. If Kendra felt she could not be spiritually fed under my leadership, then the best thing for her to do was to find another ministry where her soul would be satisfied.

"It will be hard to accept if she left, I know this may sound trite or whatever, but I'm more concerned about her soul. I'm sure we'll continue to be friends, no matter what she decides."

'It's almost like saying she doesn't believe in your ministry." Karen said wistfully.

She voiced what I had been thinking all along and was hesitant to admit or allow myself to believe.

Karen continued "If I were your life-long closest friend I would do all I could to help you be as successful as possible. But then again, she's not me, and maybe she doesn't care for female pastors, she did verbalize that long before she knew about you taking this new role."

"She has a right to her opinion, and she can worship where ever she chooses unless God directs her to a specific place....whatever she decides I won't allow it to affect our friendship one way or the other," I said weakly. "I'll continue to love her rather she stays or goes."

"Truthfully, you would prefer that she stick around?" Karen asked.

"Of course, I would I won't lie to you, but at the same time. Although Kendra's one of my closest friends, I don't want to force her to do something against her wishes just to please me. I hope I'm more mature than that."

"If you asked her to stay she would probably stay….."

"I think she would, but I'm not going to ask her to do that…I wouldn't want to put her in an awkward position. It's not fair, and it's a little selfish."

"It would be interesting trying to pastor your best friend, maybe that's her concern, you think that's it?" She asked looking in my direction.

I hunched my shoulders. To be perfectly honest I didn't think it was a personal thing. I knew Kendra had nothing against me, this was not a personal vendetta against me, this was her preference. "I'm sure I can call on Kendra if I need her," I said. Karen sensed she had touched a sore spot and quickly changed the conversation. For the remainder of the drive, I looked out the window

Throughout the neighborhood, the sounds of summer filled the air, car horns blowing, occasional police sirens and the voices of children playing in the streets. People blasting music from their cars and a group of young guys stood on the corner talking, gesturing and laughing. A serious game of basketball was taking place on a concrete playground. When we finally arrived at the church. Karen was hesitant to park her car on the street for fear of it being stolen or vandalized. I assured her it would be safe. A security guard spotted us sitting in the car. He inquired if we were visiting the church and suggested if we wanted our car to be safe and secure it would best to park it in the parking lot behind the church building.

The old church was nestled in the middle of a residential area. It was a considerably large ancient building that took up almost half the block. The church itself was surrounded by a row of boarded-up houses and a section of homes that appeared to be occupied and others that were undergoing renovations. I had to admit it was a beautiful historic building, the kind of antique structure that architects and archaeologists loved to study and preserve. The exterior of the building was a dark grey cobblestone. Around the perimeter of the building were colorful stained-glass windows of flying angels strumming harps, blowing trumpets and Mary, the mother of Jesus holding her baby boy in her arms. A concrete steeple was perched high on the slate rooftop, and a tall black wrought iron-gate enclosed the entire property. A sign in front of the church read: St. Aubin's Community Christian Church: A Church Who Serves The Community. A row of three or four steps leading to red double doors with black ironwork. Someone had pinned a note on the double doors "PLEASE USE SIDE DOOR."

We walked to the side of the building and found a door that to our surprise was unlocked. The door's hinges were severely in need of oiling because it creaked loudly as we pulled it open. The squeaking door must have been an alarm system of sorts because as soon as we opened it an older gentleman carrying a broom appeared from the hallway and waved us inside.

"Good day ladies," he said laying his broom in the corner. "I'm Reverend Wally, one of the faithful workers here at St. Aubin. You must be here to see Pastor Russell." He slowly removed his gloves and shook both of our hands.

"Yes," I answered him. "We're here to see Pastor Russell."

"Come on in. We love having visitors around here. Follow me, ladies. Pastor Russell said he was expecting some guest. He didn't say they would be such lovely guest," He smiled at us. "Come this way, and I'll show you to his office."

This amiable gentleman led us to Russell's office through the vestibule, past several rooms where we could hear children singing and playing. Reverend Wally was a talkative, elderly gentleman who ambled along because of a gimpy left leg. He was proud of his church, and it showed as he patiently detailed the activities taking place in every room we passed.

"Through that hallway is our sanctuary---and this room right here --- where the children are playing is part of our daycare program." He said pointing as he exclaimed about his church.

We politely listened and made kind remarks about each room. Every room appeared to be occupied with some type of training or educational activity. In one room adults were being tutored. In another area, senior citizens sat at a row of computers and then another room we could see Bible class being taught in a small chapel. I had misjudged this congregation simply by the disrepair of the building and the wayward people in the streets. From the adult tutoring classes and day-care program, it appeared they were doing their part to help uplift this needy and deprived group of people. I had to admit I was impressed and ashamed for misjudging the congregation simply by the looks of their edifice and the neighborhood.

When we reached the end of the hallway, Reverend Wally led us up a cramped, rickety staircase. The staircase so tight we were forced to climb the stairs in single file. The higher we climbed the staircase the more we were exposed to a structure that was sorely in need of repair. Reverend Wally led us to the top of the second landing and stood to the side. "My dear sisters this is as far as my tired old legs will carry me. If you go up one more flight, you'll see Sister Mayfield, the receptionist sitting at her desk she can help you from there."

We thanked him and continued up the last flight of stairs. Upon reaching the third and final landing, we met a lady busy typing away at a computer. She had been expecting us and immediately led us to Russell's office. As his secretary turned the doorknob to his office, I took a deep breath and braced myself for what could possibly be a hostile and unfriendly greeting. We had not seen or heard from Russell since the night of the election. A year or more had passed, and we had had minimal contact with our brother. It wasn't for lack of trying. He refused to answer our calls and ignored numerous voice messages. I wasn't sure what to expect if he would be a friend or foe.

As we stepped inside the office, Russell came from behind his desk to greet us. His resemblance to daddy was instantly noticeable; he had the same hearty laugh, a slightly receding hairline, and daddy's friendly but self-assured posture when greeting parishioners, and when he gave you that gapped tooth grin, there was no denying Russell was a younger version of our father. I was so pleased to see him smiling and his arms reaching out to embrace us. His greeting seemed genuine and absent of any anger or resentment. Maybe I was wrong in expecting him to be upset with us. Hopefully, he had let bygones be bygones and forgot the past. I breathed a sigh of relief. He laughed, hugging us both very tightly.

Karen stood back to look at Russell and exclaimed. "Vanessa, can you believe this, Russell is wearing blue jeans!"

I shook my head in disbelief. Russell in a pair of blue jeans is noteworthy because our brother never ever wore blue jeans or gym shoes. In fact, long as I've known him, he despised blue jeans and only wore them when he was forced to by our parents. We never understood how or why he developed such a penchant for stylish or chic attire. That has always been one of his many personality quirks. Neither of my parents cared that much about clothing, and Karen and I was not into style as much as he was. Russell wasn't a flashy person, but he never stepped out of the house unless he made sure he was well-groomed and presented a neat appearance. That smart and well-groomed appearance never included wearing blue jeans or gym shoes. Two items of clothing he did not care for. Blue jeans, he said were for those who worked in coal mines. And gym shoes were meant to wear in the gym or on the tennis court. You understand why it would be shocking for us to see him dressed in clothing that he detested. Maybe this was the new unpretentious Dr. Woods. Less showy and less pompous. Perhaps this was his attempt to appeal to the common man. I was glad for this change, even though it was superficial, it made me hopeful that more essential changes in his life were made as well.

He greeted us with arms outstretched and a huge smile. "Bless the Lord and praise God, my sisters. Karen, Vanessa, how good to see you both." He said in his best preacher's voice. "Come on in and have a seat." Karen and I slyly glanced at each other. Unfortunately, as soon as he opened his mouth, we knew it was business as usual. He may have changed his appearance, but his pretentious demeanor remained the same.

"May I offer either of you a cold drink, water, soda?" We both declined his offer.

"Russell," I said "You look good, really good. I love your new more laid-back look." He did look well rested, much better than I expected. He seemed to be happy unless it was all an act for our benefit. I know that sounds horrible, I'm being real I wasn't sure what to expect after what he had been through.

"Thank you, Vanessa. Both of you look well as usual."

Karen and I sat in the guest chairs, and Russell perched himself on the corner of his desk. I took a quick survey around his office. It was a rather large room. Some of the décor was a bit dated for my taste. His desk was a lovely antique piece of furniture with a matching credenza. Of course, he had plastered his degrees and other certificates on an entire wall over a beige cloth covered couch. On either side of his desk were two large windows looking out onto the street. The large windows filled the room with lots of light and faint sounds of outside activities. Along the length of the entire back wall was a floor to ceiling bookcase crammed with books, pictures frames and a flat screen television sat on the lower shelf. Behind his desk hung an abstract portrait of Jesus along with a few other nondescript works of art. Just like Russell, his office was neat and well-organized. Several papers were stacked in a pile, along with a few books and a large Bible that lay open in the middle of the desk. His credenza held a small computer, several pictures of his wife and children and a small framed photo of our entire family. Overall it was a well-organized and roomy office. It was badly in need of a paint job, new carpet and the furniture could stand to be updated, but overall not a bad set up.

"Russ, what's with the jeans?" Karen asked. "You said you would never be caught in a pair of blue jeans. Is this the new you?"

"Well, Sister Karen one can't stay the same forever. A man has got to change at some point in his life. Right?" He replied.

"I love your antique desk and the built-in bookshelves," I said, hoping to change the subject.

"Oh, thank you, all of those books aren't mine. Most of them belonged to the former pastor. But I love this office too, it's spacious, and I have everything I need right in this room."

"Do you like this church so far?" I asked.

"I love it here. This is just one of the many changes the Lord has made in my life." He said as he moved to his chair.

Karen sighed deeply. "Russ, you can drop the pastor act. You don't have to put on airs for us. It's just Vanessa and me. We've known you most of your life. There's no need to be so formal. Just be yourself."

He laughed awkwardly, "Guess I can't help it---don't quite know how to turn it off---- it comes so naturally."

"Yes, your arrogance is naturally annoying," Karen said smart-alecky.

Russell wasn't about to let that comment slip by without notice. "Arrogance? You mean my confidence and poise annoy you?"

"Russ, look we're not here to quarrel with you," I said.

"You're right," Russell said flashing us his toothy smile. "Of course, you're not. Just *what* did you come here for Vanessa? What reason could you have for coming to see me today of all days?" There was a slight change in his tone, especially the way he directed his question towards me.

"Please tell me what's so urgent that you two *had* to talk with me today. Is everybody doing well? Are your families well?"

"They're all doing well," I said. "I didn't mean to sound urgent when I called, I just needed to talk with you. I've been putting it off long enough or waiting until I felt it was a good time to talk with you about this ... issue." I said searching for the right words. "I... we, Karen and I wanted to discuss the election night and explain why we voted as we did."

"*Explain?*" He said trying his best to remain calm, but I detected a hint of anger in his voice. "I don't think an explanation is necessary. It was obvious to me and everyone else, you two voted *against* me. What's to explain? You and Karen clearly indicated to me, my family and the entire congregation of First Deliverance that you didn't think your older brother, who for years served as assistant pastor at *that church* was right for the job. I'm glad Mom and Dad were not here to see how you betrayed me."

Clearly, he was still distraught not only about the outcome of the election, but he was especially wounded by the fact that Karen and I offered no support in his hopes of being elected as pastor of First Deliverance.

"Betrayed?" I asked. "Don't be so dramatic, we didn't betray you, Russ."

"What word would you use Vanessa? Deceive? Disloyal? Any of those words work for you?"

"You're missing the point, Russ it wasn't about being loyal to *you*—it was about….."

"No, I think you and Karen missed the point."

He stood up and walked to the window with his hands in his pockets. I wasn't sure if he was still listening or if that was his way of ignoring us. I gave Karen a sign to jump into the conversation.

"Russ, we want to make sure there's no bad blood between us. We're family. Mom and Dad would want us to stick together."

"If that's your idea of sticking together as you put it... that's the kind of support I don't want or need." He was no longer trying to hide the hurt.

"Russell, let's face facts if you were supposed to pastor First Deliverance, if God had intended for that to happen, don't you think you would be there and not here? How could we prevent God's will from happening in your life?" Karen asked.

He remained quiet because he knew she was right.

"I think what Karen is trying to say is that there was nothing that we could have done to change God's mind or the people of First Deliverance. Even if we had voted for you, it wouldn't have made a difference."

"That's just the point, Vanessa! *I* expected your support, that's what families do they support and help each other. For goodness sake, you're my sisters. I thought that was a given. Guess I was wrong for assuming I could depend on my flesh and blood."

"Look, Russ we don't want to make you upset or argue with you...."

"Then why are you here? You keep saying you don't want to fight or argue. Exactly what do you want Vanessa? Did you come to rub it in my face that you're the new pastor-elect?" He leaned over the desk, looking directly at me. "Don't look so surprised. News travels swiftly in the church world."

Just as I was about to respond, loud music from Karen's cell phone filled the room. "I'm sorry, can you two excuse me for a moment," She said fiddling with her phone. "I have to take this call. I'll be back soon as I can." She left the office talking on her phone.

Soon as the door closed, he started again. "Tell the truth, isn't that why you're really here Vanessa? Come to gloat a little?"

"No, I'm not here to gloat. I'm here to apologize and to explain our actions. We, I mean I could see you were hurt."

"Oh-- I see. You want to clear yourself before standing in front of your flock as the new leader. Make sure everything is in order?"

Russ would not let go of the accusations. "It's interesting you visit me here begging my pardon a week before your inaugural sermon *Pastor Collins*." his voice dripping with sarcasm. "What took you so long?" He paused waiting for me to answer. "You or Karen didn't try calling me for months, why are you here today of all days?"

"That's not true, and you know it, I called you. Karen called you. But you never returned our calls. You wouldn't answer your phone when you saw it was one of us calling. We left you messages. We came to your house. You gave us the cold shoulder. If I hadn't seen Myra at the store, there's no telling when we would have heard from you. I wanted to call you the day after the election, I thought it would be better if I waited a while--- give you time to cool down a bit. I understand how you feel. You have every right to be upset with me."

His voice trembled a little as he spoke. "Upset is an understatement for how I felt. Try embarrassed—humiliated, the world's biggest fool, take your pick. Not only was I rejected by my own church, and my family. Those I thought loved me. You have no idea how I felt. Other than the night of Mom and Dad's accident that night was the worse night of my life. I walked out of there feeling like the scum of the earth. I vowed to never, ever set foot in that place again. You might as well have disowned me."

"Russell, what would you have done? If you thought Karen or I was in over our heads. If you felt the Lord saying to you, Vanessa's not the one? Would you defy God just to please family? You wouldn't vote for me just because I'm family. I wouldn't want you to. Because that's not showing support, that's pacifying someone as though they're a child!"

"Amateurs are pacified! I am not an amateur!" He pointed at his chest. "I worked alongside Dad as his assistant pastor learning every aspect of how to run a church, planning to step into a leadership position. What do you know about leading a congregation or running a church? Nothing! Dad wanted *me* to take his place. I know he did, he told me many times. I was the one with the experience. I was the one Dad chose. I was the one he trained. I deserved it more than anyone else. I *know* how to pastor a church--- people who don't know what they're doing---- those are the ones you pacify."

"Russell, I used to care about what people thought of me-- especially family, but I've grown a little ----- what you think of me, and my abilities no longer matter to me---- because I'm not doing it to please you or Daddy."

"You got that right! You're certainly not doing for it Daddy because he didn't think you were capable."

That really stung. Although I knew my father felt I was unable to handle pastoring *his* church, it hurt to hear my brother say the words out loud.

"Russ, I thought you had changed. You're still the same self-centered, pompous, conceited man that you've always been. It's not about you, me, daddy or who's in or who's out--- souls are at stake. Why is it always about you, how good you are, what you've done and what you deserve? God doesn't care about that... I was hoping you had changed in other ways besides your clothes, but it's obvious you still have some growing up to do." I gathered my purse and my jacket from the couch and walked to the door to exit his office.

"Don't you think my soul mattered?" He said as I turned the doorknob. "Wasn't my self-esteem at risk too? Did you ever once consider my sense of self-worth? Did that ever cross your mind?"

I looked at him in disbelief. "Russell, please! That election was not about *you* or *your self-worth*. Get over yourself, Russ. It was about selecting *God's* choice. And I would vote the same way again in a heartbeat because I don't live to please you, I live to please God. You and Daddy are just alike, assuming the church is your empire. First Deliverance was not daddy's kingdom to leave you in his will. It didn't *belong* to him. The Lord allowed him to serve as pastor. The people of First Deliverance are God's people. We serve at His pleasure. We're not there to satisfy you, or to make sure that we get what we want, that's not why the church exists."

"You got what you wanted didn't you?" he said mockingly. "Got exactly what *you* wanted didn't you Vanessa?"

"What I wanted?" I walked towards him. "If you're referring to pastoring, that's the Lord's will for my life, and I make no apologies about it. As for getting what I really wanted....well that never happened for me." I couldn't believe what I was about to say. "Russell, *you* always got what I wanted."

He had a puzzled look on his face, so I continued.

"What I wanted, was my father's admiration. To hear him say good job Vanessa or I enjoyed your teaching Vanessa--- his approval of me in ministry. That's what I wanted and ---I never got it, not like you." I sat down on the couch my eyes focused on the floor, too embarrassed to look him in the face. I had no idea if Russell was aware of how I felt--- but I knew it was time to finally confront this problem.

"I spent most of my young-adult life battling self-doubt, and feelings of jealousy, resenting you and Karen, mostly you because Daddy praised you the most… and it seemed he waited until I was around so I could see first-hand just how proud he was of you and not me. How he praised you and Karen, then when he began coaching you….I wanted that kind of attention and encouragement from him. I wanted him to evaluate my teaching skills, offer advice, give suggestions ---- Whenever I foolishly tried to force my ideas on him ---it angered him, and things grew worse between us. I knew he loved me as his child---- I just wanted daddy to compliment me, to say I did something right when it came to ministry."

He stood in the middle of the floor, arms folded across his chest looking down at me as I sat on the couch. "Poor Vanessa. Poor, poor Vanessa." He said mockingly. He pulled some tissue from the box on his desk and threw them in my direction. He sat on the corner of his desk shaking his head. "Am I supposed to be moved by your sad story? Think your depressing little tale breaks my heart because you failed to get the attention from dad that you thought you so rightly deserved?"

I had just bared my soul to this man, and he had the nerve to ridicule me and scoff at my feelings.

"Vanessa, you're not telling me nothing I didn't already know. I knew what was going on. Dad warned me to expect some resentment, especially from you. It was no secret, if that's what you came here to tell me, you might as well go home, cause I already knew. And I know that not voting for me, was your way of retaliating."

"My vote had nothing to do with you or Dad. I wasn't trying to hurt you or get back at you."

"Could have fooled me. With me out of the running, that gave you a chance to slip right into the position. You and the good Deacon Taylor had it all planned."

"Deacon Taylor? What are you talking about? Deacon Taylor and I never talked about you. You're crazy."

"Yep, I'm crazy alright. Crazy enough to believe that my family would have my back. Should have known you were looking out for you. Look, Vanessa, I've said all I want to say on this topic. It's in the past. I'm doing my best to forget about it, maybe you should too. Go back to First Deliverance and do your thing and I'll do mine."

He returned to his desk. "Unless you have some more groundbreaking news to share, I have more important things that need my attention, so if you don't mind….." He sat down at the desk and turned on his computer.

Russel and I had never had a falling out to this magnitude before. We have had our share of disagreements, but it was never to this degree. Never to the point that we could not settle an argument or iron out our differences. I hated to leave this way upset and angry, things unsettled, issues unresolved. But there was no getting through to this man. He didn't want to face the truth nor did he want to accept our explanation or apology. I was through trying. I wasn't going to waste my time trying to make him understand any longer.

I picked up my purse and jacket from the couch. I knew this was a longshot, but I decided to ask him anyway. "If you and Myra are available….. next Sunday…. Is the uhh…… installation service. I would love to see you and Myra and the kids----"

"My calendar is full for the rest of the month…" he said not even bothering to look up from his books.

Bad timing? Yes, maybe, but I had a feeling that it would be a while before I saw him again. I guess I should have expected he would decline my invitation. Why would he want to be present as I take over a job he desired? A job he desperately tried to get but was denied. It made sense for him to *not* want to be there. Perhaps I was foolish or naïve for asking him to come knowing how he felt about the whole situation. But, I couldn't help it, I wanted my brother and his family to be there, not to rub it in his face, not to gloat, nor to make him fell less than. I wanted him there because he's family, and if circumstances were different, if he had been elected as pastor of First Deliverance, I would support him, and celebrate his achievements, no matter how I felt, no matter how much it hurt.

I was not so naive as to think that all my problems in life and sometimes complicated relationships would have the proverbial happy ending. My relationship with my father did not come close to a happy ending. He died without us having an opportunity to make our peace with each other. Real-life doesn't always work out as you plan or hope, no matter how hard you try. I had hoped against hope that our visit with Russ would not turn out this way. Maybe coming here was a mistake. No, I banished that thought. I knew that was not true. Sometimes you have to do the hard thing, which could mean having an uncomfortable conversation, offering an apology, accepting defeat, etc.. I think you get my point. Besides, the Bible teaches when we have a falling out with someone, we're supposed to reconcile with them before offering God our gift of worship. Karen and I had done what was right by attempting to reconcile with Russell. But he was not ready to face the truth. He's an intelligent man, he had to realize Karen's words were so on point. If it was meant to be nothing and no one could have stopped him from his supposed destiny. Karen and I had no control over the outcome of the election, and it was our prerogative to vote however we wanted to. I knew in my heart of hearts that I did not vote against him as any kind of retaliation. I know it looks as though I was trying to make room for myself, but that's not true. I trusted God to open the door of opportunity for me when the time was right. I knew I didn't have to disparage anyone's reputation or take part in malicious activities to receive what God had promised me. The only thing I had to do was be prepared and when the time was right step into the open door of opportunity.

As I looked at my brother sitting at his desk, pretending to be absorbed in his Bible study. I realized I did not want to risk leaving Russell this way, hurt, angry, bitter and me feeling guilty and upset with him for his childish ways. This was no way to depart his office feeling despondent, and without having come to some resolution. I had not seen him in months, and if I were to make my exit now, there is no telling when we would see each other again, and if we did see each other, I would not be sure how he would receive me.

I was almost out the door when I decided to give it one final try. I left the door slightly ajar and turned to see if Russell was watching as I left the office. His head was buried in his books as though he was hard at work studying.

"Russell?" I said closing the door.

Releasing a loud sigh, he looked up from his book and placed his pen on the desk. "I thought you were leaving. What is it now?" He asked.

"This is not how I wanted our visit to end ….. I imagined our meeting happening much differently."

"Oh really? What were you hoping for crying, hugging, that type of thing?" He said with a wry smile.

"No. Not so much that. What I mean is, you're the only brother I have, and I know if I leave your office upset with you, and you upset with me. It could be a while before we see each other again. That's not what I want. I don't want to be estranged from my only brother. What I want is for you and me to talk. Not bark insults at each other."

For a few quiet moments, he sat looking at me. Drumming his ink pen on his desk, contemplating if he wanted to waste any more time talking to me or continue doing his work. Just when my patience was about to run out, he made his move.

"Vanessa, you were wrong about one thing. Dad did admire you. He admired your ability to be persistent. He used to say to me, if nothing else, Vanessa is persistent. Relentless. He said, she's like a little bull-dog, who's got a hold of your pants leg and no matter how much you kick, and shake she will not let go. I'm starting to see what he meant." He closed his books and tossed his pen on the desk. He came from behind his desk and picked up one of the guest chairs and turned it to face the couch. "Okay, you want to talk let's talk. You have a seat on the couch." He patted the cushion. "I'll sit in the chair, and we will talk. No insults, no barking. Just talking. Like two civilized human beings. Now what do you want to know?" he asked.

I decided to start with what I was most curious about, his new church. "Okay," I said laying my things on the couch. "Tell me how you became pastor of this congregation?"

P. M. Smith

"You want to hear about St Aubin's?" He said surprised. "Don't you want to discuss the election? "How I felt, my thoughts, etc.."

"I have an idea how you feel about that, let's start with how you became connected with this church, in this part of town. I'm curious how it all happened, tell me all about it."

Crossing his legs, he leaned back in his chair and began to tell the story of how he became associated with this unlikely congregation.

"Well, it's a long story, but I'll give you the short version. I had never heard of this church before, in fact I rarely come to this part of town. I didn't even know this church existed until Myra's great Aunt Verna passed. Aunt Verna was a nice older lady, a little quirky, but we loved her. She was a member here most of her life, so of course her funeral services were held here. Being good family members we took the long drive out here to pay our respects. To make a long story short. After the funeral was over everyone gathered at Aunt Verna's for the repast. So, we joined them at her house. While we're eating our meal, one of Myra's cousins remarked how the pastor of this congregation had suddenly taken ill. They discussed how gravely ill he had become in such a short time, saying it didn't look good for him. After a while the conversation turns to the church, what would happen to the congregation? Are the current ministers ready to step in and take over? Where would they find another pastor so soon? Myra and I silently listened to their complaints and concerns. Myra, of course made the occasional polite comment. I kept my mouth closed, because frankly, I didn't know the people, barely knew Aunt Verna and this may sound a little cold, but at the time I didn't care. I was tired and ready to go home. That was their problem and I assumed they would figure it out. After a while that talk dies down, we say goodbye and go home."

"A few days later I come home from work, and Myra tells me her cousins want me to speak for the next Sunday morning service. Never heard me preach a word. For all, they knew that could have been a mistake. I was searching my mind for an excuse to turn down the offer, Myra gives me one of her sympathetic looks. I knew I couldn't say no. Reluctantly, I consented, so I preached one Sunday morning and the next thing I know, a few weeks later here I am in this office with my name on the door."

"Just like that?"

"Something like that."

"An odd turn of events wouldn't you say?"

"There wasn't a lot of politicking, no deacon board or search committee to face. Just me, a few of the leaders and ministers conversing over a cup of coffee about their plans, my experience, their expectations, and so on and so forth. I think you know the drill."

"I have an idea."

"Took us about an hour or so to reach an agreement."

"Sounds like God was in the plans."

"Yes, it was definitely His doing. The former pastor suffered a massive stroke the same day Aunt Verna passed away. How is that for a coincidence?

"I don't believe in coincidences…but it is interesting."

"Yes very. Poor guy, he died within a few days and guess who officiated his services?"

P. M. Smith

"You're kidding, really?"

"God is something else, isn't He?"

We both laughed at the ironic circumstances.

"I'm only here three days out of the week. I still have my duties at the clinic. But that is how I became the leader of this church in this forgotten area of Macklin County, Michigan."

"I have a sneaky suspicion that you like it here."

"Is it that obvious?" He smiled. "I really do Vanessa. It's hard work. A lot of work, but it's good work. If you can understand that. When those brothers asked me to be their shepherd. I was dumbfounded. I thought I was unqualified for pastoring, that God didn't want me in that line of work. I asked the Lord why this church. Why these people. He said they need to see an example of a transformed life."

A single tear fell from his eye, he quickly wiped it away. I wanted to touch his hand and let him know it was ok to cry or show emotion. Instead, I forced myself to remain still with my hands in my lap.

"Evidently, God thinks you're qualified, and that's all that really matters."

"I'm finally developing a pastor's heart. Something I didn't have before. I'd like to blame it all on dad, but I can't. A lot of my failings are my fault. I said it's hard work because this area is like being in the trenches. What I like about this congregation is that they don't mind taking the Gospel to the streets. They don't wait for the people to come inside the church building. *Before* Sunday morning services they're outside walking up and down the streets passing out tracts, praying for people, distributing food to the hungry.

They're fulfilling what Jesus said in Matthew about ministering to *"the least of these."* I especially love it when I see growth in a new convert. When a man or woman embraces spiritual teaching, and little by little begin to let go of the worldly life. Those old habits become less and less important. I don't mean any harm when I say this, but I use very little of what dad taught me about pastoring. He had so many useless schemes and strategies that wasn't me, they were gimmicks, not biblical principles. I think he turned to those stunts in his old age. Here, we try to add value to the lives of everyone who steps through those doors."

"I thought this is what I would be doing at First Deliverance. Planning Bible classes and starting up new ministries, building leaders, developing a church and congregation where God's glory dwells. But, that was not to be. This is where I belong. Believe it or not, I feel at home here. This is where I belong. It has made me look beyond myself and taken away some of the pretentious attitude and lifestyle."

"Oh, is that why you changed your style of dress?"

"Kind of, serving soup at a homeless shelter in a three-piece suit and wingtip shoes was a bit much."

"Just a tad." I chuckled. "Seriously, I can't say if I've ever seen you this focused, so down to earth. You've always been a disciplined person, but now you're more modest and humble, this church suits you well."

"It has brought me down a few pegs. Who would have thought I would be suited for gang bangers, drug addicts, you name it we have seen it all. Dealing with what I used to call street people, thugs. I don't see them like that anymore. I see them as souls that can be transformed. My sermons are plain teachings about

Jesus, sometimes I don't even wear a clergy collar. They aren't for that pretentious stuff. They want to hear how they can gain strength to give up the street life and leave the bottle alone and stop shooting stuff in their veins. They don't care how I look or what school I attended. This congregation wants to know about a God who loves them and the Holy Spirit who can keep them. I'm in it for the long haul. I plan to stay here as long as God permits and I will work my fingers to the bone until I see Christ formed in these people."

Now I was crying, I wiped the tears from my face. "I know you don't want me to cry. But I can't help it. I am so happy for you Russell. I'm happy that you're fulfilled and finally enjoying your work in the church. And I'm overjoyed that you understand the true meaning of pastoring."

"I don't know how God did it, but there is a definite change in me." He said shaking his head.

"I have an idea how it was done, but you may not want to hear."

He sat up in the chair and raised his eyebrows curious to hear what I had to say. "Try me."

"There was a rather large barrier preventing you from seeing God and preventing you from becoming all you could be in Him."

"You mean your father."

"Yes, *our* father."

"You may have a point, Vanessa."

"Remember, it wasn't until King Uzziah died that Isaiah......"

He finished my thought. "....began to see the Lord. Great analogy and so true. As much as it hurt to lose mom and dad, it's so true. When God removed Dad, and the election didn't work out in my favor, my life changed."

"Drastically."

"I said earlier that I knew about how you felt about my relationship with dad, ... you don't owe me an apology not about that or your decision during the election. We've always had a great relationship. In fact, I owe *you* an apology for being selfish, aloof, and acting a bit childish."

"Russell, it's ok. We're good."

"This is the church where God has placed me, and I absolutely love being here. Honestly, Vanesa, if I were you, I would be thanking my lucky stars that Dad didn't choose to mentor you. Because his idea of mentoring was to recreate a replica of himself. I couldn't be that. I didn't want to be him, as much as I respected and loved him. We might look alike, but that's it---- besides I didn't *want* to be him. I don't have his personality, nor do I think like he thinks, but I went along with it cause at the time I couldn't see any other alternative. I admit sometimes it's a good feeling when people enjoyed your presentation or when Dad was pleased. What I despised most was having to imitate him, his leadership ways, style of speaking---it just wasn't me."

"Did you talk to anyone about how you felt?" I asked him.

"Just Myra, why do you ask?"

"I don't know---- seems like you've been holding this in for a while and relieved to get it off your chest."

P. M. Smith

"I guess it is a relief, I've never talked with anyone in the family about it, you were too young at the time, and I considered talking to Mom and Karen but never got around to it, only Myra knows how I really felt, she kept telling me if I hated it that much I should quit. The truth is, I went along with it because I had my eyes on taking over First Deliverance, being in charge so I could do things my way. Looking back in retrospect I was so immature I would have done anything he told me to do if I thought it would mean becoming the pastor. He drilled it into my head that the only way Frist Deliverance would thrive after he was gone was if I continued doing things his way. I couldn't be me and be successful."

"You could have talked to me, I may have been a little young to fully understand what was going on, but I saw your struggles, and I saw you weren't happy."

"What could you have done as a little kid?" he smiled.

"I don't know..... at least you would have gotten it off your chest."

"Yea, maybe you're right. When you were a little girl, you were the apple of Dad's eye, could do no wrong. But when you got older, ---- that's when things began to change. Dad complained about how you were getting on his nerves. For reasons, I never understood, it was his mission in life to deter you from the ministry at First Deliverance. I could never figure out why that was so important to him. It was more than him being a controlling father or his male chauvinism. It was something more, it seemed at times he was pushing me to do well to aggravate you, other times his intentions appeared to be honorable, he sincerely wanted to help me become a better preacher. He was a complex human being."

"We may never understand why he did what he did."

"He wasn't always like that you know. I saw that side of him, the controlling, domineering side --- especially as he got older it came out more and more. I call it the King Solomon syndrome. Remember when King Solomon became King of Israel? He prayed all night asking God for wisdom to lead the Israelites because he desired to not only lead well but to also please God in whatever choices he made. Dad was just like that. You might have been too young to remember when they started the church, but in the beginning, Dad did everything by the book. He was the most, humble, God-fearing example of a man I knew. But then his successes started to outweigh his failures, and that's when the overbearing side of him began to come out little by little."

I was somewhat startled to hear Russell speak of dad this way. I thought he was too enamored with him to notice or admit any of his flaws.

"I think it's part of God's plan to use men and women to add souls to His church. I used to believe it was the pastor's personality, preaching style, leadership techniques that attracted the masses to a ministry. Until I began studying the book of Acts, I saw in every case how the Holy Spirit was working behind the scenes arranging divine appointments, preparing men's hearts, guiding the Apostles through visions and dreams to those who desired to know more about God. Dad had me thinking *he* was the reason the church was thriving, his style of preaching. It wasn't until recently that I understood it's the work of the Holy Spirit, not man, it's the move and demonstration of the power of the Holy Spirit that attracts man to God."

I silently shook my head in agreement. I was thrilled to see my brother talk about God with such passion and excitement and substance.

"When a pastor or leader starts to think more highly of themselves than they ought to. They start to think they're the star of the show, so to speak. When they get to that point, I believe God backs off from that person and allows them to do as they please until they come to their senses or in the case of dad ----He removes them from their position altogether."

He looked at me to see if I understood his meaning. It was hard not to miss it.

"Vanessa, leadership in the church, is a funny thing-----you'll learn how challenging it is to keep a level head when pastoring....especially if you're particularly good at it, which I suspect you will be."

"You think so?" I asked.

"Yep, you know why I think you'll do a great job? Because you've got your father's determination and resolve that I never had. I might have had Daddy's attention, but you had the nerve to tell the man what was on your mind -- believe it or not I envied you for that."

"Come on---- I find that hard to believe…." I said.

"No seriously," He smiled a little rubbing his hand over his head. "I never told anyone this before, but I secretly admired the way you stood up to him, telling him how you really felt about him or the way he ran the church. I remember when you told the great Charles Woods that he needed to dig deeper, I said to myself, "Now this girl has nerves."

"Russell! I never told dad to dig deeper."

"You most certainly did, well, maybe not in so many words…." He laughed.

"I wasn't trying to tell him to go deeper or tell him off, that wasn't my goal. I wanted to help him........"

"I admired your courage, Vanessa. I never developed the nerve to tell dad how I felt about things --- like his pulpit antics and gimmicks to excite people. Every time I attempted to talk to him, I would trip over my words, or it would come out all wrong. I was intimidated by him, and he knew it. He knew I could never stand up to him. He also knew there were other ways of reaching people and winning souls, but he would never let me try."

"To tell the truth, I thought about calling you after the election. In fact, Myra tried to get me to call you and Karen after we left First Deliverance ----- but my pride wouldn't allow me to dial your number. I knew we needed to talk ---Vanessa, I don't think I've ever been so angry and so bitter in my life. I hope you and Karen can forgive me for my behavior these past few months."

"Of course, we forgive you, Russ." I said hugging his neck. Just as I hugged him a knock sounded on the door, Karen slowly stuck her head in the office, when she saw us hugging and smiling, she assumed it was safe for her to enter. "My timing is perfect." She said.

Russ beckoned for Karen to join our spontaneous group hug. "Karen, I've apologized to Vanessa and, now I'm apologizing to you as well. Please forgive me, I was wrong to hold a grudge against you and Vanessa. It was childish, selfish and I'm embarrassed by my selfish behavior. Please forgive me." He said tearfully.

Karen and I gladly forgave him. We sat in Russell's office talking, recalling our childhood days and of course retelling our fondest memories of mom and dad. We enjoyed our time together and decided to make a pact to meet every few months to share stories, problems, successes, defeats or just merely shoot the breeze. But most importantly to continue to keep our family bond and love for each other strong.

We said our goodbyes and Russ escorted us to the car. As he held the car doors open for us the young men standing on the corner noticed him and ran over to say hello. They addressed him as Reverend Russ. As he greeted each young man, we observed how he was so at ease with them. Laughing and comfortably calling them by what I presumed was their street names. He introduced us as his sisters, and they ran back to their spot on the corner.

Karen spoke. "Well, get out of town. The great Dr. Charles Russell Woods, II mixing with the common man. Who would have thought I would see my big brother wearing jeans and counseling gang bangers from the street?" she teased him. "I'm joking, but I'm really impressed with the work you're doing."

"These young guys need a lot of guidance." He said, "A *lot* of guidance."

"You're the man for the job." She responded. "Have they come to any Bible classes yet?"

"Nah, not yet, that's why I go over and talk to them. They're not going to come over here on their own. So, from time to time I take the Bible class to *them* and pray my light is shining so they'll see God in me. They're not as bad as they look. The sad part is when I pull up in the morning I wave at them or go over and talk for a few minutes. Eight hours later when I'm heading home, the same guys are still on that exact same corner. Some of them are standing or sitting in the exact same spot. They don't realize what a humongous waste of time it is to congregate on a street corner passing a bottle of beer. I'm praying at least one of them will give his life to the Lord."

"You've got a job ahead of you," I said. "You'll need a lot of prayer."

"You are so right, a lot of prayer," Russ responded.

"Excuse me, Pastor Collins," Karen said. "What's preventing you from leading us in prayer right now?"

"Well, nothing," I said hesitantly.

The three of us joined hands in the parking lot and bowed our heads to pray. Just as I was about to begin, we heard someone yelling for Russ. It was one of the young men from the corner. He and a young boy were running towards us.

"Hey Reverend Russ, sorry to interrupt, but it looks like you're about to pray." He asked.

"Yes, we are. You need something, or you want to join us?" Russ asked the young man.

"Can you guys say a prayer for my mom. She's been in the hospital for a few weeks."

"Sure, we'll pray for her. What is your mother's name?" Russ asked.

"Josephine Baines." He replied.

"And who is this young man," Russ asked pointing to the young boy standing beside him.

"This is my little brother Donovan." He said.

"Your *little brother*? Russ asked surprised. "How old is he?"

"I'm twelve, going on thirteen." The boy responded.

"Good to meet you, Donovan," Russ said reaching to shake his hand.

He turned to Donovan's older brother and said: "Man, don't you know the street corner is no place for a young boy." Russ chided him.

"Or a grown man...." Karen interjected.

We could tell Russ had embarrassed his young friend.

"You're right Rev... but, let me explain before you get upset, my brother had a half day of school, I just picked him up from school, and we're on our way home." He continued.

"Oh, I see," Russ said quietly. "I'm sorry, my mistake. We'll remember your mom and your family in our prayers."

"It's ok. Look, Rev I'd appreciate your prayers, means a lot to us, my brother and me." He and his little brother turned to walk across the street.

"Hold on," Russell said grabbing the young man by the arm. "Don't leave. I didn't mean to upset you. Why don't you and Donovan pray with us? And invite your friends." Russ said

"Yes. That's a good idea. Isn't that a good idea Vanessa?" Karen asked. I agreed it was an excellent idea for him and his friend to join us in prayer.

The young man was reluctant about it, maybe he didn't want to be seen praying in public or associating with religious people.

"Come on man, what have you got to lose? Don't you want God to heal your mother and bless your family?" Russ asked hoping to help him see how much *he* needed the prayers. He looked at Russ for a while and finally agreed to join us in our spur of the moment prayer meeting.

"I thought you would see the benefit of it. Let me introduce you to my sisters, Vanessa and Karen. This is Harrison Baines or HB as he is called by his friends and his little brother Donovan."

We shook hands with the young men. "Most people call me Harry or HB for short. I prefer Harry." He said with a nod of his head.

"I'm sorry to hear about your mom's illness. Has she been sick long?" Karen asked.

"Yes ma'am," he said. Stuffing his hands in his pockets. "For a while. Maybe a month or so. She's been in and out of the hospital. I wish she would get better, so things can get back to normal."

For someone who hung out on the streets, he was a clean-cut young man. He appeared to be no older than twenty-one or twenty-two. He was dressed rather neatly in khaki pants, a white t-shirt, and white gym shoes, nothing unusual stood out about him except for the colorful tattoos drawn on his arms and shoulders. As he explained his mother's illness, I wondered if his story was the familiar story we heard so many times before, a single mom struggling to keep food on the table and her kids out of jail and off the streets. Yes, it was probably the same familiar story we had heard from so many who came from single-parent homes.

"Vanessa? Vanessa?" Russell interrupted my thoughts. "Are you ready to lead us in prayer?"

Young Harry whistled for his friends to join us in the parking lot. Only three of the five young men decided to participate in our parking lot prayer session. Before we began praying, I asked them their names. Harry's friends were Jay, Matt, and Dominic. They were all so young looking. The unmistakable smell of marijuana and alcohol reeked from their clothes. I was anxious to talk to them. To learn about their backgrounds, their struggles, their hopes, and dreams if they had any. But it wasn't the time for that. Besides they were Russ's young charges. He would have the daunting task of reaching them. So much potential being wasted. My heart went out to them and their mothers.

We widened the circle to allow the three guys to mix in with us. We joined hands and prayed in the church parking lot of a busy street in broad daylight. I do not know if those passing by noticed us or thought it was strange. I don't even know if they pointed at us and wondered what we were doing. It didn't matter because I was engrossed in our impromptu prayer meeting. I was tuned into reaching God on behalf of Russ and the young men we just met. I prayed for God's blessing on Russell's congregation and for that entire area. Then I asked the Lord to remember Harry's mother Josephine and eradicate the illness that was plaguing her body and disrupting her life. Name by name I petitioned the Holy Spirit to rest over their lives. I prayed they would have a desire for godly living and instill within each of them a longing for holiness. I prayed that Pastor Russell would be a blessing to this forgotten community and that God would use him mightily to bring salvation to those who desired to know God and to prepare themselves for eternal life. At the end of the prayer, I thanked God for Harry, Donovan, Matt, Dominic, and Jay, and asked God to bless their families and to use their lives to bless others. Afterwards, they hugged us, thanked us for the prayers and returned to their meeting place on the street corner.

"Maybe, we should have our prayer meeting in the parking lot if that's what it takes to get their attention," Russ said.

"That's not a bad idea," I kidded. "I don't think I've ever seen anyone *running* to join a prayer meeting."

"I thought he was coming to rob us or something," Karen said. "I don't know about you, but I was praying with one eye open, you never know what's on a person's mind---."

Russell and I laughed at her silly remark.

"They appear to be well-mannered young men." I said. "Especially Harry, he seems to really care about his little brother."

"I think on the surface they're good guys… I've never had any trouble out of them or heard about them causing problems in the neighborhood, at least none that I can see. They're rough around the edges. What bugs me is why they have no desire to do anything other than selling drugs and marijuana. Such young lives being wasted, all that God-given potential being wasted, when I see that it bothers me that I'm at a loss about what to do, other than pray for their souls. How can I open their eyes before it's too late before they're too old or something drastic happens … " his voice trailed off.

"Russ you may not be able to do anything but pray for them and be the positive example they need to see. You can't force them or anyone else to change their way of life." Karen remarked.

"Maybe they do desire change, Russ, it's possible they don't want to be on the street corner peddling drugs, but they don't quite know how, and God placed a preacher man in this area, a man who's not afraid to get his hands dirty and wants to help all kinds of people, don't give up so soon just keep praying for an answer," I said

"We haven't given up, if we could just help one of them to see the light, just get one of those guys off that street corner, then maybe the others will follow. That one convert could be the catalyst to influence the whole group."

This was a real struggle for Russell. His desire to reach those guys was strong.

"Maybe I'll grab them and shake them by the shoulders, and tell them to wake up before it's too late. Well, ladies, that's just one of our many problems, but I'm trusting God will give us direction and wisdom. But right now, I better get back inside." Russ said hugging us both. "I love you both. Vanessa, I'm so glad we talked, and I promise to be there a week from Sunday. Look for us on the front row."

As we drove home, I could feel the love of God. Silently, I thanked God for a successful mission and how much he had blessed my brother. I even praised God for the young men who joined our spontaneous prayer meeting. What a day. And what a transformation the Lord had given Russell. Who else but God could completely transform a man's life like that? It had gotten messy for a while, but it had to get messy for us to clear the air of the confusion and come to a peaceful agreement. The stuff nobody wanted to talk about had to surface, and all those hurt feelings that we buried deep within our hearts had to be exposed and examined. Sometimes it's not until we let go of the past that we can move forward into the future.

"Hey, Karen I think I'm going to remember those guys names every time I get down to pray."

"Now that's a good idea." She said.

"I would love to see them give their lives to the Lord. I believe Russ was put in this area for a reason, don't you?"

"I do. Seems like you two had a productive conversation."

"Yes, we did. It went extremely well. It turned out much better than I anticipated. We have a better understanding of each other, and we've let go of the past."

"Bless the name of Jesus!" She said. "I told you, it didn't really involve me."

"Yea, you were right for once," I said. "God has really changed that man's life."

"I was thinking the exact same thing. He is not the same Russell, he is so much more down to earth, not so high minded."

"Kind of reminds you of Paul, doesn't he?"

"Paul?" She said confused. "Paul who?"

"The Apostle Paul silly."

"Oh, Vanessa I thought you were talking about somebody we knew."

"Remember how God changed Paul's agenda while he was on the Damascus Road? I think the same thing happened to Russ."

"Really? What do you mean… details please?" She said.

I relayed most of our conversation starting with Aunt Verna's funeral, how the pastor's unexpected sudden illness opened the door for Russell. I was reluctant to disclose everything we talked about. I left out the details about our personal insecurities and our experiences with Dad that affected our relationship. That information would go with me to the grave. It wasn't that I thought

Karen didn't need to know. I didn't want to sully her memory of Dad or Russell.

Every time I thought of how my father manipulated Russell and how he turned my own son against, me it made me ill. Family issues can be messy. I refused to focus on the damaging things my father did to me. I pushed them out of my mind, and I thanked God that we had our brother back in our lives. I rejoiced that he had his life together and finally found his place in the church. I particularly rejoiced that God was using him in the ministry. He did have something to contribute to the Kingdom of God. Like the Apostle Paul, God arrested him, humbled him and was using his life for His glory.

With one week to prepare my introductory sermon I knew I had to step up my game. I was struggling with what to say. Anyone could see that an array problems was plaguing our congregation, a growing number of issues were building up and needed addressing, but I didn't quite know where to start. Apparently, it was impossible for me to attempt to solve every problem at First Deliverance in one message. Especially, when it's my inaugural sermon as leader of a congregation. So, what do you do when you don't know what to do? Seek the Lord for direction. I turned down my plate, increased my Bible study, and doubled up on my time spent in prayer.

Our household was somewhat back to normal. Every day more and more Lawrence was coming out of his gloomy shell. The more we ignored his sulking and went about our usual activities the more he slowly began to return to his usual self.

I couldn't get those young men out of my mind that we met at Russ's church. I told Calvin about the encounter we had with them in the parking lot. I wrote their names in my Bible, and we prayed daily for them and their families. I made a mental note to call Russ to see if they had ventured to go beyond the parking lot and dare to enter the church building.

The Saturday morning before the big day I got up early as I usually do planning to use the morning time to reflect, write and pray. It was an unusually foggy morning. Brownie raced outside ahead of me. Spooked by the fog, he began barking at it and trying to bite the gray and clouds. I called to him to sit near me on the chaise lounge.

"Come here silly little dog. Don't you know you can't take a bite out of the fog? Come over here and lay next to me."

He jumped on the chaise lounge and stretched his body near my leg. The dense fog made reading almost impossible, so I closed my eyes, rubbed Brownie's head and let my mind reflect. How did my father get his inspiration for his sermons? Did he petition the Lord? Or maybe God gave him vivid dreams and visions in the middle of the night. When he was young man, he said ideas for sermons came to him without much thought or effort, he had no need for books that suggested sermon ideas. Books and things of that nature were okay, but that was not what I needed now. I needed to hear from heaven, I needed God to give me something that was designed uniquely for First Deliverance.

Calvin broke my train of thought as he entered the patio. "A little foggy out here huh?" He sat down next to me and placed Brownie's sleeping body on the patio floor. He put his arm around me, and I laid my head on his chest. "Kind of hard to read in the fog," he said patting the books on my lap.

"It's slowly lifting. It was much thicker before you came out here, so thick it scared poor Brownie,"

"Are you having visions of grandeur yet?" He joked.

"Hmm not quite, I wouldn't call them grand…every time I think of taking the pulpit tomorrow morning, my stomach does flips."

"Aww that's normal, if you *weren't* nervous, I might be a little concerned, pastoring is no small feat."

"Say that again. I've been studying the Apostle Paul's pastoral letters to Timothy and Titus."

"Maybe you should commit them to memory." He chuckled. "Then read the Beatitudes, the Sermon on the mount, the entire book of Acts …." He was cracking himself up.

I did not respond to his crazy comments.

He continued, "What kind of perks can I expect as the spouse of the pastor?"

"Perks?"

"I was thinking, maybe I could have my own special parking space, an office with my name on the door, fresh coffee and doughnuts every Sunday morning and the undivided attention of the senior pastor whenever I want, that kind of thing."

"Hmm…. I don't know, I'll see what I can do about that." We both laughed at his silly remarks.

"Vanessa, I'm not worried about you at all in this position, I know you're going to do fine. You're not the first female to pastor a church."

"True, but I *am* the first female to lead First Deliverance Church as pastor. I've been thinking about sitting down with some of the other female pastors in the city, glean from their wisdom and experiences."

"That sounds like a good idea." He said shifting his legs. "Some of the deacons have been teasing me, about sitting in the designated first pew, or making a dish for the women's potluck dinner."

"A dish for the potluck, now that's funny."

"One of the brothers said that I have to be careful not to take sides with you on certain issues, especially if they are to your benefit."

"I don't expect you to always agree with me…. I don't *want* you to always agree with me. If a sticky issue occurs, which I'm sure it will, you could remove yourself so it wouldn't appear as though you're siding with the pastor who also happens to be your wife."

"I could do that, recuse myself to keep peace and limit gossip. But I believe I can be unbiased. I'm capable of separating my feelings for you as my wife to arrive at a fair or right decision that'll benefit the church and you as well."

"It's easy to say that now Calvin, but it's different when you're in the heat of a battle or a difficult decision. I want you to be neutral and not make any decisions just to please me."

"Let's worry about that when and if it arises."

"I'm almost sure it will come up one of these days."

P. M. Smith

To be perfectly honest, Calvin was the least of my worries. He was more than capable of remaining firm in his belief and convictions. He had his own mind and was not easily swayed or led by his emotions. Even though this was unchartered territory for the both of us. His wife was also his pastor and could potentially become the topic of an issue that the deacon's board would be tasked with making the final decision. I wholeheartedly trusted Calvin's judgment in any situation, he wasn't the kind of man you had to lead around by the nose and tell him what to think or say and do. I knew he would do his best to remain impartial and vote the best possible solution to benefit the church, his pastor, and his wife.

"I feel like I should say something profound to you on the eve of your inaugural sermon, Pastor-elect Collins."

"Ok, I'll be quiet, so I can take in your words of inspiration," I looked at him expectantly.

"Would you believe I wrote you a poem?" he asked.

"No, I would not believe that. Did you write a poem?"

"No, I didn't write a poem." He laughed. "You have been on my mind, how proud I am of you pioneering the way for not only the female members of First deliverance but everyone, all the members of our congregation. It's not always easy to obey God's command, and this one is a tall order. It's an admirable profession, it's your vocation, your mission in life, and I am so proud to tell people that you are not only my wife, and the love of my life, you're also my pastor. I'm not ashamed or feel any less of a man or any of that macho stuff. My manhood is not threatened one bit. To tell you the truth, I believe we're on the cusp of something great at First Deliverance. I mean, in my gut I sense that God is about ----to just bless us until we can't stand it."

"Me too Calvin, I've been thinking about what Deacon Taylor said all week long—you know the seriousness of pastoring, the idea that souls are precious."

"Yep, but, you have a lot of help you know" he reminded me. "You're not in this alone. You've got Deacon Taylor, Dr. McClellan and the whole congregation behind you, pulling for you to do a great job."

"I sure do." I looked at him. "Calvin, despite all the awful things that happened in the past with my father, I miss him and Mom so much. I wish I could see their faces again and hear them call my name just one more time......"

"I know how you feel, but just think if they were here *you* would not be preparing to step into your destiny as Dr. McClellan put it."

"I have asked God hundreds of times if He could have found another way--- He could have changed my daddy's heart--- anything but death."

"For whatever reason, God decided this was the best way. Probably wanted to show you and your daddy who's really in control."

"Calvin if I had known that was His plan, I would have--"

He cut me off before I could complete my sentence. "What would you have done? Tried to prevent the accident? That's exactly why God doesn't tell us everything...you don't know *what* you would have done if you had known about their deaths ahead of time. It would have freaked you out."

I quietly sighed knowing he was right. I had no response, so I rested my head against his shoulder.

"Don't worry Vanessa, You'll see your parents again….. I hope." He said teasingly.

"You *hope*?" I looked up at him laughing.

"Guess what your loving husband is going to do for you? I'm going to take your unruly children out of your hair for a few hours. Been a while since I've seen my brother, so I'm going to drive out to Summerville, it will give you some alone time. After visiting my brother, we may catch a movie or go to the park, the mall or whatever they want to do. The goal is for you and Brownie to have the entire house all to yourselves until this evening when we return to pick you up for dinner. What do you think about that?"

"I like the sound of that."

"I thought you would say that. Let me get myself together ---shower and shave."

"While you're doing that, I'll make breakfast and wake up the kids."

"Sounds like a plan…please don't forget the coffee, I need my cup of coffee."

On Sunday morning Calvin, Melanie and I arrived at the church. Deacon Taylor met us at the door.

"Praise the Lord Collins family. Praise the Lord! Running a little late?" He asked smiling.

Deacon Taylor was right we were very late because the three of us had spent the morning scouring the neighborhood for Lawrence and Brownie. Calvin discovered that our son was not in his room early that morning and found his bicycle and the dog missing as well. We looked high and low for the boy but gave up after several hours. Wherever he was brooding, we prayed that he would be safe.

"Sister Vanessa, or should I say, Pastor-Elect Collins?" Deacon Taylor chuckled. "We've been waiting for you. Come on in let's get you upstairs. Got a few things to say to you before you take the pulpit."

Melanie hugged me. "See you later Mom," She said. "I know you're gonna do great." She kissed me on the cheek and headed for the sanctuary.

"Guess I better get on my post with the brothers," Calvin said. He handed Deacon Taylor the garment bag, squeezed me tightly, kissed me on the cheek and whispered, "You know I'll be praying for you when you get a moment read Genesis 21:22." He kissed me again and walked off towards the hall.

Deacon Taylor led the way to my father's office and unlocked the door. I had not been inside Dad's office since the accident. When Deacon Taylor opened the door, I almost expected to see my father sitting behind his desk talking on the phone or waving me to come in and take a seat. As I stepped into the room a wave of emotions and memories filled my mind. I swore I could smell his cologne lingering in the air and hear his deep raspy voice. I looked around at all the things he had collected over the years, books, plaques he had been given, biblical figurines presented to him as gifts. An entire wall was covered with photographs of congregants and his colleagues in the gospel. It was easy to see he was a man who was dearly loved especially by the people of First Deliverance.

His obvious popularity made my task even more daunting. I removed my gloves and stood in the middle of the office, nervously wondering what should be my next move.

Sister Mildred a young college student in our congregation, placed a cup of hot tea on the desk, turned on the light and began removing the robe from the garment bag. She hung it on the hook in the dressing area and took out the steamer to remove any wrinkles.

"Well," Deacon Taylor said. "This is your father's old office which you remember well, I'm sure." He pulled the chair out from the desk. "Now it's yours-- at least for the next year or so. Come on and try out the desk, see how it feels." I obediently sat behind the huge monstrosity of a desk. He stood in the middle of the room to get a better view. "Looks good to me. Looks real, good---though it might be somewhat too big for you. We'll have to get you a new chair that one is a bit tattered." He laughed nervously trying to cover the torn areas of the chair.

The attendant left the office with glasses and a pitcher. Deacon Taylor closed the door behind her and took a seat in one of the side chairs.

"We haven't removed your father's belongings--- I suppose it's time to clear this room. I'll get some of the brothers to box up the things, and give them to you and your brother and sister and you can do whatever you want with them." He walked over to the wall covered with photographs. "Your father loved to have his picture taken. This one right here is my absolute favorite." He pointed to a photograph of him and my father, grinning from ear-to-ear like little school boys.

"Daddy never met a camera or a microphone he didn't like," I said with a slight chuckle. "That is a very nice photograph. You should keep it Deacon Taylor—it'll make a nice keepsake for you and Sister Taylor."

He removed the picture from the wall, silently ran his hand over the protective glass covering.

"Your mother snapped this picture of Pastor Woods and me. It was right after the bank approved our loan to purchase this building. We were so excited, full of expectations for the future. We knew God was going to do some great things in this church. And He did, Sister Collins, He did many incredible, awesome miracles through this man right here." He pointed at the picture, smiling.

"Your father was my good friend, one of my closet buddies. I sure do miss him, didn't always agree with him, but he was a good man, a really, good man. We had some great times together, sometimes we would go fishing or take the wives out to dinner and then go for a long drive, the wives loved those long drives up north, we would stop at the antique shops, flea markets ---we had some good times together."

Just when I thought he might start to cry, he loudly cleared his throat and took a seat still looking at the picture.

"Oh well, enough reminiscing. Let's get back to the matter at hand." He removed a handkerchief from his pocket, ran it across his face. "Sister Collins, the board, thought it over, and we decided to increase your trial period to a year. We thought it would be fair if you had twelve months instead of six to prove yourself around here."

"Thank you," I said. "it's hard to get anything significant done in six months, I appreciate that so much. Deacon Taylor, I was hoping we could meet sometime next week if you can spare a few days. I have a few weeks of vacation time left, so I took some time off. I hope to use that time to become more acclimated to how things work. I have an idea of how it goes, but you understand---it's a little different from this position."

"Of course, sure, that's what I was going to suggest ---for us to sit down and talk, perhaps meet with some of the other key leaders and iron out some of the issues that have built up around here. Just let me know when and I'll be there."

"You know, Sister Collins, your father loved this church, which is why Clara and I decided to place our membership with First Deliverance. We were impressed how your father loved God and the people. Truth of the matter is, he loved pastoring. He really did. You don't meet too many like that. Mostly they love the position and the so-called glory that comes with it. Reverend Woods was different. He had the kind of friendly personality that drew the elderly, little children, young folk they all seemed to gravitate to him. In the beginning your father was the best preacher I had ever heard—I enjoyed the way he *enjoyed* delivering the Word. That was his specialty. He loved teaching and preaching and we loved to hear him too. Years later he changed, started doing some things that just baffled me and the board. Things that were not in the best interest of the church. We argued about some of the decisions he made—he wouldn't budge no matter how hard we tried to steer him in the right direction---so we just let him do it his way. Biggest mistake we ever made" He sighed deeply and looked around the office. "It's not a glamorous job, on the surface it may look exciting and all of that – it has its moments but it can at times be a trying, wearisome, lonely job. Dealing with people can be quite irritating. I'm sure you know this already having dealt with people on your job and the field work you've done."

He leaned towards the desk as though he was about to say something vital that I should not miss. "I'm not a pastor and I'm not going to try and tell you how to pastor, but I know that souls are precious. God expects you to do right by His people. I'll do all I can to help you, you can call me anytime. Whatever you do, don't allow what people say about you go to your head one-way or the other. I've seen many men and women start out with good intentions ----start out on the right road----soon they start believing what people say about them, good and bad. That's what messes them up every time. Truth be told Pastor Vanessa we can only be as great as God allows. And the only way to be great in God's eyes is to keep your eyes on Him. I hope you get my meaning."

I understood more than he knew. I would be a fool to refuse his assistance. He knew the people of First Deliverance better than most. "Deacon Taylor, I welcome your advice and assistance, in fact, I plan to lean on you and the other leaders a great deal. You and many others around here keep things running smoothly and would also keep me humble."

"Yes!" he almost shouted. "That's exactly what I'm saying ---- if you remain humble God will use you. I've witnessed many, many pastors and leaders start out on the right path, then become distracted by their own prideful thoughts and when that happens---it's the people who suffer. Don't allow the devil to divert you from your divine purpose. No matter what happens, Pastor Collins don't become sidetracked." He shook his finger as he spoke. "Too many people are depending on you, expecting and hoping that you will be a fine leader. My granddaughter and some of her young friends are thrilled because you have become our first female pastor. God chose you to make history at First Deliverance. I say this with the utmost respect and love--- don't squander this opportunity. Keep your head on straight ...start off good and finish well."

He stood up and walked towards the door "I'd better leave so you can collect your thoughts. The attendant will come back for you in uh, let's say fifteen or twenty minutes. Will that be enough time for you to do what you need to do?"

I glanced at my watch. "Yes, twenty minutes should be enough time," I said. I walked to the door and extended my hand to him. "Thank you, Deacon Taylor, I appreciate your support and words of encouragement. I promise I won't forget what you said. I promise not to squander this opportunity. I'd like to continue having this type of conversation in the future. I believe it will help me on this unfamiliar journey."

"Of course, I would love to help any way I can. I hope you won't forget what I've said. We'll see, time will tell, time will tell." He smiled and turned towards the door.

"Oh no, I almost forgot----" He reached inside his jacket pocket and pulled out a plain white envelope. "This," He held a thin envelope in the air. "This is the main reason I wanted to talk with you. Some time ago, years before he passed, your father gave this envelope to me. He said if anything were to happen to him I was to give this envelope to you."

To me? Why me? "Uhh, what is it, Deacon Taylor?" I asked dumbfounded, as he placed the envelope in my hand.

"I suppose it's a letter. I have no idea what's inside the envelope. I never opened it, and your father did not think it necessary to tell me the contents of the envelope. The only words he said to me was to keep it in a safe place and that I was to give it to you upon his demise."

Interesting. My father passing on an unopened envelope to me was a little strange. It was a rather unassuming business sized envelope. On the front of the envelope, he had written my name.

MY FATHER'S SHADOW

I looked carefully to confirm it was my father's handwriting. Deacon Taylor had the envelope for a while. It wasn't worn or frayed, a little yellowed, creases had developed around the edges. The envelope carried a faint aroma of cologne. What could be inside the envelope? My father was not known for writing letters or leaving notes. He preferred face to face conversations. Why after his death? Did he know when he was going to die? It was not a thick letter, it felt like a single sheet of paper. My curiosity was certainly piqued. As I was about to tear open the envelope Deacon Taylor placed his hand on mine.

"Before you open it, I need to explain something to you. Your father had one condition, he asked that you not read what's inside the envelope until afterward….." he took a deliberate pause.

"Afterwards?" I repeated. "After what?"

"He said you were not to open the letter until after you had delivered your inaugural sermon." Deacon Taylor left the office softly closing the door behind him.

I almost fell to the floor. After my inaugural sermon? How did he know? All this time my father was aware of my future destiny and he never said a word? But why write a letter? Why couldn't I read it now, why wait until after? Maybe the contents of the letter would be too disturbing and could possibly rattle my nerves. The last thing I needed was something else to cause me to become even more nervous. My stomach was doing flips all morning. Now this mysterious letter from my father did not help to calm or settle my nerves at all.

Charles Woods had been a lot of things, but a letter writer he was not. I could count on one hand the number of letters he wrote to me while I was away in school. My mother said he hated writing. His idea of a love letter was few lines quickly scribbled on a scrap of paper that he taped to the refrigerator door or the bathroom mirror. This was so out of character for him. Most of our discussions were face to face or brief telephone conversations. I was stunned and at a loss for words. I didn't have much time to think about Deacon Taylor's bombshell or to wonder what could possibly be in the envelope. All that ran through my mind was my father knew I would be in this position one day? I sat down at the desk and stared at the letter. He knew all this time. How long did he know? Why all the arguing? What was that about? Was it just a show? No, not Charles Woods, he wasn't one to waste time on frivolous game playing ---there had to be a reason for all his disputing, arguing and discouraging ways. I was so tempted to rip open the envelope, but I had promised Deacon Taylor that I would wait. I had no sooner sat down at the desk when there was a knock at the door. Before I could answer the knock, Karen and Russell burst into the room. I slid the envelope in the desk drawer.

"Praise the Lord Pastor Vanessa," Karen said excitedly.

I practically ran to them and hugged them both. This was the perfect interruption I needed to take my mind off my father's mystery letter. "It's so good to see you two."

"Vanessa, your hands are so cold, and you're shaking...." Russell gave me a questioning look. "Are you alright?"

"I'm fine, just a little nervous, come on in and talk to me for a while."

"We're not going to stay long," Karen said. "By the way, did Calvin find the prodigal son?"

"No," I said. "Not yet."

"Don't worry about him," Russell said. "Concentrate on your message. Lawrence will turn up sooner or later."

Karen went into the dressing room to inspect her handiwork on the robe. "You need anything, Vanessa? Anything I can do? Want me to stand up and holler 'amen' real loud when you get to the good part?" She laughed.

"No, please don't do that." I laughed with her.

"Hmmm --- what about your hair?" She asked picking at my hair. "What are you going to do with it?"

"Nothing, it's *already* done." I replied.

"Leave her hair alone," Russell said. "She's got more important things on her mind. Come on Karen let's get downstairs. Pastor Vanessa, we wanted you to know we love you and we're praying for you."

"By the way, love your dress, great choice" She gave me the thumbs up sign as Russell pulled her out of the office.

I was alone in the quiet office. I went to the window to watch the people as they arrived at church. What did pastor's do in their study before heading to the sanctuary? What did my father do? What kind of thoughts ran through his mind? Did he have a Sunday morning ritual before he went to the pulpit? Did mother come up and pray with him or give him words of support? As I stood there thinking it occurred to me that I had never been in his office alone. Someone was always there with me. Daddy would be sitting behind his desk or mother, and I would be sitting on the couch patiently waiting for my father to come out of a meeting or wrap up a last-minute counseling session. Now the office was empty, quiet and it was no longer my father's office. For the next twelve months, I would be the leader of a group of people. Wow! Just the thought of me being in charge was scary and exciting. *What if my father and Lawrence were right? What if I couldn't do this? What if I was in over my head?* I quickly dismissed those thoughts, this was not the time for doubt or uncertainty.

I sat down in the oversized chair that my father loved so much and began to scan the stack of papers and books that remained on his desk. Thumbing through the papers, I could tell they were minutes from board meetings and scribbles of scripture and possible sermons my father had planned to preach. Everywhere I looked in the room reminded me of him. The well-worn brown leather furniture. The faint smell of his cologne that hung in the air. Several of his fedora hats hanging on the hat rack. Even some of his shoes, robes and other personal items stored away in the dressing room area. "Daddy you were such a pack rat," I said as I thumbed through his old stuff. "Such a pack rat."

As I thought about what lay ahead of me the knot in my stomach returned. I remembered what Calvin whispered in my ear, he said to read Genesis 21:22. It wasn't a verse that I knew from memory, so I opened my Bible to find the passage. At first, I could not see how it applied to me until I came to the latter part of the verse which read…. *"God is with you in all that you do."* I am sure that's the part he meant for me to read. I read it out loud several more times; *"… God is with you in all that you do."* They were comforting words to know that the Lord supports those who obey His commands. We often talk of placing our trust in God, but it rarely occurs to us that there are times when the Lord wants to trust us too. Sitting in this office, serving God's people in this capacity is the Lord's way of entrusting me with the grave responsibility of caring for precious souls. Even though I am not one hundred percent confident in my own abilities, I know the Lord placed something in me that He could use and trust.

I looked over my notes one last time, searched a few more passages and then closed my eyes to mediate...... my mother's words ran through my mind ...*information and inspiration----help get people to heaven...* Now is the time I thought, now is the time.

A knock on the door interrupted my thoughts. I went to the dressing area to change into my robe.

As Sister Mildred and I walked to the sanctuary, we heard the choir singing. The walk through the hallway seemed longer than before. Some of the late-comers straggling in stopped me in the hallway and spoke encouraging words or wished me well. Just as we were about to enter the sanctuary one of the ushers stopped us. He said that someone wanted to talk with me.

"*Now?*" I questioned him. Who would want to talk with me *now* I thought, it must be a matter of life and death.

"Yes ma'am, they said it's urgent." The usher replied reading my thoughts. He pointed towards the chapel. I followed him to the hallway and over into the meditation and prayer chapel. The usher held the door open and motioned to the rear of the room. In the back of the room, I saw a lone figure sitting in the last pew. The room was dimly lit. I could barely make out the face among the shadows. As my eyes began to adjust, I saw the tall, thin frame of my son.

"Lawrence!" I said. He ran to greet me, squeezing me so tight it hurt my bones, but I didn't care. I was so glad to see my child. "Honey, where have you been, we've been searching for you all morning?"

"Mom, I'm so sorry." He kept his eyes on the floor, too ashamed to look me in the face. *You should be ashamed talking to me like that.* I reached up and cupped his chin in my hand gently forcing him to look me in the eye. His eyes were red. I wiped the tears from his face.

"I'm so sorry," He continued, "I don't know why I said those things. I heard Grandpa say it, and I thought he was right, but he wasn't right. He was wrong and I was wrong for repeating what he said. I had a talk with Uncle Russ, and he helped me to see my mistake, he said I shouldn't repeat everything I hear and that I'm just a child, you're my mother, and I should respect you. I'm so sorry mom, will you forgive me, mom? Please?" He hugged me again, crying on my shoulder. *How could I not forgive him? I loved him so much. I knew he didn't understand what he was saying or doing.*

I looked at his sweet little face, and Karen's remark about the prodigal son came to mind. Lawrence was very much like the prodigal son--- young, foolish, brash and hopefully humbled, humiliated and ashamed of the errors of his ways. Just like the prodigal son it appeared he had learned his lesson.

"Of course, I forgive you. You're my son. I will always love you no matter what. But, don't you ever run away from your family and if you ever speak to me like that again, I don't know what I'll do to you. And another thing, if anyone comes to you with some lies or foolishness about me, your father or Melanie, you come to your father or me, and we will discuss it together as a family. Do you understand?"

MY FATHER'S SHADOW

"Yes, ma'am" he said. "I'm sorry. I feel so stupid for saying that stuff, I still can't believe those words came out of my mouth. If you want to be a preacher or a pastor for the rest of your life, it's alright with me."

"Thanks for your permission," I said sarcastically. "Come on, we're holding up the service. Go on inside, your father saved you a seat."

"I love you, Mom. Grandpa was wrong, you're gonna be the best pastor we ever had." He kissed me on the cheek.

"I love you too Lawrence." I turned to go inside the church when I remembered the missing dog.

"Lawrence, where is Brownie?" I asked him. He turned around and showed me Brownie's little face peeking through his mesh-covered back-pack. As soon as Brownie recognized me he began barking.

"Lawrence, you can't have a dog in the church." I made him give the back-pack to the usher who took the dog upstairs to my office. Lawrence and I walked into the sanctuary together.

Deacon Taylor gave a very brief introduction and then turned the podium over to me. The congregation politely applauded. I looked over the sea of familiar faces. The flips and flops in my stomach started to increase. The palms of my hands were clammy with sweat. Most of the faces were people I had known since forever. Others were unfamiliar faces I could not recall as members of First Deliverance. I scanned the audience for my family and my friends, took a deep breath and plunged into my sermon.

"Thank you, Deacon Taylor for such a warm introduction," I said my voice cracking and my knees literally shaking. "I would also like to thank the entire board of directors for this opportunity to serve this great church. I would be remiss if I did not recognize my dear husband and my family whom I love with all my heart. I thank God for the elders, associate pastors and ministers who make up our capable ministerial staff. I would also like to acknowledge some someone we all know and love, my brother, Pastor Russell Woods, his wife Myra and their family."

To my surprise, the entire congregation gave him a rousing standing ovation. Russell and Myra blushed with pride. I think I even saw Myra wipe away a tear or two. I was very proud of First Deliverance for showing such love and warmth to my brother and his wife. When the applause ended, Russell pointed to the row behind him. Sitting directly behind Russell were several of the young men we prayed for in the parking lot of Russell's church: Harry, his little brother Donovan and his three friends Jay, Matt and Dominic. I asked them all to stand so the congregation could welcome them with applause and explained that they were Pastor Russell's young friends and hopefully one day would become future members of his congregation.

"I would also like to thank God for this church, this congregation, together we have weathered many storms, but we stuck together just as God and my father would have wanted. All that we've gone through both the ups and downs, it is evident that God has blessed us with His favor, mercy, and love." I was again interrupted with applause and shouts of "Praise God and thank you, Jesus."

Once the applause died down I continued....

"I was torn about what to say to you this morning. I wrestled with it for the past week or so. I believe I heard the Holy Spirit leading

MY FATHER'S SHADOW

me in this direction. So, I ask that you pray with me this morning as we turn to the book of Psalms the 18th chapter. We'll read verses 1 through 6 and then verses 21 through 30. My focus this morning will be verse 30. This is a beautiful Psalm of David. In fact, these words were penned by David after he was delivered from conflict with King Saul and his men. If you read the entire passage, you will see throughout most of the Psalm David writes of his appreciation and love for God. Because God like a mighty Warrior delivered him from the clutches of King Saul who was desperate to take David's life. So, David does what any, appreciative person would do who was facing certain death, surrounded by strong enemies, running for his very life and God rescues him in the nick of time. He sings the praises of his Deliverer, his Strength, his Rock. David extols and exalts the greatness of God His Savior. Because God, once again has come to his rescue in a time of need and trouble.

These words of praise and celebration are easy to write and quote when one has experienced a great victory like David or when one has defeated his enemy or overcome a hard-fought battle. When everything is going well on the job, the family is healthy and whole, children are well behaved, and the spouse is as sweet as pie. Words like these roll easily off the tongue when all is well with one's soul.

What happens when life turns sour and becomes an unbearable bitter pill? When your days are filled with anguish, night after night your pillow is wet with tears? When the battle you're going through seems like it will never end? When those you love, are taken from you --- suddenly, no warning, no notification whatsoever. What happens when life's complications and difficulties become your everyday routine? Then what? Do you remain like King David in a praising mode? Does your mind continue to reflect on the goodness of God?

Perhaps you become like me and foolishly begin to question the actions of God. *"Why God"* or *"why me"* or *"what am I supposed to do now*" or the classic *"what did I do to deserve this?"* Maybe you've never been there or, perhaps you've never had a reason to question God about a detrimental occurrence or undesirable person He has allowed to intrude in your life.

In my arrogance and pride, I dared question God about a tragic situation. Rather than turn to others, I thought it best to go to the Source. The only One who could have prevented it from happening. The only One who could look through the annals of time to see it occurring long before it became a reality in my life. As I lay on my bed tears streaming down my face, heart heavy and sad. I asked God why, and His reply was exactly what I needed. It calmed my spirit and shut my mouth. I asked God why and He directed me to this Psalm 18 and the thirtieth verse. The words seemed to jump off the page; specifically the first part of that verse ….. "As for God His way is perfect" as I laid on the bed meditating, the Lord said to me, "All my ways are perfect."

"All my ways are perfect." That was God's response to a troubling situation I thought was out of His control. I was certain He had made a mistake. Not me Lord, how could you allow *this* to happen to *me*, I'm your child, I thought I was special in your sight. The words came back even stronger and louder: "All my ways are perfect." Who can argue with that? Who can dispute those words when God is the One speaking? God has never made a mistake. What faults or errors can you find in Him? Since God is a perfect God, then all of His ways would be perfect too. How dare you question the God who sits on the center of the universe? The God who speaks galaxies and stars into existence? I asked myself what have you created Vanessa? What have you spoken into existence? How dare you insinuate that God does not know what he's doing, that He's not in control. Everything the Lord does is right, just and fair because He is sovereign. All of God's ways are perfect.

Ladies and gentlemen, saints and friends, do you know how hard it is to be perfect? To do *everything* perfectly and never make a mistake? To live a flawless life? To never think wrong or have an inappropriate thought? To never misspeak? To never second guess yourself? Every decision you make is always right, to succeed at everything you attempt to do? Who lives like that? No one, but God.

For you and I to live a perfect life would be extremely difficult and impossible. But for, God it is a small feat. The scriptures tell us "… with man it is impossible, but with, God all things are possible" Even perfection. Because He is perfect in all His ways, perfectly holy, perfect in wisdom, perfect in love, perfect in judgment, He is always perfect, I've never known Him to make a mistake.

The loss of a loved one is His perfect will. Chaos and confusion in your life is the ideal time to experience His perfect love. Uncertain about the next step to take? Seek His perfect knowledge. God is perfect in all His ways. Even the hurt, pain, sickness in our lives is a part of His perfect plan for our lives. He knows exactly what He's doing when trouble comes knocking at our door.

First Deliverance it is no mistake that we are experiencing these difficulties at this time. It was no mistake that we lost our former leaders at the hands of a drunk driver. That was God's perfect will for this ministry. It is no mistake that you are where you are in life. It is no mistake that things are jumping off every time you turn around. It's no mistake if you're in the perfect will of God.

When hard times come, or you get the urge to question God about some awful thing you're going through. Just remember these words, think of them before you speak, before you charge God foolishly, you'll save yourself a lot of trouble. You'll be able to sleep at night if you just remember that…. God is perfect in all His ways.

If He is imperfect, flawed or defective in any way then He ceases to be God. You and I, we are far from perfect. We are extremely flawed. You and I have to do a thing over and over and over again until we perfect it and even after all that practicing we still are prone to make mistakes. Not God. He does something once and it is done perfectly forever."

This morning God is challenging you and me to accept His perfect will for our lives. He's inviting us to experience His perfect love. A love that understands you when others don't. A perfect love that never fails even though you may fail Him. A love that will be with you in the thick and the thin. Without doubt, without questioning what He allows to happen in this congregation, this ministry, in your family and in our individual lives. From this day forward this will be our mantra, "All of God's ways are perfect."

Say it with me, all of Gods ways are perfect. Obediently the entire congregation raised their voices and we repeated the words together. "All of God's ways are perfect."

In sickness, in health; "All of God's ways are perfect."

In good times or bad: "All of God's ways are perfect.

I paused as the congregation praised God with their applause and shouts of joy.

When the applause died down, I continued, "Acknowledging God's perfect will, helps to maintain your sanity, deal with stress and provides peace of mind."

"Let's not forget Psalm 18:30. I have come to look at it from a new perspective. It came at the appropriate time for me. Keep it at the forefront of your mind. Tape the words on your bathroom mirror if necessary, so you can be reminded of it every day. Never forget it especially when you find yourself in a tight spot or facing an unfortunate dilemma. I can't promise you there won't be tears or you won't feel sadness or pain from time to time. But knowing this will help you understand that God has you in His perfect will even during the most troublesome times."

I closed my Bible and scanned the audience, my eyes fell on Russell's young charges. "It is impossible for man to experience the perfect, enduring love of God until he makes the decision to give God complete control of his life. Why not allow the Perfect God to control your imperfect life? I promise you He will never make a mistake. He will never steer you in the wrong direction, and He will never leave you. I'm praying there is someone here this morning who desires to experience perfect love from a perfect God. If so, come down the aisle, and we will pray with you." I extended my hands, as the choir began softly singing.

I almost lost my composure when Russell's young friend Harrison, his little brother Donovan and a woman I presumed to be their mother came forward.

After the service, I warmly greeted every parishioner, welcomed every visitor, embraced some, laughed and joked with others, listened to the advice from the seasoned members, hugged the little children and the young ladies who enthusiastically greeted me and gave me their support and words of approval. I took the time to acknowledge everyone who came across my path. After all of this handshaking and greetings, I was mentally and physically exhausted and more than ready to head home.

Sister Mildred helped me pack up my things and poured me a steaming cup of herbal tea. I thanked her for her assistance and released her to go home to her family. In the back of my mind was the letter from my father. I could not wait to read it. I sat down at the desk and retrieved it from underneath the stack of papers inside the desk drawer. Turning the envelope over in my hand, I chuckled at the irony of how my father, though he had passed a couple of years ago, was still very much involved in my life. I searched through the drawer until I found a letter opener. I ripped open the envelope, and a single sheet of paper fell onto the desk.

Dear Vanessa,

If you're reading this letter that means several things have occurred: First, I like the Apostle Paul have "...fought a good fight, finished my course." Which means I've gone on to glory to be with the Lord. Secondly, it also indicates that congratulations are in order because you have preached your first sermon as Pastor of First Deliverance Church.

Don't fall off your chair. I know you're surprised to hear these words from me. (I would love to see the look on your face.) You were aware that I was opposed to any female succeeding me as pastor, even my own daughter. I didn't hide my beliefs from you or attempt to sugarcoat my words. That was how I felt until the Lord showed me differently.

I've always had high hopes for all three of my children. I love each one of you equally but individually. I wanted you all to be whatever you desired to be, and I planned to be actively involved in whatever way I could to help you achieve your goals in life. I held true to this promise until you went away to college. I think that's when our relationship started going downhill.

Vanessa, please don't take it personally. It was never a discredit to your abilities, but more to your gender. I must admit I had some very misguided beliefs that the Lord later corrected---- He allowed me to understand that He has the option to use whomever He chooses.

You presumed I didn't see your abilities. I would have had to be blind to not understand how God was using you evangelizing in the field and at First Deliverance and to miss the undeniable gifting that He divinely imparted to you.

Here is what you must understand about me. I'm from the generation of men who believe in their sons following in the father's footsteps, taking over the business, running the corporation, etc... After I started pastoring that's what I desired for Russell. For my son to assume the leadership of our church whenever I decided to retire. It was a cultural-male thing. Passing the baton to my son, who would hopefully one day pass it on to his son. I discovered that God is not too fond of our cultural traditions and He's not obligated to follow them. Some time ago, He corrected my way of thinking. I was planning to tell you and your mother but never got around to it.

You're probably wondering why did he write a letter? Why not sit down and have one of our knock down-drag-out-discussions --- well because I saw that the more I opposed your ideologies, the more determined you became. You were doing it more so to prove me wrong, but mostly I think what kept you going was that you knew God's plan for your life and nothing and no one could deter you from it...not even me, your loving father.

You don't know how much I loved to see that strong determination in you. A resolve and willpower I longed to see in my son..... but that is neither here or there. God gave it to you. He gave you the strength and strong-mindedness to stick with His will for your life even though others criticized, overlooked you, laughed in your face. You ignored it all and kept going despite the ridicule you received.

P. M. Smith

When I finally decided to reveal the truth to you, how my beliefs had changed. The thought occurred to me, my challenging you were necessary in helping you reach your potential, the same way my father challenged me— with tough love. I saw in you the undeniable persistence to be something in the Lord. What I mistook for arrogance and an attempt to have authority over men, God revealed to be genuine conviction, passion and a strong desire to fulfill His will.

Vanessa, understand I have always believed in you, and inwardly I was so proud that you never backed down from my criticism and seemingly harsh words. Giving up without a fight is not in your DNA ----if you ever thought about quitting I never saw it. If the thought ever crossed your mind to throw in the towel, you hid it very well.

What I did see in your eyes was a disappointment in me as a father who had a responsibility to mentally and emotionally support his child. The pain and frustration on your face caused me much hurt. With my own eyes, I saw you turn disappointment into strength because no matter how I tried to discourage or dampen your spirit you would not give up. It only provoked you to work all the more to prove me wrong. I applaud you for sticking to your guns, and I also ask you to forgive me for my cruel words and unkind behavior. I was wrong. I am ashamed. But it was done with the intent to help you develop a thick skin, a quality you will find extremely helpful in the coming days, as you will see when leading a group of people.

If I were with you today, I would caution you that the responsibility you're about to take on is of great significance. An honorable work that God expects you to labor in both day and night. Expect to take the parishioners calls at three in the morning, to make endless hospital visits, bury their dead, oversee marriages, counsel, lead and mentor those who sit under you. These are just some of the duties expected of someone in your position.

There will be days you will not feel like preaching, or you'll want to padlock the doors of the church, but keep going, don't allow exhaustion and fatigue even failure make you quit. Push through the exhaustion because souls depend on you. God depends on you.

Pastor Vanessa, my dear daughter, work hard, labor until sweat pours from your brow and your body aches. In other words, give it all you've got because God's people are worth it! Don't ever give up on a single soul. No matter how many times they make the same mistake. Your responsibility is to never, ever stop praying for the weak and the strong. Remain patient and show them the love of God, especially when you feel they don't deserve it. Pray, labor, teach and preach until you see Christ formed in the people who sit before you, that is the purpose and duty of an undershepherd.

Always remember your heavenly Father is your greatest supporter because He chose you. He alone knows what you are capable of and He promised never to leave you, nor forsake you.

Tell your dear, sweet mother I love her so very much. Give my love to Karen and Russell.

Vanessa, I love you with all my heart. I believe in you, and I know that with God's help you will take First Deliverance to heights I only dreamed of.

Vanessa, my baby girl, "…be strong in the Lord and in the power of His might."

Love your father.

I was completely speechless. I reviewed the handwriting once more to make sure it belonged to Charles Woods. I sat in my chair and wept. This was the most beautiful and heartfelt letter I had ever received. My father wasn't crazy after all. He wasn't some mean, chauvinistic, narrow-minded old man so entrenched in his philosophies that even

God Himself couldn't make him change. I wanted to scream thank you, God. Thank you, Lord God in heaven! I don't know how it happened, don't even care—I just wish he had told me these words—but I guess a letter is acceptable---I would have loved to have had this conversation with him. To look him in the eye and hear the words from his own mouth. I would have to settle for the written word which is better than nothing at all. I would rather have this letter than go through life thinking my own father saw me as a failure. The part I was most drawn to was the paragraph where daddy apologized and admitted his belief in me. It's sad to say, but I never imagined hearing or reading those words from my father. The part that touched me the most was where he wrote, "Your heavenly Father is your greatest supporter......" This was a stark reminder that if the whole world doubted my abilities, even my own father, it should not deter me because I could always depend on my heavenly Father who created me and knew me better than anyone else. I held the letter close to my heart and thanked God for allowing my father to finally realize the church belongs to God and He has the power and wisdom to use whom He wants whenever He wants.

I carefully folded the letter and placed the envelope inside my purse. I considered showing it to Calvin or Russell and Karen. I knew one day I would let them read it---maybe not today, but soon. It's only fair that they know that our father was not the cruel, vindictive man we thought he was. There was a purpose to his madness after all….to help me become what God had already ordained. The scripture is undoubtedly true when it says, "all things truly work together for our good."

Calvin and I planned a family potluck dinner to celebrate my parent's memory. We invited Russell, Karen, and their families. Kendra, Dr. and Mrs. Solomon. We had a house full of people, children and teenagers swimming in the pool, playing with Brownie. While the adults sat under the pavilion laughing, talking and enjoying the food. I ran up to my bedroom to retrieve a gift for Russell. Calvin was sitting on the side of the bed putting on his shoes. "Thought you were downstairs." He said.

"I was. I need to get something from the closet." As I walked by him, he grabbed me by the waist and pulled me close. "Not so fast Pastor Collins. Have I told you how honored I am to be your husband? An excellent message this morning, very thought-provoking. I know God is perfect in all of His ways because He gave me you."

"Oh-- so you were listening?" I joked with him.

"Of course, I was, I wasn't quite sure where you were going with it at first, but then you really brought it home –just fantastic! I can't wait to hear next week's message."

I put my arms around his neck. "I can always count on your support, can't I?"

"You sure can---there are two things I'm good for--, well actually three, my support, my honest opinion and my undying love." He kissed me.

"You know I am so blessed to have such a sweet husband."

"Yes, you are, and to think you were going to marry that other guy." He teased.

We laughed and shared another kiss.

P. M. Smith

"Vanessa, if your father heard you this morning he would have been moved by what you said."

"Hmmm, you're probably right," I said thinking about the letter. "You know Calvin, I don't know what I would have done without you these past few weeks, it has been pretty rough around here, don't you think?"

"You mean that stuff with Lawrence and your brother? That's nothing, keep pastoring for a while, you'll find yourself saying like Jesus said,' how long must I suffer with you people'…"

We laughed at his words, but in the back of my mind I knew he was right, this was child's play compared to what possibly lay ahead.

Our alone time was not to last long---we heard footsteps on the stairs. Brownie darted into the bedroom and squeezed himself right between our legs. He cocked his head to one side as he looked up at us. He was closely followed by Melanie and Lawrence. Since the door was open they barged in the room Melanie falling onto the bed spoke first, "Sorry to interrupt this love fest, but everybody's asking for you two."

"We'll be down in a minute," I said.

"Yea and I'm ready to eat," Lawrence added.

"As always," Calvin replied. "Hey, can't you two see we're trying to have a moment here?"

"Sorry Daddy---- but my stomach is starting to growl a little too." Melanie said.

"I guess we'd better get downstairs," I sighed. I put on my sandals and followed the kids outside.

"I'll be down in a few," Calvin hollered. "Hey, take the dog with you."

After everyone had enough to eat and appeared to be relaxing. I stood and tapped my glass to get everyone's attention.

"The past couple of years has been a rather difficult time for our family. Losing our parents, our children losing their grandparents and for others, friendships were suddenly terminated. We're here today to celebrate and remember the lives of two lovely people Charles and Iris Woods. They weren't perfect, but they taught us what they thought to be right. They loved God, and I know they loved each other and each one of you."

The entire group broke out in cheers.

"They were such a great team and an example of love to Calvin and me. They touched many lives, and they will be remembered for a long time to come. I think you'll agree that it is important to keep their memory alive in this family. They are sorely missed. This is something I hope we will often do, it does not have to be the same type of event or at the same location, but we want to have some kind of get-together that will help us to remain a close-knit, loving family. Mom and dad would want us to overcome our differences, resolve conflicts and do whatever it takes to remain a loving family, as we depend upon and support one another. Right now, I'm going to take my seat and allow you all to share your memories of mom and dad."

It was quiet for a while until Lawrence stood up.

P. M. Smith

"Well, I don't have a lot to say, just that I miss my grandparents. I miss them a lot. I think about how Grandpa took me to the pier, taught me how to fish. One of my favorite memories is when me and Melanie watched baseball games with Grandpa. He loved baseball ---we were little kids back then, both of us could fit in his big recliner chair. We would eat peanuts while watching the game and Grandpa would throw some of the shells on the floor purposely just to irritate Grandma. It was funny when she finally caught on to what he was doing. She hit him over the head with her broom, and then he would chase her around the house. That was hilarious, me and Melanie laughed until we cried. I miss those times we had together. They were great grandparents. Grandma was a great cook. She would make anything we wanted, especially on my birthday, she made the best German chocolate cake. Next, to Dad, my Grandpa was my closest friend-----." He began to cry. Calvin rushed to his side and put his arms around him. It was a beautiful scene as he comforted his son.

A few others spoke recounting their fondest moments of mom and dad. Some of the moments were comical, and some brought tears to our eyes. When everyone had had their say, I called for my niece, Zoe.

"We have a video of mom and dad we want you to see, but before we look at the video. Little Zoe has something she would like to say." I looked down at her, "Are you ready?" she nodded her head. She came forward carrying a large gift box that was almost as big as she was.

"Uncle Russell, we want you to have this because you're special to us, we love you, and we're glad you're the patriarch of our family." She looked up at me, "Did I say it right?" she asked. I smiled and nodded yes.

She presented Russell the huge gift box. He lifted her and the gift box in the air. We clapped and cheered more than usual hoping he understood that her words were sincere. We *did* love him and we were *glad* he was our brother.

Russ looked at the box for a while very cautious about opening it. Karen urged him, "Don't be afraid Russ--open it." He untied the ribbon and threw the lid on the ground. For a few moments he stood looking at the contents of the box, smiling at Karen and me his eyes wide with glee.

"We want to see too." Someone shouted from the back.

Finally, he removed a fashionable, gray and white pillbox hat. He put the hat on his head. "How did you know this was just what I wanted." He laughed and passed the hat to Myra, his wife. It was a perfect fit, and she looked gorgeous in it.

Russell continued digging through the box. "Are you sure there's something in here for me?" He questioned. Throwing tissue paper all over the pavilion floor.

"Keep looking Uncle Russ," Zoe said. "You'll find it."

After searching through what seemed like an endless amount of tissue paper Russell finally pulled a clergy robe from the inside the big box. His eyes were wide and his mouth agape in astonishment. It was a black robe with turquoise embroidered designs in the shape of a diamond on each sleeve and around the hem. The front and back of the robe had a single pleat that extended the length of the robe. Russell hugged the garment to his body smiling his biggest smile.

"I don't know what to say. I know this is Karen and Vanessa's doing. I love it. I love it. I love it. Thank you so much."

"Try it on Russ," Calvin yelled. It didn't take much coaxing to get him to try on the robe. He did look handsome and scholarly. He and Myra modeled their gifts together.

"Alright, Russ---- look like you're ready to preach man." Calvin hollered again. Russell struck a pose in his new robe, Melanie snapped pictures as he hugged Myra for the camera.

"You know I'm not one to talk much…." Russ began. We all laughed at this comment, he was more of a talker than anyone we knew. "But, I think in this atmosphere of love, and warmth I feel it's necessary for me to speak since we're all together. As you know, these past few years have been very interesting, they've been dominated by a great deal of anguish, pain, distress, some of the suffering I couldn't prevent, most of it I admit I brought on myself. I guess what I'm trying to say is, that I wished I had handled things differently, if I could do it over again I would not have pushed you all away or blamed you for my failings. I apologize for how I dealt with the troubling situations, it wasn't one of my best moments… and I want to thank you all for loving me through it all. I know that sounds a little strange, but you could have forgotten about me, you could have kicked me to the curb, deservingly so, but you didn't, and for that, I am extremely grateful…." He dropped his head as he began to tear up. Melanie sitting nearest to Russ, grabbed a napkin from the table, and put it in his hand. As he wiped his face, she hugged him, causing him to cry even more. A space of silence fell over the room while Russ had a much-needed emotional release. With all that he had been through in the past couple of years, public rejection, the loss of our parents, all of this was a massive blow to his dignity and self-esteem. It was amazing he had not suffered a mental break down. Having a good, long cry was the start of his healing process. Like Mel, I wanted to go to him and hug his neck, but Calvin's firm hand on top of mine let me know to stay put in my seat.

Once Russ composed himself, he continued as Mel clung to his side. He looked down at her and lovingly placed a kiss on her forehead. "God has blessed this family with so much love and grace, we're not perfect, we have our battles, but the grace of God helps us to resolve them. As I sat around observing how you were enjoying each other, the delicious meal, friendship, laughter this whole scene made me think of "…..*but the greatest of these is love.* The greatest thing in life a man can possess is love, despite how he's mistreated, the losses he experiences, as long as love remains he can make it. Because love covers a multitude of faults, I understand that more than ever because I saw how your love covered my faults. Love kept us together no matter what disagreements we may have had. I especially felt the love this morning when First Deliverance greeted my family and me with smiles and open arms, everybody I spoke to was genuinely glad to see us, there were no disparaging remarks, no phony gestures, just real brotherly love. I felt the love then, and I feel the love right now among all of you. I hope we continue to have this deep affection for one another. Especially during the tough times, those are the hardest to endure, and that's when love is needed most. Thanks again for the lovely gifts, I love you all."

When it seemed no one else had anything to say Calvin and Lawrence set up the laptop and projector screen to view the video montage of our parents. It began with still photographs from mom and dad's wedding. Pictures of my mother holding her children and grandchildren. There were clips of my father preaching of course, scenes of them at various church and family gatherings.

We had a good laugh at a scene of my parents doing the tango in our living room. I remember the day this was filmed. It was one

Christmas when I was a little girl. I remember it so well because, Russ, Karen and I pooled our resources to purchase mom and dad monogrammed matching bathrobes as a gift. In the video, they showed off their gifts as I filmed them strutting around the house in their new bathrobes.

The last scene was a clip of my father filming my mother in the kitchen. She was at the stove pouring a cup of coffee, and by the look on her face she didn't want to be bothered with him or the camera. She kept waving him away as she tried to enjoy her cup of coffee and a magazine she was reading. We could hear daddy in the background trying to get her to say something to the camera. She paid him no attention as she poured cream and then put sugar in her coffee cup.

"Come on honey bun say a few words to the camera. We'll show it to the kids later." Mother continued to ignore him and walked around him exiting the kitchen. He followed her continuing to sweet-talk her. *"Aww--- come on Iris, say hi to the kids or sing something."* When they reached the living room area Mother finally turned around and said to Dad: *"You're not going to leave me alone are you?"* We heard Dad say *"No."* She placed the coffee cup on the table.

Daddy said, *"Sing just a little bit of your favorite song --- I promise I won't laugh."* It was quiet for a while, as mother stood with her arms folded scowling at the camera. Then her mouth began moving but, we heard very little sound.

"I can't hear youuuu." Daddy said in a sing-song voice. *"A little louder pleaseeee?"* With her arms still folded and the most unpleasant look on her face mother began singing: *"The cross of Jesus is love, the cross of Jesus is love, took away my sins, made me whole in Him, the cross of Jesus is love."*

My mother never had a very melodious voice, in fact, most of the time she sang terribly out of tune. Hearing her singing on the video she sounded pretty- good. The longer she sung, the more her face softened until she unfolded her arms and began to feel the words of the song. Soon Daddy was singing with her from behind the camera. He had the camera moving to the beat of their song. My father turned the camera, holding it at arm's length so we could see them both singing and swaying together. The video ended with the two of them arms around each other singing *the cross of Jesus is love.*

As the video ended, we cheered loudly and had a good laugh at my parent's attempt to harmonize their voices. Calvin and Lawrence put away the video equipment. We started up our various conversations. But the kids did not want to let the song go. They clapped their hands and danced around the pavilion singing "the cross of Jesus is love." At first, we watched as they sang and danced around, then at some point, I'm not sure when or how it happened, but their singing, clapping and the joy they exuded became contagious, soon we were waving our hands in the air, dancing and clapping as we joined in singing along with them about the love of Jesus.

P. M. Smith

The cross of Jesus is love,
The cross of Jesus is love,
Took away my sin, made me whole in Him,
The cross of Jesus is love.
The cross, the cross, the cross, the cross,
The cross of Jesus is love.

The power of Jesus is love,
The power of Jesus is love,
His power is real, strong enough to heal
The power of Jesus is love

The Words of Jesus is love
The Words of Jesus is love,
It's a way for sinners to be set free
The Words of Jesus is love

"The cross of Jesus is love,
The cross of Jesus is love,
If you wanna be free, live eternally
The cross of Jesus is love,

The cross of Jesus is love,
The cross of Jesus is love,
The cross of Jesus is love,

EPILOGUE

My father's letter from the grave has prompted many imaginary conversations with him. in my mind, he and I have discussed his unexpected letter explaining his change of heart, the ups and downs in the life of a pastor, I've even conversed with him about how our relationship fluctuated over the course of my life. Unfortunately, these conversations as I said are just figments of my imagination. One of my greatest desires is that my father and I would have *actually* had this final conversation face to face. I suppose in a way we did through his letter, though it was a one-sided conversation. Perhaps it was better this way because whenever we talked, our discussions often turned into heated arguments, and something would have been said or done that one of us later regretted.

My first inclination about my father's letter, after the initial shock had passed, was that it was a creative and loving choice to write a letter of support and love for his daughter. Every time I read his words I smile on the inside. As I read his words, I hear them in his deep-toned baritone voice. Sometimes I cry, sometimes I laugh, but I always feel my father's love as I read the words he wrote just for me. I must admit his letter did clear up a lot of things. I am thankful that I have tangible proof of my father's apology, support, and explanation that I can treasure for the rest of my life.

I do wonder from time to time if we had not debated, argued and deliberated would I have become the person I am today? Would I have been prepared for ministry? Or developed the thick skin needed to deal with multiple personalities of a large congregation? Would I have learned how to believe in myself despite being continuously rebuffed by someone I loved and admired? I am confident that this must have been God's plan because He allowed it and used the outcome for good. *All of God's ways are perfect.*

For whatever reason, I felt it was not time to share the letter with a lot of people. Calvin and my sister Karen are the only ones who know of its existence. I'm sure you can imagine the shock on their faces as they read the unbelievable words penned by my father. I may allow Russell and my children to read the letter one day. Calvin believes it will be a good idea for Melanie and Lawrence to learn how their grandfather admitted and corrected his mistakes. Perhaps when the time is right, I will show them the letter. For now, I keep it safely tucked away in a secret place in my home office.

Now that some of the drama in my life has subsided, I have a greater understanding of why Mom and Dad were taken from us so suddenly. It's apparent that God had to move them out of our lives so we could see *Him* more clearly. Removing my father created an opportunity for First Deliverance to discover additional avenues to serve Him. It also allowed Russell to become a stronger godly man and find his true calling in service to God. Lawrence brought out some issues that troubled his young mind. I wish he had approached them differently but, you can't choose how problems are ironed out and corrected. My parent's death brought our family closer, uncovered some hidden grudges and forged new paths for First Deliverance to expand our ministry base.

If you're wondering how I fared during my trial period as pastor. Let's just say it wasn't bad, neither was it great. Little by little things are on the upswing. Of course, mistakes were made, fortunately, I learned from them all. I am extremely delighted to say that after the twelve-month trial period, the congregation unanimously elected to retain me as their Senior Pastor. So, I must have done something right. The scripture Calvin gave me is a constant reminder *"God is with you in all that you do."*

It took some time for some of our leaders and members of the congregation to adjust to my leadership style and to the fact that a female was now their pastor. We continue many of my father's traditions which have become an integral part of our congregation. Although there are times, I find myself wondering what would my father do in some situations. More often than not, God has graciously come through and guided the leaders and me through numerous sticky situations.

Calvin is thoroughly enjoying his role as the "first gentleman" of First Deliverance. He remains a reliable support system for our family and me. There are times when I can literally feel his prayers. Of course, I never divulge to him all that goes on behind the scenes in various meetings, consultations, discussions, etc. I do appreciate being able to pick his brain, cry on his shoulder and of course bend his ear from time to time. His wise words keep me grounded, and are a constant reminder of what's really important. Most of all I am grateful to God for a husband who is both accepting and supportive of my role in God's Kingdom.

Kendra and I remain the best of friends to this day. For a while, she kept her membership at First Deliverance. Kendra was true to her word, if the Lord allowed she would join another local assembly. A few months after I was installed as pastor she informed me of her decision to join another congregation. God did not leave me in the dark concerning Kendra. I was fully prepared for the decision she made, it came as a shock to others, but I had already accepted that her joining another church could be a possibility and graciously gave her my blessings. Despite her absence from First Deliverance, we manage to keep in touch. I still consider her one of my closest friends.

Later that year Dr. & Mrs. Solomon became members of our congregation. Mrs. Solomon has been such a blessing to this congregation. She was divinely led to initiate a women's weekly prayer band, that was an immediate success, and I believe one of the catalysts that sparked a revival and even greater unity at First Deliverance. She and I have become quite close. We still get together to share stories about my parents and to talk about God's goodness. I think she enjoys talking with me because in some ways I remind her of my mother. Whenever she visits, I expect a boatload of vegetables from her garden. Some of which I keep for my family, the rest I donate to the church's food pantry. I continue to enjoy our conversations about the endless stories of her life, her garden and her love for God. I have come to value our friendship so much. Who would have thought Mrs. Solomon and I would one day become such good friends?

Gradually, new ministries and ideas are being introduced to the congregation. We expanded our missions program by partnering with a local bank to supplement our scholarship program. Some of the bank's VPs and managers mentor our students of all ages to help them achieve their educational and career goals. Audrey agreed to head our global outreach efforts. She is seeking to take the Gospel to the unchurched parts of the world. It is a monumental task, but she is passionate about outreach and has a creative mind for acquiring funding.

One of the first significant additions to our ministry was establishing the Charles P. Woods Center for Biblical Learning. An anonymous donor provided enough funding to purchase a plot of land to erect this magnificent institute of learning. Deacon Taylor, Sister Clair Robbins, and Calvin spearheaded the project. After a year and a half of planning, praying and laboring over the building structure and interior design the center was finally complete. On opening day, we made a big deal out of it. A committee was formed to plan a ribbon cutting ceremony, we invited the mayor and had a ceremonial unveiling of the enormous sign displaying my father's name in huge block lettering. Dr. McClellan was more than happy to serve as the director of the learning center. He put together a great team of advisors and instructors to develop challenging Bible curriculum for anyone desiring to enhance their Bible knowledge. No one is exempt, from little children to senior citizens. Thankfully, our teachers and instructors volunteer their services. For those who are financially strapped or unable to pay for classes, we have developed an unspoken bartering system. The impoverished person can take the course of their choosing if they provide a service to the learning center or to the church. We don't want to deprive anyone of the opportunity for spiritual growth. If someone is willing to learn more about the kingdom of God, we are more than willing to provide the necessary instruction.

From time to time guest lecturers and teachers are invited to instruct specialized classes. Russell has taught lessons for aspiring pastors and ministers in training. Dr. Solomon lends his skills to instruct biblical principles for young men. Even Melanie has volunteered to teach a course on how to create and maintain a blog page. I am very excited about the Biblical Training Center, and the best part is that the members of First Deliverance love it as much as I do, their response has been overwhelming. One of my favorite things to do is to peek in and observe the young children as they recite scripture and learn biblical doctrines, it warms my heart to see their increased love for God's Word. This is proof that one is never too young or too old to learn and memorize the Word of God.

The Bible learning institute has not changed the culture of First Deliverance. We remain a hand clapping and foot stomping kind of church. We continue to rejoice in the God of our salvation. In fact, I encourage rejoicing and praising God like King David with complete abandonment. But I also emphasize that studying, living and applying the Word is just as vital in the life of a Christian.

This was the first phase of the vision God had given me for First Deliverance. I am praying and hoping that these additional ministries will continue to whet our appetite for the Word, allow us to get closer to Him and help us to become a more impactful congregation in our city and in our community. My mother was so right when she said .... *God will use the vision He has given you to take the church even further.*

I know without a shadow of a doubt that God is pleased with the growth and development occurring at First Deliverance. He is pleased with the atmosphere of love and warmth displayed not only among the congregation but also in our family.

Through this whole ordeal, I have discovered a great deal about life, myself and human nature. What stands out most in my mind is the lesson that a little bit of rejection and tough love is good for us all. The Christian life was never intended to be a life of comfort and pleasure. Yes, the Bible promises joy unspeakable, an abundance of love, peace and all the bountiful blessings that God will provide as we obey His commands. The Bible also reveals that these virtues are sometimes acquired when God sends pain, affliction or some misfortune into our lives. A little discomfort now and then not only has a way of humbling you, but if we endure it God's way, without complaint or retaliation, then adversity no matter how much it hurts, no matter how embarrassing or uncomfortable the situation may be, God supernaturally uses that painful experience to strengthen us in our weakest moments. That's why the scriptures states "…… my strength is made perfect in weakness….." These moments of weakness not only make us like His Son Jesus, these pitfalls of life have a way of drawing us even closer to our heavenly Father, where we gain strength and more of God's grace.

My heart's desire is to walk closely with my God. Just like my grandfather, Percy Lafayette Woods and even my father, who risked the early years of his marriage seeking to obey God's will. I want what they wanted, to know God in the most intimate way and to serve in His divine kingdom until my dying day. I know I have a long road ahead of me before I reach their level of commitment. A road that is paved with disappointments, regrets, successes, and triumphs. Only God knows what the future holds for this great congregation that I am privileged to serve. I am excited and so encouraged to stay with God.

One other thing I have learned firsthand is that God keeps His promises and that He has a place for us all in His kingdom. We don't have to cajole anyone, use bribery, or clamor for anything God has promised. He'll bring it to pass in His own time and in His own way. Our only challenge is to be prepared when it's time to be used by Him. And never forget that God is perfect in all His ways.

Psalm 18:30

"The End"

Printed in the United States
By Bookmasters